EXTRAORDINARY ACCLAIM FOR
JULIA WALLIS MARTIN'S EDGAR NOMINEE

A LIKENESS IN STONE

"A thoroughly chilling and atmospheric first novel . . . Martin teases readers with a clever plot and a hypnotic voice."

—*Orlando Sentinel*

"This fast-moving, well-written first novel effectively combines the police procedural and psychological thriller genres. Characters and dialogue are realistic and compelling; Oxford and the southern English countryside are vividly described."

—*Booklist*

"Provides plenty of creepy psychological suspense . . . Martin's atmospheric prose explores the life-scarring burdens of guilt, betrayal and obsessive love within a finely turned and suspenseful plot. A highly promising debut."

—*The Herald* (Portsmouth, NH)

"A LIKENESS IN STONE is an intense read that grips the reader from the first pages. With cleverly turned phrases, Martin brings a chill to the reader. Crafty and well-constructed, this is a tale not easily forgotten."

—*Romantic Times*

"A LIKENESS IN STONE combines the best of the British police procedural with a chilling psychological drama into an incredibly well-written and exciting debut novel. Bill and the rest of the cast are all top-rate characters, but it is the cleverly designed story line which constantly forces readers to re-evaluate what they think is going to occur that turns this book into something special. Keep an eye out for Julia Wallis Martin because if this novel is any indication, she has a great career ahead of her."

—Harriet Klausner, bookbrowser.com

"Chilling . . . Absorbing and genuinely surprising."

—*The Guardian* (London)

"A compelling psychological thriller with echoes of Barbara Vine and Minette Walters. Well-written, intelligent and chilling, it demonstrates an assurance unusual in a first novel."

—*Manchester Evening News*

"Full of dark suspense, a gripping psychological crime debut that cleverly combines the themes of guilt, love, and betrayal with loyalty and cunning."

—*South Wales Argus*

"Complex and compelling. This is an unbelievably good debut novel."

—*Coventry Evening Telegraph*

A Likeness in Stone

Julia Wallis Martin

St. Martin's Paperbacks

FOR MARENGO

First published in Great Britain by Hodder and Stoughton, a division of Hodder Headline PLC.

A LIKENESS IN STONE

Library of Congress Catalog Card Number: 98-10286

ISBN: 0-312-97077-3

Printed in the United States of America

St. Martin's Press hardcover edition/May 1998
St. Martin's Paperbacks edition/August 1999

10 9 8 7 6 5 4 3 2

1

Vaughan didn't know precisely what it was that attracted him to diving, but, whatever it was, he never seemed to tire of it. Maybe that was because his stint with the navy had enabled him to experience some of the most impressive diving environments the world had to offer, or maybe it was just that he was addicted to the rush of adrenalin that pumped through him when water closed over his head.

He had felt the familiar rush a few moments ago when he and Saunders had entered the reservoir at Marshfield, but he had felt something else, too – a sinking sensation that wasn't entirely due to the tanks pulling him down. It was more an instinct than a feeling, a sixth sense that came to him whenever he was working in a stretch of water notorious for its ability to extinguish human life.

His first reaction was to wonder whether to junk the dive – but, not unreasonably, once they hit the surface, Saunders would want to know why. Like himself, he was an ex-navy man, so Vaughan didn't really want to have to say he just felt there was something wrong. He was hardly likely to be impressed and Vaughan didn't want him thinking that maybe he was losing his bottle; but the feeling, the instinct, was strong, and, although there was nothing to suggest that this reservoir was any more dangerous than many they had dived in, there was a peculiar stillness to the water, a certain gloom that couldn't entirely be explained by the lack of light.

Above them, the skin of the water was broken by rain, and

the sky producing it was doing little to penetrate the depths and light their way. It was oppressive, but at first Vaughan couldn't quite put his finger on why. And then it came to him: the thing that was strange about this particular reservoir was the lack of fish. No dark, slow carp gliding like shadows into even darker shadows and becoming one with them.

An instructor had once told him to let an absence of fish serve as a warning. It was unnatural, and could usually be attributed to pollution or predator. Consequently, when he had once been diving for pleasure off the coast of Mozambique, the realisation that, quite suddenly, the fish had disappeared had frozen him to immobility. He had tried to sense from the feel of the water what it was that had frightened them, and when a Bull shark had loomed towards him everything he had ever heard about them flashed instantly to mind. He knew, for instance, that they rarely attacked with the ferocity of the Great White but cruised round their victim, taking a foot, and then perhaps a hand, and possibly severing a leg just below the knee before losing interest, leaving the limbs to rot and the victim a torso.

He had panicked then and had thrashed for the shore, certain that at any moment he would feel the mouth closing on one of his limbs; but the terrible pain had never come. Instead, he had felt a dull thud against his right leg and had collapsed on the beach, sobbing with fear and afraid to look at what he was certain would be a stump.

There had been blood, but no stump – just shredded skin where the shark had brushed against him, its skin like glass paper.

Vaughan had been deeply ashamed then, ashamed that people on the beach had heard him crying like a woman, and he had tried to block the memory out. But the stillness of the water had logged itself into his memory, under 'useful information', and he felt it now as the house came into view. It was marked on records kept by Thames Water – and the old water authority before it – as having been submerged when Marshfield became a reservoir. With luck it would produce some saleable items and make the dive worthwhile.

They circled it slowly, each of them noticing that the door frames and windows had rotted away, the glass having fallen to become covered by silt, and, in his search for a suitable entrance, Vaughan looked up, the weight of the water making what should have been a quick, automatic movement a heavy, thoughtful process. He reached out to touch the walls and feel how the lichen had given a soft covering to the brick, and then he pushed upwards, Saunders behind him.

As they swam over the roof, he looked down and, in seeing the tiles pass beneath him, he had a feeling that was the nearest he could come to describing an out-of-body experience. It was something he had felt before, but never quite so strongly, and was the sort of sensation a person might have in a dream: that of rising out of the material body and wondering whether death would be like this.

The weight of the tanks pulled them down at the back of the house, and, after pausing for a moment to consider their options, they dived through a window, the gentlest of efforts easing them through and into a kitchen that had been left partly furnished. There was an old oven still plugged into the wall, a cupboard containing tins minus their labels, and clothes left rotting in a washing machine.

At some point, the kitchen had been modernised with Formica-topped units that had warped in the water. The sink was stainless steel, the greyness of the metal melting into the greyness of a wallpaper that rubbed away to the touch. Flimsy net curtains billowed with their every movement, and Vaughan touched one gently. It fell from the runner and draped on his arm, falling apart and drifting to the floor even as he tried to free himself from it.

He was afraid. He didn't know why, but there had been occasions when he had dived to sunken vessels, and once in the living quarters he had experienced the same unease, as though the former occupants might materialise, ethereal things, no more than an imprint on the water.

He got a grip on himself, and after signalling to Saunders he led the way to a room off the kitchen, finding it fully furnished. A Bakelite clock on a brick mantelpiece led his eye to a cheap framed print still hanging over the fireplace: a doe-eyed woman leaning against a tree, the water distorting the scene so that tendrils of her hair appeared to float through the glass towards him.

He pushed away and swam over an armchair to reach a long narrow hall. At the far end, a watery light showed where the door had been and it lit their way to stairs that disappeared into darkness. He hesitated, and now came something that made him feel that he really was in the middle of some bizarre dream – he swam up the stairs.

On the landing, he paused to get his bearings before flipping his way slowly into the first of several rooms. It was empty and he backed out, signalling that they should try the next. This one yielded a mattress dumped by a far wall, a clock radio beside it and a pile of what might have been blankets.

Unwilling to be left there alone, he followed Saunders into a bathroom that was small and tiled, the cupboard over the sink having nothing to offer but a pack of razors, a toothbrush.

They left it together, flipping effortlessly into the master bedroom, a pair of ghosts whose presence moved the water, which in turn lifted the sheets from the bed so that they rose in a childhood fantasy of horror. He saw them out of the corner of his eye but couldn't bring himself to turn his head a fraction, afraid of what he might see in the way that a child is afraid of looking into a mirror as he runs past.

He fixed his attention on a tall fitted wardrobe, reached it in a few slow strokes and tried the knob. Tarnished to blackness with time, it fitted into his hand neatly, the brass having oxidised to a roughness that brought the shark's skin to mind. There was a knack to it and he struggled with it before the latch lifted, but finally he managed to open the door, the weight of the water making hard work of what should have been a simple task. He stepped back as it fell from hinges that had rusted through, and when the silt had settled, he stared at what it concealed, Saunders directly behind him, his view of the wardrobe obscured.

It wasn't real. He decided that almost instantly. It had been left there for a joke, and if he were to touch it his hands would confirm what his mind knew to be true: that the face was one of those masks people wear to parties at Hallowe'en. It would be plastic, stiff and unyielding, not flesh, soft and rotting as his eyes would have him believe.

He reached out, took hold of the lower jaw as if to pull the mask from a stuffed-stocking head, and wanted to deny that it had come away in his hand; that what he was holding was a piece of corpse, long dead. And then came the rush of bubbles, a yell carried to Saunders' ears by water that distorted the sound, but did nothing to diminish the horror it conveyed.

2

By the time he left the office, the traffic nosing its way out of Oxford had come to a complete standstill. Roadworks? An accident? Gilmore didn't know. He only knew that tonight he would walk into an empty house; that what Sue had taken when she left was merely the handful of things she had brought when she had moved in less than a year ago, but that the house would echo regardless.

He hadn't loved her. He knew that. Maybe she had known it too, the observation that it was hard to live with a ghost being a conclusion she had come to within weeks of their having first met. *Who is this woman, this woman you never talk about?*

He could have lied to get her off his back. He could, for instance, have said it was any one of the women who had preceded her, and he might have added that each of them had left him a note on the fridge.

Why the fridge? he wondered. Was it its position in the sparse kitchen, the certainty that if left there it would be seen? Or was it merely the fact that the magnetic snowman that clung to the enamel was ideal for securing a note?

Not that he needed one. He knew the signs. With all of them he had known, sometimes weeks in advance, that they were about to vacate his life. *You never say what you feel.*

Initially, she had accepted his reserve, but, as her feelings for him grew, she had started to try to get through, as she put it. He could have told her she was wasting her time, just as he could also have told her that ultimately there would come a day when he would drive home to find the house dark, cold and devoid of the Sue who had finally joined the long list of women who had given up on him.

He caught his reflection in the windscreen, the face looking unfamiliar, distorted by the glass. It was the face of a man in his prime, the kind of face that attracted women easily because it gave the impression that he had everything under his firm, unflappable control.

Ironic, really.

The traffic moved and he eased along behind the car in front, heading home, but only by degrees, taking the longer routes, shooting off down side roads he'd never seen before, reluctant to face the fridge.

Eventually, inevitably, he pulled into the drive of a semi that was identical to every other red-brick, three-bedroomed box in the crescent, and he felt, as he always felt: that it wasn't home. He had lived there for several years now, yet his attitude towards it was similar to that of his attitude towards the women who had lived there with him – he could have left at a moment's notice, and without a backward glance.

He parked in front of the garage, locked the car, and entered the house to find the door to the kitchen closed. He couldn't remember having shut it, or why he had done it. Maybe it was the look of control that peered out from the white plaster face.

In a moment of decisiveness, he pulled sharply at the thin, lined paper. It whipped from under the snowman, leaving him undisturbed, and, without reading it, Gilmore screwed it tight and threw it into a pedal bin. He knew the contents by heart in any case. It wasn't as if he'd read it over and over: merely that it would be like every other note that had ever been left on the fridge. Only the signatures differed.

Unusually for him, he poured himself a drink and took it into the sitting room. The furnishings were plain, comfortable, and now devoid of the female touch, and as he sank into the sofa he used the remote in order to catch the news.

Later, he was to have no recollection of what came before

the item relating to Marshfield. He remembered only that the slate-grey water seemed, for a moment, to have risen without warning to swallow him whole, and then it was gone, a different item of news wiping it from the screen to leave him listening, without comprehension, to accounts of other catastrophes, disasters that would presumably devastate others in the way that Marshfield had devastated him.

He turned it off, sat there, and suddenly thought of Sue and her whining accusation: 'Who *is* this woman?'

On evenings like these, wintry, cold, and typical for November, he had sometimes felt like answering that question. The trouble was, he could hardly picture her face now, but he could remember things about her. He could remember, for instance, that her hair had been short, dark, and moussed into an urchin look, and that she had been thinner than he would have liked. He could remember also that she had possessed a self-assurance that is common among women who are not only beautiful, but clever; and, since she had been reading English at Somerville, there could be little doubt that she had indeed been clever.

Why couldn't he forget her?

He didn't know, just as he didn't know why he had never been able to bring himself to go to the police and tell them what they had failed to drag out of him twenty years ago.

He had sometimes longed to do it, but the consequences would overwhelm him. And so he lived this lie, this lie that was smeared on the surface of his existence like a suffocating veneer, distorting what lay beneath it so that nobody saw the nature of what it concealed.

3

It had come, as Driver had hoped it would, during his lifetime, the broadcast providing what his dimming vision had denied him the option of reading in the press: that a body had been found at Marshfield. And in a wardrobe, of all places.

It didn't sound right to Driver. There had been thousands of acres of marsh to bury it on, marsh that was about to be submerged by a reservoir built by the water authority – so why hide it in a wardrobe?

He went to the kitchen, looked out across a small, neat square of lawn to the retirement bungalows opposite and spoke to the memory of his late wife: 'Mary,' he said, 'they've found her.'

There was a ghost by the sink, methodically clearing the dishes from breakfast, a ghost who didn't look up, her hair no longer crisp, her figure no longer neat. *Didn't I tell you they would?*

'But you'll never guess where,' said Driver. 'All these years, it's been down there, just waiting. He hid it in the house!'

He couldn't understand it. If he'd even suspected that Gilmore would do something as stupid as that he'd have sent divers down at the time of the investigation, but twenty years ago he had stood on the embankment to stare into the water and come to terms with the fact that the body was buried on the marsh – a marsh that, like the house, was now completely submerged. He had therefore believed his chances of finding it to be nonexistent.

He went into the hall where he phoned Thames Valley Police, the number coming to him automatically.

'Put me through to the incident room.'

'What's it in connection with?'

'Marshfield,' said Driver.

As he waited for the connection, he recalled that he had suspected from quite early on in the investigation that Gilmore had killed her. He could see it in the way he'd shrunk away, not so much from the questioning, but from some dreaded scene that flickered continually across his field of vision.

'You killed her.'

'You seem very sure.'

'I'm sure.'

A voice broke into his thoughts, a quick-talking, stress-filled voice that snapped, 'Incident room.'

'Who am I speaking to?'

In the incident room of Thames Valley Police, papers in one hand, a file in the other, the phone jammed under his chin, a detective answered, 'DI Dalton. And you?'

'Driver. Formerly DCI. Thames Valley.'

The name rang a bell, and in seconds, Dalton had pulled a face from some distant memory. 'Bill?' he said, and, cautiously, Driver replied: 'Do we know one another?'

'You retired in 1980, or thereabouts.'

'That's right.'

'I'd just joined the force.' There was no immediate response and Dalton pictured him scouring his memory for some recollection, so he added, 'You won't remember me, but I remember you.'

Driver caught the warmth in his voice. 'I daresay I'd know you if I saw you,' he said, half apologetic, and Dalton replied: 'Doesn't matter. What's the problem?'

'I heard an appeal for anyone with information about the remains found at Marshfield to contact Detective Superintendent Rigby at Thames Valley.'

'He's out,' said Dalton. 'What have you got?'

'A probable ID on the remains.'

There was a pause before the inevitable, 'What's your number?'

Driver gave it and Dalton added, 'Give me a name and I'll pull the case file.'

'Warner,' said Driver. 'Helena Warner.'

4

One of the advantages of living above a newsagent's shop was the certain knowledge that the daily paper would arrive.

As always, it was pushed half under the door at the top of the stairs, a door that had once led to a back bedroom but now served as the entrance to her flat, and one of the first things Joan did when she got up was tug it through gently so as not to tear it.

She took it into a room that had once served as a bathroom but was now a kitchen. Boxlike and cramped, devoid of its cast-iron bath, it now contained a Baby Belling cooker, lino that was ice to unsocked feet, and a stainless-steel sink that was stained beyond redemption.

The plain plaster walls were half hidden behind cupboards that were too big for the space they occupied, and from force of habit she avoided catching her head on one as she made tea by spooning a dried tea-and-milk concoction into a cup and pouring boiling water over it. It didn't taste too bad once you got used to it and it saved her having to buy milk.

She took the tea and the paper through to the main room where the couch was also a bed, switched on a bar of the electric fire, and folded the paper into a manageable tabloid size.

The headline jerked her to full consciousness. It wasn't the horror of it – in a life spanning thirty-seven years, several of which had been spent as a reporter with the *Manchester Evening News*, she hadn't exactly been shielded from the horrors of life. Murders happened, and bodies were found all the time. She read about them, heard them reported on the news, thought it all a shame, but carried on in much the way most people carry on, their lives unaffected, the victim forgotten, sometimes within a matter of minutes. But this was different.

She paged through the paper, looking for a continuation of the story, and found it in the centre pages, where a picture of the reservoir dominated.

She had never seen Marshfield like that. She remembered only the still, flat land and the birds that rose from the reeds.

She put her tea down on the carpet, picked her way around soiled cups and plates that had stood on the floor for days, and pushed the curtains open. Outside, the sky was a blanket of grey, a cloudless, unbroken, colourless mass producing a barely perceptible rain. Condensation had run down the pane to settle in pools on the sill and she wiped a circle with the back of her hand, feeling it wet and cold.

A bus stop stood opposite, children in school uniform playing the fool, darting into the road in front of slow-moving cars that scattered them onto the pavement like marbles.

Thirty years ago, she had played the same game on a similar road less than a mile away, and she had known this house even then. In those days, the ground floor had been a launderette, the owner living in the flat she occupied now. But she had presumed that when she grew up she would move away.

Of course, she hadn't known then what she knew now: that she would *never* move away. That after university, and what had turned out to be an unsuccessful association with the *Manchester Evening News*, she would move back to Warrington, to within a stone's throw of where she had been born.

She hadn't always been so resigned to it though. In the days when she had lived in student accommodation she had presumed that, sooner or later, her lifestyle would change; though whether this would be as a result of a successful career or marriage she had neither known nor cared. Her main concern had been to succeed and success would have been a good job, her own house, a partner, maybe children. But none of those things had happened.

Sometimes, when she let it get to her, she had to admit that it wasn't so much the fact that none of those *specific* things had happened as the fact that *nothing* had happened – merely the passage of years, years during which she had simply grown older and less successful; years during which she had slid down the hill of a recession that had made it increasingly difficult for her to sell her work.

She moved away from the window and back to the couch, and picked up the paper. From a professional point of view, she felt that the story had been well reported. Not that she was an expert. She might have worked as a reporter for several years but she hadn't been cut out for it. She was far too slow, far too precious about what she wrote, and far too introverted to stand much of a chance of getting a scoop on a story. She had been the type of reporter who covered golden weddings and twin births, and, like a fool, she had given it up to go freelance.

The money and the work had been irregular enough to keep her on income support ever since, but now and again she filled in a form to state that she had received payment for an article and a portion was duly deducted from her giro to take account of it. She didn't know why she bothered.

Coming back to Warrington had made her feel a failure. It wasn't the town. The town itself had a lot going for it. It was just that she had hoped for more, that was all. Even just a little more – someone to share her life with, and a moderately successful career that produced enough income to live on in a place that was – she looked around her – better than this.

Her life had been virtually devoid of male company. She had to face facts. She was fat. Fat people who could accept themselves tended to find partners. Fat people who wished they were dead tended not to. But at the end of the day there were certain advantages to living alone. There was nobody to complain about the fact that the flat was unbearably hot in summer and insufferably cold in winter, that it was possible to determine the days of the week by the food she cooked on each given day, or complain that the couch was too narrow for two to sleep on in any degree of comfort.

She consoled herself with the thought that writers were often notoriously unhappy in their private lives, particularly those who were reduced to writing features for downmarket magazines, and, whenever she felt bogged down by the frustration of writing features that rarely sold, she worked on the Book, that mysterious, ethereal, pageless thing that flickered on the screen of her computer like a ghost.

Sometimes, it appeared as if of its own volition. She couldn't recall having pulled it up from the files list but it would materialise as if commanding her to work on it. And she would work on it. Adding a paragraph, wiping it out, adding another, and forgetting to save it – only she didn't forget so much as make the subconscious admission that what she had written was something she would rather delete for all sorts of complex reasons. She had intended it to be a sort of tortoise-and-hare story, the beautiful, clever antagonist eventually being totally outshone by the plain, hardworking protagonist, and, as with most first novels, great chunks of it were largely autobiographical.

The plot was of a type that was frequently used by writers of mass-market fiction: her protagonist had spent years living in the antagonist's shadow, but had overcome almost overwhelming odds in order to build a chain of clothes shops from which she made a fortune. It was to have culminated in the protagonist's marrying the antagonist's lover, and, if Joan had been able to adhere to the general theme, it might have worked quite well; but her tendency to digress had been holding her back for some years.

The trouble was, the truth kept creeping in. Not only had she named her protagonist Joan and her antagonist Helena, but certain scenes appeared on the screen when they had no right to be there, like the scene depicting the occasion when Helena had arrived on the doorstep to tell her she'd got into Oxford. She had looked much as Joan imagined a figure from the Bible might look after experiencing a vision of Christ. Her eyes, her skin, her entire personality seemed radiant somehow, as though something had changed from within. 'You'll never guess,' she said. But that was just the trouble: Joan could always guess. Joan had her down to an art. 'I've won a scholarship to Somerville.'

Joan, who knew her every move, her every trick, had stepped aside to allow her in, and Helena had followed her into the kitchen, dodging the cat as it shot through her legs and made for a flap in the door. 'Well?' said Helena.

'Well what?'

'Aren't you going to congratulate me?'

Joan had felt a peculiar ache at the back of her throat, as if someone were pressing his thumbs against her oesophagus and trying to strangle her from the inside out, and it occurred to her, not for the first time, that to be in any way associated with Helena was rather like submitting oneself to an ongoing and particularly agonising torture. This demon who came in the guise of a friend was there to torment her for the sins of unattractiveness, poverty and intellectual dullness, and she came to the conclusion that she had neither the strength nor the knowledge to perform whatever ritual was necessary to exorcise it.

From the dim-lit hovel adjoining the kitchen, her mother had called, 'Who's that?' and Joan had replied, 'Helena.'

'Come in, love.'

Helena had poked her nose into the only downstairs room, the stale air within keeping her in the doorway. 'I was just telling Joan I've won a scholarship to Somerville.'

Her mother said, 'Did you hear that, Len?'

Without taking his eyes from the television set, her father had said, 'Where's that then?'

'Oxford.'

Joan had remained in the kitchen where the smell of gas from a cooker lit by matches was almost inviting. She filled the kettle, put it on the hob, and heard Helena say, 'I'll write. We mustn't lose touch.'

I'll bet you will, thought Joan, bright, chatty letters, full of your own success.

The letters had come, crammed full of happiness, and Joan had written back: 'Dear Helena, you can't imagine how glad I am that you love your accommodation, adore your college, find the work easy to cope with and have met some fantastic men – I too am having a wonderful time . . .'

A wonderful time, thought Joan.

The loneliness of those three years would stay with her forever. The miserable digs. The way she gained weight. Masses and masses of weight. It hung on her still, the shame of it, the heat of it, the soul-destroying fact of it. All food is fat. She knew that now. A truth she would take to the grave.

She had expected Helena to forget her. Soon, the letters would stop coming, she was sure of it. But on the contrary, it was as though Helena knew, intuitively, that every time Joan received one of her letters, she screwed it up with rage, so she kept them coming, the elegant writing depicting a life that was hopelessly closed to lesser mortals.

It was some time after the first half-term that she mentioned a lover, somebody she had met through a friend. At first, Joan took little notice, but, when Helena began to mention him in every letter, she took a greater interest. This man of hers sounded so very like the type she wanted for herself, and she built a fantasy around him. They would be introduced, their eyes would meet, and they would know that each was meant for the other.

She held, of course, not the slightest hope that this fantasy would ever become a reality; and yet, when Helena invited her to a party in Oxford saying that he would be there, she decided to go.

In the book, she had written that, at the party, Helena's lover and Jo had fallen in love, but that, for a variety of (largely implausible) reasons, they couldn't let the fact become public knowledge. In reality, it had been a little more complex than that.

Joan was under no illusion about Helena's reason for having

invited her. She had just wanted to show her what she was missing, stuffed away in Southampton. Even so, she went. She wasn't sure why. Maybe she just wanted to flagellate herself one last time. She didn't know. Whatever the reason, she went to the party.

The party where Helena died.

5

It was late afternoon by the time Rigby returned to the station, and one of the first things he saw when he walked into his office was the message relating to Driver. It had been pinned to a file pulled by Dalton, a file that was inches thick and bound into submission by thin blue tape, the name Helena Warner in the top left-hand corner.

After reading the message, Rigby had mixed feelings about it. On the one hand, it was useful to have ex-coppers coming forward with information. On the other, he knew from experience that they could make real nuisances of themselves if you let them. He left his office and poked his head round the door to the incident room, finding the blinds, like the windows, tight-closed against an afternoon that was both grey and bitterly cold.

'John,' he said. 'This message.'

Dalton looked up from a mass of paperwork scattered in what appeared to be total disarray on the desk he had chosen to work at. 'Which one?'

'Driver,' said Rigby. 'Former DCI.'

'What about it?'

'Should his name mean anything to me?'

'Before your time,' replied Dalton, and the words carried an edge that wasn't lost on Rigby. He was young for a DS, a product of the Accelerated Promotion Scheme, and sometimes resented by men who had put in the number of years people like Dalton had served. But there was no edge to Dalton's voice, and Rigby merely replied: 'I take it he handled the investigation into her disappearance.'

'So he says. And it's his name in the file.'

Rigby hovered in the doorway and more to himself than to Dalton, he added, 'And he thinks we've found her at Marshfield.'

'He thinks there's a pretty good chance.'

'Did you look at the file?'

'Glanced at it,' replied Dalton. 'He was convinced she was murdered and buried at Marshfield before the house was submerged.' As an afterthought, he added, 'He was also convinced he knew who the killer was.'

'How likely is it that he was right?'

Dalton cast his mind back to the few occasions on which he had met Driver. He wasn't a man given to jumping to conclusions or bending the facts to get a result. 'If Driver thinks he had his man, chances are he did.'

'So what went wrong?' said Rigby.

'Phone him,' said Dalton. 'Find out.'

Rigby returned to his office, picked up the phone, and dialled Driver's number. It was answered almost instantly, and he got the uncomfortable impression that Driver had been standing there, waiting for the call.

'Detective Superintendent Rigby, Thames Valley,' said Rigby. 'Mr Driver?'

'Speaking,' said Driver.

'You phoned with information.'

'The remains found at Marshfield,' he replied.

'What about them?' Rigby asked.

'Helena Warner.'

Rigby picked up a pen and started to write as he spoke. 'Dalton pulled the case file. It looks extensive.'

'Let me save you time,' said Driver.

'When?'

'How about now?'

Rigby, who hadn't eaten since breakfast, felt home beckoning. He let it beckon. 'Six do you?'

Driver merely replied, 'Forty-seven, River Walk, Riverview Estate. Know it?'

'No problem,' said Rigby. 'Six.'

6

Riverview Estate was one that Rigby was not familiar with. The rows of neat retirement bungalows housed the elderly, and, as far as he was aware, there were few incidences of joyriding, hooliganism, or vandalism reported anywhere in the vicinity. There was no river either, the nearest being the Thames, and that was several miles away.

He parked outside a bungalow identical to those that surrounded it in every respect but one: Driver was clearly no gardener, and the patch of lawn that fronted the house stood out by having no border.

There were medium-sized pots standing by the front door, terracotta and devoid of soil. They had no doubt been bought with every intention of there being geraniums to follow, but the geraniums had never been planted, and at some point one of the pots had cracked as a result of frost.

He rang the bell, but the door was opened before he took his finger from the push. 'Rigby,' he said, showing his ID.

He looked like a kid, thought Driver, but then, anyone under fifty probably looked young when you were knocking on seventy. Well-dressed, intelligent-looking; no doubt the product of one of these new-fangled schemes that sends graduates shooting up a ladder Driver had to climb rung by painful rung, year after frustrating year. His voice held a tinge of resignation as he checked the ID, stepped aside, and said, 'Come in.'

The voice, thought Rigby, held traces of a northern accent,

much softened by years of living in the south, but there was nothing soft about Driver. Dalton had mentioned he must be getting on, but he looked fitter than Rigby had imagined.

He stepped over the threshold and followed him into a room where Driver indicated the couch, leaving the armchair free for himself. 'Sit down.'

Rigby sat, and as he did so noticed shelves that were fixed above a sideboard. They were crammed with books of a type that would once have been essential to the work of a copper of senior rank, most of them outdated, and he wondered why Driver hadn't thrown them out. A reminder that he had once served a useful purpose in a life that was as good as over, perhaps?

'That's a fair collection.'

Lowering himself into the armchair, Driver replied, 'Tools of the trade, once.' And Rigby suddenly saw himself at some point in the future, sitting in a bungalow, long retired and probably long forgotten. It was a worrying apparition. 'Good of you to phone.'

'Least I could do,' replied Driver. 'You'd have done the same.'

True, thought Rigby, particularly if he had nothing but the past to occupy his mind. 'You read it in the paper?'

'Heard it on the radio,' said Driver. 'Looks like the divers got more than they bargained for.'

Casting his mind back to the look that had been on Vaughan's face as he described what he'd found, Rigby merely nodded. 'He won't forget that in a hurry.'

'Why were they diving?'

'Trying their luck,' replied Rigby, and he recalled that if he hadn't already been aware that it was Vaughan who had found the body, he would have known anyway. Of the two men, he looked the colder, and he looked deeply shaken, as though the water had drained more than mere heat from him.

'Did they have permission?'

'They're employed by the water authority.'

'They were on a job?'

'No,' said Rigby. 'Day off.'

'They must like diving a hell of a lot to want to do it on their day off,' said Driver. 'What were they looking for?'

'Anything they could sell.'

'And there's no chance they were mistaken? It *was* a body, down there?'

Rigby replied, 'Vaughan only recently retired from the navy. He's seen bodies before. Besides . . .'

'Besides?'

'We sent a couple of *our* divers down. They confirmed it. We're planning to bring it to the surface.'

'When?'

'Tomorrow.'

The knowledge that police divers had confirmed it satisfied Driver. He said, 'I've always thought the chances of that body ever coming to light were next to nil. Seems I was wrong.'

'What's the background?' said Rigby, and strangely, now that it came to it, Driver wasn't sure where to start. He had thought that, if ever it came to it, he would know precisely what to say to the person heading the investigation if the case were ever reopened, but now the moment was here he wasn't too sure.

Eventually he said: 'In 1975, I investigated the disappearance of a student from Somerville College, Helena Warner.' Rigby made no response. He knew that already. 'Over the years, I'd investigated the disappearance of quite a few students. You know how it is. Girlfriend trouble. Boyfriend trouble. Worry about exams.' Rigby nodded. He knew. 'But the minute I started to piece her last movements together, I knew she was dead.'

Rigby didn't ask how. Some men could sort, instinctively, the runaways from the murder victims. It was a gift, of sorts. A sixth sense. 'Did you have a prime suspect?'

'Gilmore,' said Driver, softly. 'A first-year student at Worcester College.'

Driver fell silent, and Rigby prompted him. 'What made you go for him?'

Casting his mind back to the way in which Gilmore had gradually disintegrated as the investigation progressed, Driver replied, 'He nearly had a breakdown. Touch and go. Not because of anything *we* did, you understand, but because of something *he'd* done. Big difference.'

'How old was he at the time?'

'Nineteen.'

Rigby knew well enough how some people reacted if they were repeatedly questioned by the police on a serious matter, especially if they were young and they had no previous convictions. 'Some people can't take it,' he suggested.

'It wasn't that,' replied Driver. 'Given time . . .'

'What happened to time?' said Rigby.

'We ran out of it. Nothing concrete, and all lines of enquiry exhausted. We had to drop it.'

'Frustrating,' said Rigby, quietly. 'How convinced were you that he'd done it?'

'Totally.'

'Why?'

'Call it instinct – call it what you like. Whatever it was, it told me something else . . .' He leaned forward, the springs of the chair old and fighting him every inch. 'She died a brutal death.'

7

Before the 1939–45 war virtually destroyed the whole system of domestic service, Chaggfords had been staffed by a cook, three housemaids, a chauffeur, a groom, a footman and a butler. These days, Cora Bowerman made do with the help of a paid companion/help, although it would still have been within her financial means to keep the house fully staffed.

She had been born there in 1921 at a time when the kitchen garden had looked out onto fields, but gradually suburbia had encircled the house so that she could hardly remember what it had been like to walk out of the gates and find herself in a country lane. It seemed to her that a row of terraced houses had always stood opposite, and behind them, a Sainsbury's superstore. Beyond that was the A40 and beyond that Cora had no idea. She was lost now, the suburbs surrounding Oxford having changed beyond all recognition.

Only the house seemed familiar, and safe, and even that was because most of it had been shut up for years. Not that there had been any conscious decision to close various parts of it off. On the contrary, the closing of so many doors had been a gradual thing: a process that had taken place over a period of seventy years, a natural consequence of realising that certain rooms had been left unused for some weeks and then months and it dawning on one that they would never be used again.

It was time to leave. To go away. Forever. So much of what was said about elderly people wanting to cling to the houses they had lived and loved and borne children in was rubbish.

Cora knew of too many who couldn't wait to move to a smart new bungalow that took a fraction of the time to clean. Not that she felt that way about Chaggfords. She would be sorry to leave it. Of course she would. But it was time to go. In her younger days, it had seemed bright and full of life. Now, it was a cold, echoing place full of dark corners, groaning water pipes, creaking floorboards and draughts that defied all efforts to eradicate or redirect them, and, since her companion was nearing retirement age, Cora had decided to throw in the towel and spend what remained of her life living somewhere small, warm and alone.

The problem had been what to do with Chaggfords. She was an only child who had never married, and she had managed to outlive all but the most distant of her relations. Consequently, the job of deciding whom to leave it to had proved tricky.

She wasn't sure what drew her to the decision to donate it to Churchill House. Perhaps it was because the consultant psychiatrist, Dr Thurston, had become a friend, or perhaps it was because, as a girl, she had accompanied her parents when they had called on the family who owned it before the war. Whatever the case, it had somehow seemed an appropriate course of action, and she had made the gift on condition that Chaggfords would be used to house patients who were being eased back into the community – a sort of halfway house, she supposed.

There was a catch, of course. There had to be a catch. Nobody could expect to receive a highly valuable property without there being a catch.

She walked with the hesitancy of the frail from the sitting room to a hall of such vast proportions that it was conceivable that it might one day house the bones of a large dinosaur. But it would never house a dinosaur. Not if her wishes were respected, for standing in the corner furthest from the door was a stone plinth. It had once supported a statue of her late father, Group Captain Richard Bowerman, DSO, DFC. Pillar of the community. Captain of industry. *Destroyer of dreams.*

She plucked a bottle from its hiding place in a rosewood

cabinet and returned to her room with it, sitting down and feeling the chair she had left only moments before still warm on her back.

Arranging for the statue to be demolished had given her a certain satisfaction, but it was going to give her even more satisfaction to erect a statue of the man her father had prevented her from marrying, a statue that had been commissioned several months ago, and was now complete.

It had been sculpted by a patient of Dr Thurston's, and in a modest – some might say almost self-effacing – way she felt herself to be qualified to choose a sculptor, her education and background having prompted one of the more prominent auction houses to employ her for a period after the war. But it was not that fact alone that persuaded her to commission him: it was the fact that Wachmann might once have managed to capture her heart in the days before it was given to the man whose statue he then went on to sculpt.

She had told him what she had never been able to impress upon her father: that James had come from a respectable, working-class family; a quiet man, a thoughtful man, and the rather shy product of a local grammar school. What he had ***not*** been, despite what Cora's father had insisted to the contrary, was a fortune hunter. He was merely what his obituary had said he was, a young RAF pilot who had given his life for his country.

There had been plenty like him when Cora was in her twenties. Some of them as young as eighteen; others, like James, a few years their senior and staving off jokes about the reflexes slowing now they were growing old.

Old, thought Cora. What would any of them have known about growing old? So few of them got the chance to find out. Certainly not James, at any rate, who had given his life for his country but who mightn't have had to if not for her father ensuring he flew on every conceivable bombing raid. If he was awake, he flew. That was how one of James's friends had put it. Night after night, he flew and flew and flew.

Until, one night, he flew away forever.

She was too old to care what people might think if they came to the house at ten in the morning and smelled drink on her breath. She toasted the ghost she had never seen but whose comforting presence she felt in every corner of the house, and as she drank she imagined herself unveiling the statue.

At first, people would be staggered in the way they so often are when confronted by a work of art that is larger than life, and it would probably take several moments for the subject matter to register. Once it did, the majority would no doubt assume that what they were looking at was a statue of her father sitting in the cockpit of a Lockheed Hudson, and then she would tell them it was a statue of the man she might have married if not for her father.

She knew it would surprise, possibly amuse, and perhaps even shock some people. And she wanted to do just that. Of course she did. But those were secondary reasons for commissioning the work. Her primary reason was far simpler.

She had one photograph. That was all. Just one black-and-white photograph of James. And before she died she wanted the chance to run her fingers over the contours of his face and touch his lips with her own, to bury her head in the nape of his neck and weep in a way that she had not been able to weep over a mere photograph. For that, she needed his likeness. His perfect likeness in stone.

8

Wachmann stood at the window in Dr Thurston's consulting room. From here, he had a view of the coach house that had been converted into a studio for his sole use. It stood at the back of Churchill House, itself a former stately home, its graceful, confident architecture entirely in keeping with the surrounding Oxford colleges.

Within the walls of the coach house, and hidden even from Thurston's analytical eye, was the statue commissioned by Cora. Complete now, and dreadful in its beauty, it would change his life forever. He didn't know how he knew that. It was an instinctive thing, a knowledge that, once revealed, would unleash a series of events that would prove utterly beyond his control. He would be famous, he supposed, but that wasn't what drove him. He had long since given up fantasies about making his name in favour of fantasies that revolved around fulfilling his potential. Whether dead or alive, he would be remembered for his talent. Above all, he would be remembered for the statue commissioned by Cora.

There had been many occasions during the past few months when Thurston had asked if he might be allowed to see it, but Wachmann had kept it hidden. 'Not even Cora has seen it yet.'

'When will you let her see it?'

'I persuaded her to wait until the day we intend to unveil it.'

'And when will that be?'

'The day that Chaggfords is officially opened for multiple occupation.'

He had managed to stave Thurston off, somehow persuading him that, if he were to take even the briefest look at what Wachmann had come to consider to be his greatest work to date, he would smash it, on principle. 'No one must see it,' said Wachmann. 'Not until I'm ready.'

The coach house was built from stone that was as grey as the sky that had hung over Marshfield, but the vines that crept up the walls were a blaze of crimson. It was all such a contrast to flatlands that had been devoid of any such vulgar display of colour. They had been a watercolour production, the river rising and falling in accordance with the season, the tide, and the rainfall, the reeds on its banks like the tips of so many fingers breaking through the water.

It had inspired a piece that was currently being exhibited in one of the better-known galleries, *Hand of a Drowning Man*. It was tasteless, he knew that, but it was also saleable, and Thurston, who found it interesting, had referred to it a moment ago.

'What made you sculpt it?' he said.

Wachmann turned from the window to face a room that seemed filled with what could only be described as a golden glow. The effect was contrived, too obvious, the result of a modicum of artistic ability. Interior designers, thought Wachmann, were like the majority of modern poets: they tended to live too long.

'The hand is mine,' he said.

'What are you reaching out for?' Thurston asked.

'Someone who never comes.'

Thurston, his suit expensive, his manner determinedly unthreatening, replied: 'The hand wouldn't happen to be drowning at Marshfield, by any chance?'

'Not that I'm aware.'

'Shall we explore the possibility?'

'What's the point? We've discussed Marshfield *ad infinitum* over the years.'

It was an evasion Thurston had no intention of allowing him to make. 'You read the papers. You knew the remains had been found.'

'I didn't, actually. Remains of what?'

Thurston ploughed on, regardless. 'A body. Probably that of a woman.'

'Dangerous places, reservoirs. She must have fallen in.'

Thurston couldn't help himself. He laughed. 'I doubt very much she fell inside a wardrobe.'

It was Wachmann's turn to smile. 'I suppose not.'

'So what do you make of it?'

'I find it depressing.'

Thurston gave him the look he reserved for patients who were being less than forthcoming. 'You find everything depressing, Richard. Isn't that why you're here?'

'You tell me.'

'I might be able to do just that if you tell me how you feel?'

'Feel about what?'

'About the fact that remains have been found hidden in a wardrobe at your parents' former home.'

'I don't know.'

'You must feel something?'

'All right,' replied Wachmann. 'I feel . . .' He searched for a word, and spoke the first that sprang to mind. 'Numb.'

'What kind of numbness?'

'How many different kinds of numbness are there?'

'Well,' said Thurston, getting into his stride, running a hand through hair that was perfectly groomed and perfectly brown despite his fifty years. 'Numbness can stem from horror, grief, shock, disbelief, fear – which do you think it is?'

Wachmann was getting the picture. 'I suppose I'm shocked,' he admitted. 'I mean, it sort of proves she went back to Marshfield after the party, doesn't it?'

'Does it?'

With an edge to his voice, Wachmann replied, 'She left the

party with Ian and Joan. I followed in my own car. I saw Ian drop them off at Somerville.'

'And you're sticking to that?'

'It's the truth.'

'Even though her remains have been found?'

Wachmann answered abruptly. 'I think that's enough for today, Dr Thurston.'

'Sit down, Richard.'

'I don't want to. I'd really rather get on with some work.'

Thurston stood up, walked across to him, and put a fatherly arm across his shoulder. 'I'm not a policeman, Richard. I'm not here to judge or punish. I'm merely here to help, and you know that whatever is said between us is totally confidential. I couldn't go to the police even if I wanted to.'

That wasn't true, and Wachmann knew it. There was certain information that a psychiatrist had a duty to tell the police if it came to light, but he wasn't about to enter into an argument about ethics. He merely wanted to get out of there. Thurston's line of questioning had been a sharp reminder of what it had been like to be questioned by Driver, and it wasn't a memory he particularly cared to resurrect.

Trust Helena to be found. He might have known she'd never let any one of them live in peace, not in the long term. What was the last thing she'd said? It came to him in the instant he recalled the terror that prompted the threat: 'They'll find me . . .'

'Sit down,' said Thurston, again, so Wachmann sat in the plushly upholstered room, staring at the stone-mullioned windows and seeing only the sky thickening with a mist that would cover the parklike grounds by mid-afternoon.

'The police intend to bring the remains to the surface.'

'I'd rather not know.'

'You may have no choice,' said Thurston. 'If it's established that they are indeed the remains of Helena Warner, they may want to question you. I thought it better to prepare you in case they turn up on the doorstep.'

He had a point, thought Wachmann. Driver would be

long retired, but, if the police decided to reopen the case, no doubt he could expect a visit from his successor in the not too distant future.

'Tell me,' said Thurston. 'If it transpires that they are in fact Helena's remains, how will you feel about that?'

After a pause, Wachmann answered truthfully. 'Well, assuming, for a moment, that they *are* . . .'

'Assuming,' said Thurston, playing along.

'It won't surprise me.'

It wasn't the response Thurston had expected. 'Why not?'

'She wasn't the type to stay buried,' said Wachmann, simply, and he found himself wondering what effect the discovery of Helena's remains was having on Gilmore. It was possible he had spent the past twenty years preparing himself for the possibility that one day the remains would be found, but personally Wachmann doubted it. Gilmore had struck him as being the type of man who wouldn't be able to face the idea. Each time it entered his head, he would push it out. He would do what he'd done from the start. He'd run away.

Joan, of course, would exhibit the kind of guts Wachmann could admire in a woman. She might still protect Gilmore, she might not. It much depended on whether she still had feelings for him, he supposed.

He cast his mind back to the weekend of the party and recalled that he had been warned before her arrival that he would find her a bit of an oddball. 'Now, you have to be nice to Joan,' Helena had said, and that, alone, had been enough to seal her fate. She had fitted Helena's description of her to perfection, a person who had somehow managed to turn unattractiveness into an art form, a clumsy, besotted, insensitive woman, with no sense of style or colour, her accent thick, the vowels flattened.

To do himself credit, he had at least tried to find something appealing about her, but to no avail. Joan just *was*, he decided.

He had found it entertaining when it had dawned on him that she had a thing about Gilmore. On the morning of the party she had padded after him, following him round the house, driving him crazy, Helena barely able to hide her amusement. Eventually, Helena and Gilmore had disappeared to escape her, and, having been deprived of the object of her desire, Joan had turned her attention to him. 'What did you say you were reading?'

Wachmann had been struggling through the living room with a box of booze destined for Marshfield. 'Fine art.'

'Do you paint?'

He supposed it wasn't as stupid a question as it first sounded. There were students of fine art who hadn't lifted a brush in their lives and didn't intend to, but he wasn't one of them. 'I have been known to make the occasional effort.'

'What kind of stuff?'

Stuff? thought Wachmann. How can she refer to an artist's work as stuff? He struggled with the box and panted, 'All kinds.'

He made it to the door, opened it with one hand and managed to hold on to the box with the other, Joan sitting on the couch, watching him as if barely noticing he could do with some help. 'What's your favourite?'

'Favourite what?'

'Painting.'

'Mine, or somebody else's?'

She thought it through for a moment and said, 'Yours.'

Without thinking, he replied, 'I painted some butterflies a while back. I'm fairly pleased with the way they turned out.'

Butterflies, he thought. She'll think I'm out of my mind. He almost explained that they weren't the kind of butterflies one might expect to find on a birthday card, but he really couldn't be bothered. Besides, he couldn't explain without showing it to her, and he didn't intend to do that.

'Show me,' she said.

'Tomorrow, maybe. I'm a little busy right now.'

'Go on,' she pleaded. 'Show me now. It won't take a minute.'

'It's up in my room. You probably won't even like it . . .'

Before he could stop her, she'd made for the foot of the stairs and was climbing towards his room. 'Don't go up there,' he called, and, putting down the box, he plunged after her. Already, she had opened the door, and he charged in behind her, staggered by her audacity.

'What a neat room. I thought artists generally lived in chaos.'

'Most artists try to make sense of the chaos they live in.'

'You wouldn't think so, not with the kind of stuff most of them produce.'

'I doubt you know much about what any artist produces.'

The comment was either lost on her or ignored by her, he wasn't sure which. He felt violated by the way she had penetrated his room, and he stood in the doorway, willing her to leave.

She turned, and for a moment, he thought she might oblige, but she merely said, 'Where is it then?'

'Where's what?'

'This painting of butterflies.'

He wished he'd never mentioned it, and, more to get rid of her than to satisfy her curiosity, he walked towards the bed, pulled a canvas out from beneath it, and leaned it against the wall.

She looked at it, tipping her big fat head this way and that like an overlarge, clumsy bird. 'They look like a woman's inner thighs.'

'That's the intention,' said Wachmann.

'And you've painted butterflies right up next to her . . .'

She was so crude, thought Wachmann, so utterly incapable of expressing herself with anything even approaching charm. He couldn't help comparing her reaction with Helena's sultry response of 'Paint some on me.'

She had slipped out of the wrapover skirt before sitting on the bed, a slip of silk barely hiding the mass of pubic hair, and he had rooted in a drawer for coloured inks, had pulled them out, and had dipped the tip of a fine sable brush in each of the bottles in turn to produce butterflies identical to those in the painting. When they were finished, he had held a mirror to her thighs and she had looked at them in the reflection.

'Satisfied?' he said, and she pulled the slip of silk to one side. 'This is the most beautiful butterfly of all,' she replied, and the soft fluted lips of her vagina were wet, inviting, glittering like the wings of some exotic species.

'What are they?' said Joan.

'Red Admirals,' said Wachmann, and then she did something that caught him out completely, something that surprised and disturbed him more than anything Helena could have done: she looked up at him, her eyes overlarge in the thick-lensed glasses, and said, very softly, 'They're beautiful.'

It was perhaps that comment alone that prompted him to sketch her from memory in the months following the party. It was not, perhaps, his most realistic piece of work, but then he hadn't sketched her as she appeared to the outside world, but as he saw her from that day on, a sensitive, feminine soul trapped by some cruel trick of fate in a body that disgusted her. He felt her pain, and portrayed it.

He had intended to send it to her as a gift, but there had been something about her obsession with Gilmore that frightened him, and he had been afraid that she might turn her attention on him if he did. If that happened, he would, at the very least, reject her, and he didn't want to hurt her. She didn't deserve that.

She looked round the room, the walls crammed with pieces of work, some of them executed on scraps of paper Sellotaped to the wall, others having been framed and thoughtfully hung. 'What's it like to be you, to see things as you do and to be able to portray them so that others can see them too?'

He covered the painting, eased it back under the bed, and pulled a folio out from behind the headboard. He laid it flat on the floor, untied the strings and invited her to look.

She thumbed through the sketches, and when she came, as he knew she would come, to a sketch he'd made of Gilmore, she stopped thumbing. He hadn't known what to expect. Shock, perhaps. Helena might have laughed. Helena might have suggested that *ménage à trois* that Driver suspected had existed between them, but Joan merely said, 'Does he know?'

'No, and neither do you. It doesn't mean I'm gay. It merely means I'm capable of appreciating a good body, male or female.'

'I'd love to have it.'

'I can't allow that.'

'He'll never see it, I swear.'

'It isn't that. It's just that I'd be encouraging you to continue longing for something that will never be yours.'

He'd hit the nail squarely on the head, and she was embarrassed. 'I didn't realise it was so obvious.'

'Believe me, it's obvious.'

He didn't say anything further, thinking it might be better to leave her to get used to the idea that she was making a fool of herself, and a few moments later she said, 'I know I'm not attractive.'

He wasn't about to try to persuade her otherwise. It would have been a lie, and she would, in any case, have seen through it. He flipped the folio closed, tied the strings, and put it behind the headboard as she added: 'And I know he'll never leave Helena for me.'

'He'll probably never leave Helena, full stop.'

'What man in his right mind would?'

Wachmann thought back to the fluted lips of her vagina, the coarse, almost vulgar smile behind those fabulous eyes and the coarse, almost vulgar sexual act that he had committed as one might commit any crime, there having been about it a sense of danger tinged with shame, self-disgust and a desire to obtain similar gratification should the opportunity to do so ever arise.

'Come on,' he said, 'we'd better load the car.' And after she left the room he locked it behind her and followed her down the stairs.

9

The morning, after Rigby's visit, Driver stepped out of the centrally heated bungalow and breathed in air that was charged with minuscule particles of ice. Twenty years ago, he had stood on the bank of the reservoir and, despite the fact that the entire country had seemed to be at the mercy of a summer described in the press as one of the hottest since records began, Marshfield had been cold.

He wasn't sure why. There was no adequate reason to explain the chill in the air, the way in which the water had seemed to absorb the heat of the day, and, if it had been cold during summer, Driver was certain of one thing: it would be bloody freezing now. He had therefore wrapped up warmly, but doubted it would make much difference on a morning spent standing on the bank to watch as the remains were brought to the surface.

There was a lot of standing around to be done on a job like this, but he thanked his lucky stars he was a spectator and not a diver. Not only would he do anything rather than submerge himself in freezing water with poor visibility, but he wouldn't much fancy handling remains that had been submerged for any length of time. Mind you, it wouldn't be the first time he had seen a body that had decomposed in water and he knew what to expect. With luck, the remains would be skeletal, but, if Vaughan's description was anything to go by, it was rather more likely they would resemble a child's worst nightmare.

He didn't want to think of Helena like that. In each of the photographs supplied by her parents, she had come over as being something of a stunner, and it didn't seem right that a body so alluring in life would be so repulsive in death.

He walked towards the car, Rigby's words coming back to him as he described what Vaughan had found: 'The jaw came away in his hand. He won't forget that in a hurry.'

Driver could imagine.

A mile after leaving the A40, Gilmore turned onto a tarmac road signposted for single-lane traffic only. It wound its way round what had once been the back of Marshfield, and he followed it to within sight of the copse that had sheltered the flood plain from the north. Now it sheltered the water, a vast expanse that stretched from bank to bank like so much sheet metal. Dull. Grey. Still.

From his vantage point, he could see a crowd held back by a cordon, a crowd miserable under a rain that was finer than dust, a barely perceptible, yet somehow relentless, downpour. They stood almost perfectly still, watching the police, forensic and media, and it wasn't the cold that made them stand like that, thought Gilmore: it was the air of threat that was peculiar to Marshfield.

It was this air of threat that the media had picked up on, this saleable air of threat that would line their pockets, and photos of the house as it had once been had already appeared in the papers. He wasn't surprised to see them. Any reporter worth his salt would have made straight for the local archives, but the archives wouldn't provide evidence of what the house might look like now with its lichen walls and silt-covered floors, so readers had been forced to use their imagination and visualise, from interviews Vaughan had given to journalists, precisely what he had seen.

A flicker of light in the water drew his attention and enabled him to locate the divers' approximate position; but, unlike those who were trying to picture them moving around the interior of a house they could only imagine, he was able to visualise what they were seeing with some degree of accuracy. He had furnished that house; had spent the weekends there with Helena.

He felt a sudden pain behind the breastbone and attributed it to the memory of the way she had sometimes looked up at him. He had thought he had forgotten her face. Now he knew he would never forget it. Not really. It might escape him for years at a time, but it was there, ready to surface, to smile, to die.

He left the path and threaded his way through the trees until they thinned, the water stretching before him, devoid of translucence or any variety in shade. It was so completely still, so utterly opaque, it could have been concrete poured from hill to hill, the greyness broken only by the launch now skimming through the water.

Ultimately, the divers would bring the body to the surface and tie it to the outside of the launch, having bound it first in something resembling a white plastic sheet. He had seen it all before. Other stretches of water, other bodies, a fascination for such scenes having enticed him to stand, observe, and wonder whether the day would come when he would witness the same thing at Marshfield.

He made his way to the front of the cordon and remembered what it had looked like the last time he had stood at this spot. There had been no reservoir then, merely the wide shallow river that spread like a spilled drink over land that it rendered unfarmable for the most part, and it was the very wetness of the land that had provided a sanctuary for birds and plants, many of them rare. They, like their habitat, were gone now. Gone for good.

Some yards to his left and on the other side of the cordon stood a man he recognised from a photo in the press: Rigby, thought Gilmore, his tall, lean frame remarkably similar to that of Driver – or, rather, Driver as he had been twenty years ago. Then his eyes were drawn back to the water as the divers surfaced. It felt to Gilmore as though they had been down there an age, but in fact the whole operation had taken less than twenty minutes, and, after they signalled the launch, he witnessed, from a distance, the way in which the remains were strapped to the side.

He stood transfixed as the launch powered its way to shore. It was as though the man at the helm had decided to land as close to the cordon as possible in order to entertain the crowd, but he stopped several yards from the bank for fear of grounding the launch, and it was left to the divers to slip into the water, untie the remains, and carry them to shore.

They laid them on the bank, and the crowd pushed forward, uniformed men holding people back as best they could.

Gilmore stayed where he was in the knowledge that, if he were to look, he would find it difficult to believe that the tangle of bones belonged to a face he had once touched with fingers that had marvelled at the texture of the skin. It would look fragile, he decided; fragile in the way that the wing of a bird looks breakable to the touch, and mentally, he dressed the bones of the face with flesh, much as a forensic scientist might dress a skull with wooden pegs and precisely the right depth of clay to reveal an identity.

He turned to leave, head bowed against the rain, and found there was someone in front of him, somebody blocking his path with the stubborn persistence that he himself used when blocking the past from his mind, and as he looked up his initial irritation was replaced by a stab of shock.

'Small world, Ian.'

He wondered why it hadn't occurred to him that Driver might be there. Such had been the media attention, he should have realised the possibility existed. Their eyes met, locked together, and held for a moment, Gilmore faltering first.

He fought the urge to run, to escape, knowing, even as he experienced the momentary panic that there *was* no escape. Not really. However far he ran, Driver would find him, ready to make good on a prophecy made in the interview room at St Aldate's.

'I'll break you, Ian. Maybe not today. Maybe not for many years to come. But one day . . . I'll break you . . .'

10

Gilmore had gone, the crowd having closed over him like a wave, but Driver went down to the cordon and shouted to Rigby and Dalton. They left the remains and approached the cordon that he, like any other member of the public, was obliged to stand behind, and Rigby said, 'Didn't know you were here.'

'Didn't want to bother you,' said Driver.

Didn't want me to tell him not to come, more like, thought Rigby.

'What's the problem?' he asked.

'I just saw Gilmore.'

'When?'

'About two seconds ago.'

'You sure it was him?'

'Positive.'

'Cheeky bastard,' said Dalton. 'Where is he?'

'Gone,' said Driver. 'Took one look at me and evaporated.'

Don't blame him, thought Rigby. Driver was probably the last man on earth Gilmore had expected to see at Marshfield, but then he supposed that Driver could probably say the same. 'Happy reunion, was it?'

'He looked a bit surprised,' admitted Driver. 'He probably thought I was long dead.'

Rigby made no comment. He also made no move and Driver added, 'Don't you want to go after him?'

As Rigby and Dalton led him through the cordon towards the remains, Rigby replied, 'We need to confirm the ID before we start getting excited about Gilmore. Besides, there's no point asking him questions that failed to pin him down twenty years ago. I'd rather leave him alone until we've got something new.'

'We've got a body,' said Driver. 'That's something new, and in your position, I'd have brought him in yesterday.'

'You're not me,' said Rigby, and Driver left it. There was no point antagonising Rigby, and he had to accept that he'd retired, that Marshfield was no longer his case.

Rigby said, 'Don't worry, Bill. We know where he is. If and when the time comes, we'll pick him up, no problem.'

'Oh?' said Driver.

'He never moved from Oxford.'

Rigby said nothing further and, exasperated, Driver said, 'Is it a state secret, or are you going to tell me where he's living?'

'Milton,' said Rigby. 'Housing estate, fairly recently built.'

'Does he work?'

'Software company in Abingdon.'

Driver was surprised. He had expected more of Gilmore, he didn't know why.

Rigby added, 'You realise that, even if dental records prove this is Helena Warner, it won't be enough to crack Gilmore's story, not unless Poole and Wachmann change their story.'

'Poole and who?' said Dalton.

'Wachmann,' said Driver.

'Where did they fit in?'

'Joan Poole was a friend of Helena's, if you could call her that . . .'

'And Wachmann?'

'Wachmann was also a first-year student at Worcester. Gilmore read classics. Richard Wachmann read fine art. They shared a house in North Oxford.'

It hadn't made sense to Driver. Why forsake the relative

luxury of college accommodation in favour of a cold, inconvenient, two-bedroomed house in North Oxford?

He and a junior officer, Slater, had gone there to speak to Wachmann when Gilmore was first held for questioning. 'Nice place,' Driver had said. 'How long have you lived here?'

'Since the beginning of the Easter term,' said Wachmann. 'Where's Ian?'

'Down at the station.'

'Again?'

'Again,' confirmed Driver.

'Why don't you leave him alone?'

Driver had wanted to reply, 'Because he's a killer', but thought better of it.

'What kind of bloke is Gilmore?'

'What kind of question is that?'

'You know him, share a place with him; you must have some opinion.'

'You've lost me,' said Wachmann. 'What's he like in what way?'

Driver let a pause hang between them. 'Let's start with drink,' he said. 'Does he drink?'

'Sometimes. Not often.'

'Too much?'

'Sometimes. Not often.'

'And when he drinks, how does it affect him?'

Wachmann, resigned to it, bored almost, replied, 'It makes him drunk.'

Ignoring it, Driver had said, 'Then what?'

'He sleeps, mostly.'

'Ever known him to get out of hand, get aggressive?'

Wachmann replied, 'Now you mention it, he does have a habit of murdering people after the second glass of wine, but other than that he's delightful.'

Driver had asked for that, he supposed. He left it, and wandered into the kitchen, Wachmann following, unwilling to leave him in any part of the house unwatched and no doubt wondering what Slater was doing in the upstairs rooms.

From here, it was possible to see the full extent of a garden that was both long and narrow. It swept towards the canal, a mooring jutting out into the water, the timbers rotting. Gilmore would see that each time he looked out from the bedroom above the kitchen.

Slater had searched that bedroom, and what he had found behind panels – roughly constructed to form a false back to a cupboard – had been some of the hardest pornography Driver had ever encountered.

He had shown it to Wachmann. 'Take a look. Go on. You must have seen it before?'

Wachmann had flicked through it rapidly, the expression on his face telling him all he needed to know. And yet, even then, and for reasons Driver had not been able to fathom, he had tried to shield Gilmore. 'We rent the place. You can't hold Ian responsible for magazines that a previous tenant hid at the back of a cupboard.'

'Really?' said Driver. 'Expensive stuff like that, you'd have thought whoever owned it would have taken more care.'

Wachmann had made no comment. 'Come on,' said Driver, 'they belong to Gilmore, right?'

No answer, but Driver had seen a flicker of fear. 'What has he got on you?'

'Nothing.'

'You're covering for him, you and Joan both. Why?'

Wachmann had turned away from him then. 'I have a tutorial.'

'It can wait.'

'I've got exams at the end of this term.'

'You might not be at liberty to take them.'

There had been no response.

'Come on, Richard. I'm getting to like this story, so let me have it again. What happened after the party broke up?'

Wachmann's agitation had pleased him. 'I've *told* you. I drove myself home.'

'Anyone with you?'

'No.'

'You didn't get lucky at the party?'

'No.'

'Good looking bloke like you – not gay, I take it?'

'No.'

'Didn't think so,' said Driver. 'So you drove home. What about Gilmore?'

'He dropped Joan and Helena off at Somerville. Then he came home.'

'Helena didn't come back with him.'

'No.'

'Bit odd, that, don't you think?'

'I don't see why,' said Wachmann.

'They were lovers,' said Driver. 'I'm not an educated man, Richard, so you'll have to excuse my crudeness, but I would have thought he'd have preferred to bring Helena back here with a view to getting his end away rather than dropping her off at college.'

'It was late, and anyway, there was Joan to consider.'

'She could have stayed here – slept—' Driver was going to say 'Slept with you?' but thought better of it. Besides, he'd seen Joan. Chances were, Richard wouldn't have taken her up on the offer even if she'd made one. '. . . Slept on the couch,' he finished, and Wachmann, who realised what he had initially intended to say, ignored the comment with something approaching contempt.

'Good-looking woman, Helena,' said Driver. 'Bet you wouldn't have minded a bit of that.'

'You disgust me.'

'Oblivious to her looks, were you?'

'I didn't say that.'

'So you fancied her then?'

'I didn't say that, either.'

Quietly now, Driver taking him to one side as if suggesting they should keep this strictly between themselves, he said, 'Not a *ménage à trois*, I take it?'

'You've lost me again,' said Wachmann. 'I'm reading fine art, not French.'

Driver laughed and left it. 'So Gilmore wasn't drinking that night?'

'Christ,' said Wachmann. 'How many times?'

'As many as it takes,' said Driver. 'Where are you going?'

'Like I said, I've got a tutorial.'

Wachmann had grabbed his jacket and had stormed towards the door.

'I haven't finished.'

'Arrest me then. Or fuck off.'

Driver had chosen the latter option for the moment, experience having told him there would come a time when Wachmann would show more respect of his own accord. That time might come in an interview room, or in a court of law, but Driver had been certain it *would* come.

He took his leave of Rigby, walked through the trees to his car, and felt, rather than saw, the reservoir fall away as he drove up the hardcore road.

Those magazines. Somehow, he hadn't been able to imagine Gilmore getting a kick out of stuff like that. He didn't look the type. But he didn't look the type to kill, either, and whatever else Driver might or might not have been certain about, he was at least certain that Gilmore *was* a killer.

11

The Sunday paper Joan was in the habit of reading carried a full-length article complete with photograph of the reservoir, and it brought it home to her that, after two days of dwelling on what had been found at Marshfield, she still didn't know how she felt. She had always suspected that one day the body would be found, but she had also suspected that its discovery wouldn't affect her in any way.

She was therefore surprised when it came as a shock, and even more surprised when she wept for a moment. The tears had just seemed to come, spilling down her cheeks.

She looked round the flat and wondered what Helena would have made of it had she seen how she was living. She could even imagine herself saying, 'It's only temporary, Helena, just until I get on my feet financially and can afford something better,' because, even now, she would be apologising for the fact that she was poorer, dumber and plainer than Helena. If she were alive today, Helena would no doubt have a wonderful flat, a wonderful job, and a wonderful marriage.

But she wasn't alive. She was dead. It was there in black and white, and, although she had known it for years, seeing the discovery of her body reported in print had somehow managed to bring it home to her.

She stood up and went to the window. Her living room would once have been a bedroom and from it she had a view of the council houses opposite. They marked the beginning of an estate that sprawled for miles, and over the past few years she had come to accept that, like her parents, she would probably end up living in one of them. It was a fate preordained, like the colour of her skin and the inexplicable bouts of depression that were apt to descend on her for months at a time.

She moved away, sat down, and picked up the paper again. The article said that the police hadn't been able to establish an identity yet. She could have saved them a lot of trouble by contacting them to give them Helena's name, but they would want to know how she knew and that would take some explaining. She could hardly say she had helped to hide the body. She could imagine the response: 'Why didn't you tell someone? Your parents, or the police? Why did you keep quiet?' Why, she thought, does *anybody* keep quiet under such circumstances? Why does a man who has used a prostitute who is later found dead refuse to come forward so that the police can eliminate him from their enquiries? Why does anyone refrain from admitting that, while they were enjoying an illicit meeting of some sort, they witnessed an accident, a robbery or anything else that would require them to say precisely what they were doing at the time?

She couldn't go forward. If she were to do so, sooner or later it would come out that, although she had met Gilmore only the day before, she had ended up in bed with him on the night that Helena died.

She could imagine what Driver would have made of that if he'd known.

He had been a man of integrity, a man who had standards, a man who intended to discern the truth and pursue the consequences of that truth, and he had visited her several times at her parents' home.

That she lived in vaguely squalid surroundings hadn't bothered her at the time: the clothes strewn over the end of the bed to spill onto the floor like a corpse, a tartan leg clashing with a paisley arm, the rag of a hat like a bludgeoned head. The smell of life gone stale.

Joan hadn't noticed the staleness until her mother had shown Driver upstairs to the bedroom she and Cathy shared, but the expression on his face had shamed her and she had opened the window a fraction, the noise from the traffic filtering in, the slap of tyres through rain.

He must have seen many such rooms in his time, rooms he perhaps associated with deprivation or a criminal underclass; rooms she associated with a childhood spent living in a way that was natural to her immediate family, a way that had appalled and yet fascinated Helena, as though she had unearthed a sub-species.

She knew it was filthy, of course, and then, as now, she had intended to do something about it; but now, as she looked around her, she realised she would never do something about it.

It had disgusted Driver. But he wasn't there to moralise, to advise, or to despair: he was there to inform her that he suspected she knew more about Helena's disappearance than she was admitting to.

She had made the right noises, had pretended to an indignation she didn't feel and an anger she couldn't muster. And she had wondered whether he knew that she felt her knowledge of the circumstances surrounding Helena's death to be a form of power, something to be held in the palm of her hand like a life force ready to take on flesh.

'You lived here long, Joan?'

'All my life.'

'So how did you come to meet Helena?'

It was a fair question, and what lay beneath it wasn't lost on her. Driver had wondered what had drawn them together, their backgrounds being so different.

'We met when we both got a place at the local grammar.'

'And you've been friends ever since.'

'Best friends.'

'But you're at Southampton, reading for a degree in . . . ?'

'Journalism.'

Driver digested the thought, no doubt weighing her up and finding it impossible to imagine her having sufficient about her to make a success of it.

'Do you intend to live in Warrington after you graduate?'

'No.'

'Why not?'

There was the sound of voices from the room below, voices that had been raised in direct competition to the volume of the television. 'I want to get out,' she said quietly.

'I can understand that,' said Driver, and maybe he could, thought Joan.

She had known, instinctively, that his background was similar to hers. Another northern town, perhaps, but the estate he'd been born on probably much the same. She couldn't quite place the accent, but the occasional colloquialism sounded familiar, some Manchester suburb perhaps, one she didn't know, but one where similar values were held by people who came from a culture akin to her own. It made her afraid of him, and she guarded her every comment in case he proved capable of reading the subtext to get to the truth of the matter.

'So, Helena went to Oxford in a blaze of glory, and you toddled off to Southampton.' He digested the thought, looked up, gave a quick, bright smile, and said, 'How did you feel about that?'

Clever, thought Joan. Astute. 'I was very pleased for her.'

A silence developed, one that had no doubt told Driver all he needed to know. 'You were pleased.' The fixed smile remained firmly in place. 'That's nice. I expect she was pleased for you, too.'

'Naturally,' said Joan, a little more coldly than was perhaps wise, but she'd said it, there could be no taking it back, and it hadn't been lost on Driver, who added: 'And after you graduate, you'll be looking for a job.'

'Yes.' It came out flat.

'Think you'll get one easily?'

'No.'

'That's realistic,' said Driver. 'Jobs are hard to come by. Not that I speak from experience, I'm happy to say. I joined the force straight from school.' He leaned forward a little, as if to impart a secret. 'Twenty years' experience.'

The comment wasn't lost on her. He meant it as a warning, and she took it as such.

'I've investigated quite a few disappearances in my time.' The smile was still fixed. 'I pride myself on knowing, you might say instinctively, whether what we're looking for is a runaway or . . . a murder victim.'

'Must come in handy,' said Joan.

'Oh it does,' replied Driver. 'It comes in essential, does that.'

'I don't see how.'

'No?'

'No,' said Joan.

'Well now,' said Driver, 'let me explain. If I think we're looking for a runaway, I tell my superior officers there's no point throwing resources at it, especially when the person we're looking for is over eighteen. Old enough to make their own decisions, do you see?'

Joan saw, and Driver continued: 'If, on the other hand, I think we're looking at a murder victim, I pull all the stops out.'

'And what do you think you're looking at with regard to Helena?'

'You tell me,' said Driver. Joan declined, and he added, 'When did you last see Helena?'

'I told you. She invited me to a party last weekend.'

'How did you get there?'

'By train.'

'When did you arrive?'

'Friday.'

'When did the party take place?'

'Saturday night.'

As if he didn't already know, Driver said, 'Whose party was it?'

'Richard's.'

'What was it in aid of?'

'Nothing in particular.'

'He just decided to throw it?'

'That's right.'

'How many people turned up?'

'About twenty.'

'Did you know anyone other than Helena, Ian and Richard?'

'No.'

'No one at all?'

'No.'

'What time did it break up?'

'About two in the morning.'

'Unusual, wouldn't you say?'

'I don't see why?'

'Student parties,' said Driver, 'tend to last all night.'

'Not all of them. Besides, the water authority had erected notices warning people that the water was rising. We thought there was a risk it might rise faster than any of us anticipated and that we wouldn't have time to get out of the house if it did.'

'Then why have a party there at all?'

'It was Richard's party. Ask him,' said Joan, and she knew what Richard's answer would be. He would point out that he was born in that house, that he had been brought up there, and that he had the right to say goodbye in his own way, in his own time. If that time happened to be perilously close to the moment when his childhood home was to be submerged, that was his business.

'So it broke up at one in the morning, and then all four of you came back to Oxford.'

'Correct,' said Joan.

'Where did you and Helena spend the rest of the night?'

'Somerville.'

'Why not with Richard and Ian?'

'There wasn't room, at least . . .'

Driver seemed to know what she was going to say, that Helena might well have been more than welcome to sleep with Gilmore, but that, even if Joan had been inclined to jump into bed with him, Richard would hardly have been likely to be delighted by the prospect.

'You could have slept on the couch.'

'I chose not to.'

'Fair enough,' said Driver. 'So what did you do when you woke the following morning?'

'We skipped breakfast, got up late, then went to the house for lunch.'

'And after lunch?'

'Ian drove to Surrey. Look you know all this . . .'

'Why did he go home?'

'To collect some tickets to a concert at the Free Trade Hall.'

Driver considered this for a moment, just as he had considered it every time Joan had mentioned the tickets. It was almost a ritual with him, the pause, the look of mild bewilderment, the incredulous tone of voice when he eventually said: 'Why didn't he ask his parents to post them?'

'I don't know.'

'It would have taken him anything up to two hours to drive to Surrey.'

'I suppose it would, yes.'

'A bit drastic, don't you think? I mean, why not buy more tickets? Surely he would have been better off doing that than spending a fortune on petrol.'

'I don't know,' said Joan. 'Ask him.' And she knew that, once Driver became aware that the tickets had cost over £30 each, he would realise that a student strapped for cash might well choose to drive home and get them rather than replace them, so, as alibis went, it wasn't a bad one.

'How did you spend the rest of the afternoon?'

'At the house with Helena and Richard.'

'And that evening, you caught the train back to Southampton.'

'Helena waved me off,' said Joan.

'And that was the last time you saw her.'

In a tone that was dangerously playful, Joan sighed, and replied, 'I'm rather afraid it was, yes.'

'Be careful, Joan,' said Driver, softly, and his tone made her feel afraid.

'I meant it was the last time I saw her, that's all.'

Driver, his face expressionless now, said, 'Any idea where she might have gone after she left the station?'

'No.'

'She hadn't mentioned any plans for the evening?'

'No.'

'So you don't think she went to see Gilmore?'

He'd hit a nerve. 'He was in Surrey. You *know* he was, so why the fascination?'

'Why the fascination?' said Driver. 'Good question. I suppose it might be fair to say he's a fascinating man.'

'I'm glad you think so.'

'I do,' said Driver. 'And so do you.' It was so sharp an observation it shocked her for a moment. 'Tell me about Gilmore.'

'I don't know much about him.'

'Really?'

'Really,' said Joan.

'Did you find him attractive?'

'We only met the night before the party.'

'That doesn't answer my question.'

'I didn't really notice him, to be honest.'

'I think you did.'

'Well you're wrong.'

As if he hadn't been listening, Driver merely said, 'Would you have liked to have had sex with him?'

She was cautious about the reply. Suitably embarrassed. 'I'm a virgin, Mr Driver.' And before he could probe further she added, 'Anyway, let's face it, I'm hardly in Helena's league.'

'Meaning?'

'He wouldn't have looked at me.'

'He might have done, with Helena out of the way.'

'People like Ian don't look at girls like me.'

'You do yourself a disservice.'

'I do myself an honest appraisal. Isn't that what you came for, honesty?'

Driver changed tack rather than answer. 'So, if you don't think she went to see Gilmore after she left the station, where do you think she went?'

It was tempting to insinuate that she might have gone anywhere, with anyone, but Joan didn't succumb to it. 'I think she headed back to college. Whether she ever got there, I can't say.'

'What would she have intended to do when she got there? Any ideas?'

'Worked, in all probability.'

'Why do you say that?'

'She was aware that she had to maintain the standard of her work if she hoped to get a good degree.'

'You keep referring to Helena in the past tense.'

'So do you.'

He had smiled. It was a thoughtful smile. 'So Gilmore was in Surrey.'

'We've been through all this.'

'And he didn't intend to return to Oxford until the following morning, which was . . . ?'

'Monday.'

'Ah yes. Monday.'

He had it down to an art, the same questions, the same order, right down to the sudden, feigned loss of patience and the edge that crept into his voice.

'Let's start again, shall we. What happened at Marshfield?'

'I've told you.'

'Tell me again. From the beginning.'

'Dear God,' said Joan. 'How many more times?'

'As many as it takes.'

She repeated, word for word, what she had told him before,

and when she came to the end of it Driver allowed a silence to develop.

She sat with the silence, and he looked at her, and he smiled, and he said: 'I don't believe you.'

'That's your privilege.'

'No, not my privilege – my gut feeling.'

Leaning forward, conspiratorially, Joan had said, 'And what does your gut feeling tell you about Helena?'

Leaning towards her, his smile equally conspiratorial, Driver had replied, 'It tells me she died at Marshfield.'

'So where's the corpse?'

'Corpse,' said Driver. 'It's an odd word for a friend to choose. You were her friend, I take it?'

'Devoted,' replied Joan. 'So where is it?'

'Buried on the marsh,' replied Driver.

'Why don't you look for it then?'

'You know why.'

He was right. She knew. The water had risen; the house was submerged, and Driver was convinced they'd never find it. It wouldn't occur to him that they might have hidden it in a wardrobe. Nobody in their right mind would do such a thing if they had acres of marsh at their disposal, but what if the police were to search the house?

She couldn't resist asking: 'Why don't you send divers down to the house. You might find it.'

'No point,' replied Driver. 'We won't.'

And that, thought Joan, was perfect. She said, 'If you say so . . .'

'I do,' replied Driver.

'Then if I were you, I'd give up.'

It had been the wrong thing to say to a man like Driver. He had dropped all pretence at civility then, his words softly spoken, but crawling down her back. 'Not me, Joan. I'll never give up.'

The threat had hung heavy between them, Driver rising to his feet as he'd delivered a final warning:

'I'll be back.'

12

True to his word, he returned, and, each time, she'd repeated what she had told him before. His only response had been, '*You're lying.*'

How had he known she was lying?

He was right though. She had, of course, been lying, and during one of the customary silences that had followed this observation, he had broken with tradition to ask her what she was thinking. His approach had been almost paternal, and Joan, who had experienced precious little caring and protection in her life, had been caught off guard.

'Ian,' she admitted, regretting, instantly, the momentary weakness that had led to the admission.

'Do you think about him a lot?'

'No. I was merely wondering how he was taking Helena's disappearance.'

It was the nearest she could safely come to asking how he was, how he was coping, whether he was cracking under the pressure.

Driver merely responded with, 'He never asks about you. I daresay he doesn't give much thought to you other than to wonder whether you're backing his story.'

It was unexpected, and the truth, the brutality of it, hurt her. She doubted she had been able to conceal that momentary stab of pain from Driver, particularly when he added: 'He doesn't even *like* you, Joan. Why cover for him?' She made no response, and he added, 'What happened between you that night?'

'Nothing,' said Joan, and she found it remarkably difficult to lie about *that*. Part of her would have denied his very existence if that was what it took to protect him, but another part of her wanted to tell the world that they'd made love.

She wasn't ashamed of it. On the contrary, it had been tender and brutal and highly sexual. At times, she believed it had been the only truly sexual experience she had ever had. It was just that she was afraid that, if the police viewed her behaviour as promiscuous, they might very well choose to believe she had had more to do with Helena's death than she was admitting to.

She hadn't known what to expect of sex. She certainly hadn't expected it to hurt, although she had read somewhere that it could, and, by the time he'd realised sex was what she wanted, he was wild with rage and had hurt her quite a lot. And when he had said, 'What would you do if she caught us like this?' she had realised that, even as he was making love to her, he was thinking of Helena, but strangely enough, it hadn't seemed odd. She cared, of course, but she was so used to Helena taking precedence in all things that she wasn't particularly surprised.

She wondered whether he had guessed that, for her, it was the first time. Probably not. Men have highly preconceived ideas about what motivates women to behave as they do, she thought, and he would have told himself that virgins don't behave like that. They don't throw their virginity at a virtual stranger.

But he wasn't a stranger. Not to her. Over the months, she had come to know him intimately through Helena's correspondence. It would be absurd to say that she had fallen in love with him through Helena's eyes, but she had come to know what he liked, what he did, what he wanted. She could have told him things about himself that his own mother wouldn't have known, and, looking back on it, she supposed he would probably have been horrified had he suspected that

Helena was in the habit of confiding the most intimate details of their sex life to some former schoolfriend.

That said, those intimate details had comprised but a small part of the letters. The rest was taken up by her description of Oxford, and it all sounded so – so totally unlike Warrington, that was all. The climate was warmer, the winters were shorter, the people were taller and thinner and smarter. It was all a far cry from the damp and the gloom, the lack of a job and her own dim existence.

Looking back on it, she realised, of course, that Helena's letters had merely served the same purpose as the type of romantic fiction that whisks a woman into a fantasy world where she is the heroine and the tall, dark stranger is the man she has longed for every night of her life. It was certainly true that Joan was able to imagine what it might feel like if Gilmore were to make love to her, and her throwing her virginity at him had merely been the consummation of a relationship she had allowed herself to believe existed between them.

It had been a mistake, of course, but then to surrender one's virginity outside marriage usually is, as she had discovered when he had pushed her away, dressed himself, and left the room abruptly.

She wondered what he would think if they were to meet after all this time. Twenty years down the road, she had lost what little allure she possessed at nineteen, her plain, round face having thickened, the crêped skin that rested on her lashes being accentuated by thick-lensed glasses, but then she had never been anything to shout about. Fact of life. One she had learned to live with.

She also wondered how he was reacting to the discovery of the body, turned to the back page of the newspaper, and found a continuation of the article. Above it, there was a photograph, a face in the crowd held back by a cordon, and it answered her question. She hadn't seen him in almost twenty years, but it was him all right, and the realisation that he had had the audacity to witness the body being brought to the surface seemed staggeringly bizarre. And then it struck her as funny and she started to laugh. But it wasn't funny. Not really. She shouldn't laugh.

She had tried to contact him during the months following Helena's disappearance, but without success. The following October he was to have started his second year at Worcester College, but it transpired that he hadn't gone back and the college wasn't willing to divulge his home address on the grounds that it was confidential.

She had written to him care of the college, but her letters had been returned, unopened, and ultimately she had been grateful they hadn't reached him. When writing them, she had taken such pains to make them appear casual, but it was all too easy to read between the lines and she realised now that he would have known immediately that she was infatuated with him. But at least he would also have known that, although they had met, made love, and parted within the space of two days, she had developed feelings for him. To call those feelings love would be absurd. She knew that. But, at the time, she had believed that what she felt for him was love, which was why it was so very hard to come to terms with the fact that the brief, sexual act that had meant everything to her had meant nothing to him. *She* had meant nothing to him.

It had taken her years to see that.

13

The farmhouse looked what it was, semi-derelict, uninhabited, the buildings surrounding it covered with ivy, hidden by trees, and melting into the scenery as if the earth were reclaiming it.

A van pulled into what once served as a driveway, flattening the grass under tyres devoid of tread. More a riot of colour than a vehicle, its bodywork depicted signs of the zodiac in blue, red and gold, and, when the side door opened, a woman emerged, the child on her hip struggling to be set down.

He slithered from her grasp, his nails snagging on a full cotton skirt that was threaded through with silver, jumped to the ground, and ran to a bearded, braided father, whose ivory-pierced ears were a fantasy of texture to the small, delicate palms of his four-year-old child.

'This it, Dad?'

'This is it.'

He scooped the boy into his arms and plonked him onto the roof of the van where the sun and moon shone skyward in luminescent paint. 'Home,' he added. 'For a while, at any rate.'

The woman shivered, cold in an acrylic shawl. 'Where are we?'

'Burford.'

'Where's that?'

'Still in Oxford, just.'

She glanced around at countryside that undulated into the distance. 'Bit remote.'

'Good. No one'll bother us.'

They made for the house, its chimney cracked, the walls as thick as the stone of the barns that surrounded a yard at the back.

'We'll have to break in,' he said. 'Shouldn't be a problem.'

She wasn't listening. She had stopped in front of the house as if considering whether what they were doing was wise. 'I dunno,' she said. 'I've got this feeling.'

She got no response. He knew about her feelings. The only thing he could say in their favour was that at least they wore off, given time.

He lit a fire, and smoke billowed into the room, the result of a combination of blocked chimneys and damp wood. It got on their lungs, caused them to cough, and threw out little warmth.

'I'm cold,' she said.

He pulled a mattress of sorts across the floor. 'We'll manage, for tonight.'

The boy clawed at her skirt. 'Is this where we live now, Mum?'

'For a while.'

'I'm hungry.'

She wasn't listening. Ivy trailed across the windows. It clawed at panes that were held by putty that crumbled to the touch. Here and there, a gap in the vines gave a view of the barns to the back. They looked ominous. Abandoned. Watchful. 'I've still got this feeling.'

He indicated the mattress. 'Sit down. It might wear off.'

'Can I go outside, Mum?'

'All right then, but stay at the back.'

The boy ran towards a door that led to the kitchen, the sink porcelain, the floor flagged, and once he'd gone his mother sat cross-legged on the mattress. 'I hate this place.'

Time of the month. Cycle of the moon. Women were bloody strange, and that was that. 'I'll make some tea,' he said.

He filled a pot with water from a container brought in from the van, boiled it on the fire, and poured it into mugs, one teabag between them. She looked tired, he thought, a great deal older than twenty-four. If not for the kid . . . But that was just it. He couldn't part with the kid. All that stuff about flesh and blood, there was more in it than you gave credit for when it came down to it.

He sat on the mattress beside her, reached out, and tried not to feel the mild irritation she caused him by pulling away.

She lay down, and he settled beside her, feeling the mattress damp, but a faint warmth emanating from a body that was temporarily out of bounds. He drank the dregs of her tea, the teabag bobbing around in the bottom of the mug, lay down beside her, and closed his eyes for what seemed a very short while.

When she woke, so did he, the stirring of her body arousing him, until he remembered; then he checked a watch that no longer worked, for time that didn't exist.

'Where's Bo?' she said.

There was no noise, no running or shouting or calling for them to come and see where he was, what he was doing; but, when they sat up, they saw him in the doorway, his face solemn, his wide hazel eyes unblinking, unseeing.

'What's wrong?'

He ran to his mother, crawled onto the silver-threaded skirt, and buried his head in her breasts.

She stroked his hair and touched his face with the tip of a finger. 'What is it?'

There was no reply, just a desire to get as close to his mother as possible.

His father stood up, strode across the room, and ran through the kitchen to the yard.

The barns formed a quadrangle here, the only exit a gate

that led to the fields beyond. The entire area was covered with dead grass, the stems knee-high, the path that had once led through it overgrown.

Bo had made a trail through the grass, one that led to a small wooden door set into the wall of a barn. It was slightly ajar and wide enough for a child to slip through, and, as his father pulled it open, the topmost hinge gave completely, the door falling to reveal a narrow passage.

It opened onto an interior that was littered with obsolete milking equipment and a trough that was positioned in front of some cast-iron stalls. It was filled with foul-smelling water, and he could see nothing through the film of slime that sat on the surface like oil; but telltale drips on the side spoke of his son's having dipped his fingers in, only to pull them out, and he did the same. There was something in there, something that felt like soap.

No, he thought, not soap, some soft thing having stroked his fingers, the movement of the water having caused it to caress them. For a moment, he couldn't work out what it was. And then it came to him, the shock immense, the realisation that his son, young though he was, must also have realised instantly what it was.

Hair, he thought. Sweet Jesus. *It was hair.*

14

Dalton, who had been on the point of leaving the incident room, reached for the phone, half despising himself for the brief temptation to leave it ringing. 'Dalton,' he said.

In front of him, the desk he had claimed as his own was neat, the paperwork that had tied him to it for the better part of the day having been dealt with, and he pulled a notepad towards him as he said, 'Where?'

He wrote rapidly as the details were conveyed, his pen flicking across the page as though controlled by some supernatural force. 'You sure there's no mistake?' he said, and a voice replied: 'A patrol checked it out. There's no mistake.'

Dalton ended the call, replaced the receiver, and dialled Rigby's home number. He had gone off duty earlier than usual, something about his wife's birthday and taking her for a meal with the in-laws. Rather him than me, thought Dalton.

Much as he expected, he got the answering machine, and after the tone, he said, 'Frank, it's John.'

Almost instantly, Rigby's wife plucked the receiver from the holder. 'Hello?'

'Sheila,' said Dalton, 'I need to speak to Frank. It's urgent.'

There was a pause, a silence that spoke volumes, and then a note of resignation in her voice as she replied, 'I'll get him.'

The evening was about to become a write-off, and she knew it. 'I'm sorry,' said Dalton.

There was no reply, just the sound of a receiver being put by the side of the phone and then the click of heels on a wooden floor that was polished and varnished and warm. He pictured her walking into the living room, the skirt short, the legs long, the mid-brown hair soft and loose. Rigby was a lucky bastard; no denying it.

He heard voices, then Rigby took the receiver, his voice aggressive.

'This better be good?'

'We've got a body,' said Dalton.

There was a pause, and then, 'Where?'

'Barn in Burford.'

He gave the location, and waited while Rigby made a note of it. 'Contact McPherson,' Rigby said. 'Ask him to meet us there.'

After ending the call, Rigby stood in the hall a moment.

Murder was rare in Thames Valley, the few that occurred tending to be drug or domestic related. What with the find at Marshfield and now this, he was getting more than his fair share, and his immediate reaction was one of uncertainty.

He suddenly thought about Driver. Maybe he hadn't had the opportunity to blaze an academic trail through the exam requirements of some Accelerated Promotion Scheme, but Rigby couldn't help but envy him his experience.

15

It was 9.30 p.m. and the gloom had given way to an almost complete darkness. Rain lashed down on the windscreen with such force that the wipers made no impression, and Rigby's car bumped along the road, slowing to a crawl as it grew increasingly rutted.

He didn't mind the rain so much. He preferred it to the ice that would follow once it stopped and the temperature dropped, and he hoped his wife had reached the restaurant safely. He imagined the air of enjoyment she would manufacture in order to appease her parents, and considered resigning from his job to get a milk round. *I love you.* Those were the last words he'd said to her before diving into the car and heading for Burford. They were always the last words he said before leaving her on any occasion, partly because they were true, and partly because he was aware that a copper's job was growing increasingly dangerous. No telling what might happen, not these days.

'Sometimes, I worry that you won't come home,' she sometimes said, 'that one day someone will knock on the door and tell me you've been killed.'

It was a thought that crossed Rigby's mind more often than he cared to admit, but his only response was to pull her close, tell her he loved her, and add that he'd be back in one piece, no worries.

He put these thoughts aside and concentrated on the road. Burford was an area he didn't know well, and the narrow country lanes all looked the same, particularly in visibility that was reduced to a minimum by darkness and lashing rain.

There was a glow up ahead, and as he rounded a bend his suspicion that it was attributable to headlights was confirmed. Dalton, and a team of scenes-of-crime officers were already at the scene.

He pulled up in front of a cluster of vehicles and parked tight into the hedge, Dalton running through the rain towards his car as he climbed out of it.

'Who found it?'

'Squatters.'

'Where are they now?'

'Down at the station. Nowhere else to go.'

That was a job for Social, and Rigby didn't allow himself to dwell on it now, or on the questions he would put to them later. He turned as a car pulled up behind his own and recognised it as belonging to McPherson. The pathologist climbed out of it and Rigby noted that he, at least, was dressed for the weather. He pulled up the hood of a waxed-cotton coat as Rigby and Dalton approached him, Rigby saying, 'You got here fast.'

'A mere matter of geography,' said McPherson. 'Let's take a look.'

They made for the barn along a path that was overgrown, the grass and weeds slapping wetly against their legs as Dalton conveyed the details of how the body had come to be found.

As Rigby made mental notes of what he was being told, he took stock of the barn. It was of a type that was found all over the Cotswolds, the stone it was built from two feet thick, the wooden doors having long since rotted away. The roof was tiled, the edges of the slates jagged, their grip on life at best precarious. But other than that it was solid, and they entered via the passage as the child had done.

Scenes-of-crime boys had already rigged up lighting and, as Rigby and Dalton followed McPherson in, they saw cast-iron stalls set into the floor, and a stone trough in front of the stalls. It was a feeding trough, thought Rigby, and he visualised cattle standing in the stalls, sticking their heads through the vertical bars and reaching down for food while somebody milked them.

He peered into it and saw water covered by scum. It stank, and he backed away to observe as McPherson took samples before seeking and finding the means to drain it from the trough.

It ran into a channel and slopped down the drain, thick, slow-moving, a stinking mass of rot, and as it inched away it seemed to Rigby that the body was slowly rising to the surface.

'Jesus,' said Dalton.

Once the body was fully exposed, McPherson took samples, the gloves and mask giving him the appearance of a surgeon, the instruments that pricked and scraped and plucked seeming somehow barbaric. Rigby watched him and couldn't help feeling that what lay in the trough could not, at any stage, have been human, as though it was of monstrous origin, as though there was something about it that wasn't of this world, and it wasn't the way in which it had decomposed that horrified him: rather, it was the fact that it had about it an aura of absolute death that he hadn't come across before. 'Male or female?' he said.

'Female,' replied McPherson.

'Strangled, drowned, what?'

'I've currently no idea, but, as bodies go, this is more interesting than most.'

'In what way?'

'It's in the early stages of saponification.'

Saponification. It sounded like the kind of word that ought to be sounded through the bass notes of a harmonica.

'Saponi-what?' said Dalton.

'It's something that sometimes occurs when a body is left in water.'

'What causes it?'

'The body fats solidify and form a waxy substance. It clings to the bone and helps to retain the shape of the body. Often, as in this case, the extremities don't contain sufficient fats to enable the process to keep them intact, so they decompose as they would normally.'

Almost involuntarily, Rigby looked at the long white arms, the way in which they tapered to skeletal fingers as though someone had taken a knife and stripped the flesh. 'How long does it take?'

'Anything from three months onward.'

'And how long can a body stay intact in these circumstances?'

'Once the adipocere is formed it can remain stable for years.'

'Can you tell just by looking how long this has been here?'

'I'll have to do tests to confirm it, but I'd say we're looking at several years, at least. The flesh bears a resemblance to soap. If you touch it, you'll see what I mean.'

Rigby had no intention of touching it, not with his fingers, not with gloved hands, not even with a pole if he could help it.

McPherson added: 'In the later stages, the flesh bears more of a resemblance to chalk.'

'These tests,' said Rigby. 'How long do they take?'

'A couple of hours. You'll know by morning.'

'Keep me informed,' said Rigby.

He left the barn with Dalton and they made for the house, entering via the kitchen and finding white-suited Scenes-of-crime people taking it apart with infinite care. It was as though they intended to pare the entire house down to bare stone with nothing more than tweezers to help them. Chances were, it would yield nothing of value, but you could never be sure, and you had to cover your back.

There was a toy on the windowsill. A Power Ranger. 'How's the kid taking it?'

'Hard to say,' said Dalton. 'He knew what he'd found. No doubting that.'

Rigby imagined the four-year-old fingers dipping into the water and fumbling with a shape that didn't belong there. He also imagined him in the years to come, waking suddenly from a recurring nightmare that didn't make sense – that would *never* make sense.

'Someone'll sort him out,' said Dalton, but Rigby wondered about that.

There was a pattern on one of the window panes, a pattern made by the fingerprints of a child who had stood with his face pressed close to the glass, looking out at the barn. 'Poor little bastard,' he said.

16

Cora, who could picture the Jacobean hall as it might have been two hundred years ago, wondered what her ancestors would say if they could see it now. The panelling was still intact, but, if she looked down from the gallery, she could see the top of a concrete support that rested on the foundations. Its flat grey surface was level with the floor of the hall, a square of concrete which would ultimately be concealed by the plinth and statue it was designed to bear.

It seemed to her that the house was taking on a new identity, a new life, and she was glad now that she hadn't accepted an invitation to live with her former companion while work was in progress. She had wanted to remain to the bitter end, not merely because she was interested in the way in which the conversion was being carried out, but because she felt she had a duty to stay, particularly since the house was currently filled with people she didn't know.

Most were builders, and it wasn't so much that she mistrusted them: on the contrary, she enjoyed their company, and was amused by the deference they showed her, a deference that arose from their considering her to be a batty old dear. And so she was, but what did it matter? What did anything matter now?

She left the galleried landing and descended a flight of stairs that had once been used only by servants. They led to the cellar, and once there she caught sight of Wachmann rooting around in a room that had once been used for storage purposes. She watched him for a moment, witnessed the way in which he lifted objects of interest and replaced them with a gentleness unusual in most men. It was a gentleness that James had possessed, and that was another reason for remaining at the house. A close physical proximity to Wachmann reminded her of so many things about James, things she had almost forgotten.

She threaded her way towards him and he turned at the sound of her approach. 'Mind you don't fall,' he warned, and Cora avoided the Georgian firedog minus its partner. It lay among other, miscellaneous items, items she recalled from childhood: a blacking-box, a bellows, a block of soap the size and weight of a brick. How often had she seen Alice sweep across such blocks with a scrubbing brush, Alice who seemed forever stooped at the foot of a flight of stairs; Alice whose arms were pale for lack of sun, her hands those of a much older woman, the fingers swollen, the knuckles raw. 'If I fall, I fall,' she said.

In front of her, the concrete support seemed a monolith of sorts. Smooth, vast, and deathly grey, it had about it the look of a vault awaiting some form of inscription. 'It's horrible,' she said.

'No one will see it from the hall.'

'I still don't see why it was necessary,' said Cora.

'The floorboards wouldn't have supported a statue and plinth the size of a small van.'

'The statue of my father wasn't supported by anything.'

'It was smaller,' said Wachmann, 'and the plinth was positioned over one of those.' He pointed up to where a lintel ran above their heads, and noticed small, iron hooks screwed into the beam beside it. For a moment, he didn't know what they were, and then he realised that this had once been a coldroom of sorts, and that game would have been left on the hooks to hang, sometimes for weeks on end. He said, 'The lintel was a strong enough support for your father's statue, but it wouldn't have been enough for the statue of James.'

Cora turned away, and, with a perception that surprised her, Wachmann added: 'You don't like this room.'

'It's just a room,' said Cora. 'A cellar, like any other.'

'To me, perhaps, but not to you. What do you see in it, Cora?'

Shelves stacked with preserves and tinned foods, glassy-eyed birds staring down from the hooks; the look of disbelief that was on my mother's face. 'Nothing,' she replied, but she fixed her attention on a zinc-lined box lying by the bellows, and Wachmann, who was sensitive to such things in a way that reminded her of James, touched it. It could almost, he thought, be a coffin of sorts, and he lifted the lid, half expecting the body of an infant, a stillborn, newborn thing. 'What was this used for?'

'Ice,' replied Cora, and it was as though fingers of freezing air seeped up from it to curl around her body. She heard her mother's voice: 'What have you got in the box, Cora?' and her own reply of 'Don't lift the lid. Please, Mother, don't lift the lid,' but she had lifted the lid to find the child concealed.

She had placed her trust in the thickness of the walls, but her faint cries for help from a God she didn't believe in had filtered through an airbrick to be heard in the garden above – a garden where her mother was walking, a mother who could differentiate between the cry of a snared animal and that of a woman giving birth. Agony, thought Cora, all is agony – and she recalled how very primitive it had been, how utterly cruel, like lying in a cave, cold, naked, hungry, and gnawing at a bone. Perhaps, thought Cora, death will be like that.

A feather, discoloured, but clearly that of a pheasant, lay beneath the lintel, and, in casting her mind back to the last time Chaggfords had land enough to shoot over, Cora realised it must have been there this past fifty years or more. She doubled back, picked it up, and said, 'For my album: life in the great old house . . .' Then she left the cellar, Wachmann following as she climbed the stairs to a room that had once been allocated to kitchen staff.

Cora remembered it as it had been when it contained the large rectangular table they sat round at mealtimes. Now, the staff furniture had been replaced with a bed, the rosewood cabinet and two comfortable armchairs. 'Come in,' she said, sensing rather than seeing Wachmann behind her.

He stepped into the room. 'This where you've been living for the past few months?'

'Yes.'

'Why down here?'

She couldn't answer that. She didn't know him well enough to reveal what she had revealed to Dr Thurston: that as a child she had frequently fled to the servants' quarters in order to avoid her father. 'I don't really know. I just feel comfortable here.'

She opened French windows that led to a kitchen garden. It was a wilderness, the grass and nettles now higher than she could ever remember. Soon, it would be uprooted, and its fragrance would be supplanted by the sharp tang of asphalt. A skip would arrive to take the debris away, and one of the first things to go would be the desecrated statue of her father. It lay on its side in the undergrowth, a metal rod protruding from the neck, the head some feet away, the face minus its nose.

Wachmann touched the stone, finding it soft, breakable. 'It's a strong face.'

'He was a strong man.'

He broke a piece of wax from the plinth and revealed an initial. He looked up, their eyes meeting, but Cora declined to confirm what he suspected to be the case: that, on each anniversary of the date that James's plane had been shot down, she had held a Service of Remembrance. He could visualise her lighting the candles, sticking them on the plinth, and watching, over a period of years, the wax drip down to obliterate the inscription.

They made their way back to the house, Wachmann rubbing the fragment of wax through his fingers, feeling it crumble. Dust to dust. It would melt in the sun come spring, but not before.

He stepped into Cora's room and closed the french windows, windows that led to a patio so overgrown that only the hardness beneath a soil breathed onto the paving by wind could give it away. Weeds had taken root, had grown up against the windows, were pressing their frondlike fingers to the glass. Left to their own devices, the day would have come when they pushed out the panes and entered the room to grow. They did not know their reign was coming to an end, thought Wachmann; did not know that tomorrow, or the day after, machinery would tear them from the soil. Perhaps, once the statue was revealed, a different machinery would do the same to him.

Cora indicated the few possessions she intended to take when she went: the last of her really good clothes, the rosewood cabinet, an armchair she rather liked, the piano she never played. Photographs, of course, mainly of the family, but one or two of horses her mother had bred and an oil that depicted Slipper, the King Charles who had slept at the foot of her bed for most of his fourteen years. 'This is it,' she said. 'This is the sum total of my life, of anything that means anything to me. It's all I'm taking.'

'What about the statue of James?'

'It's to stay.'

'Why?'

She didn't reply for fear that he wouldn't understand how she could go to the expense of commissioning something vastly expensive, and then proceed to leave it behind within days of its being unveiled. It was to stay at the house, protected from the possibility of vandalism. All she asked was to be allowed to see it when it was unveiled, and then, like James, she would fly away. Forever.

17

Gilmore sat at his desk, paperwork strewn across the surface, the subject matter of no more interest to him than the people he worked with or the company he worked for.

His office was five miles from Oxford city centre, and if he looked out he could see countryside sliced through by the A40. But he didn't look out. Not often. Vast expanses of land had an adverse effect on him these days. They reminded him of Marshfield, the low-lying land around Abingdon tending to flood at certain times of year, and that too reminding him of something he'd rather forget.

As a rule, he kept to his desk and kept his mind on his work, and he knew about the software he supplied. He knew what the users needed from it, and could solve their problems without having to apply what one of his tutors had once described as a fine mind. But the fine mind had belonged to a boy of nineteen. Gilmore was thirty-eight now, and he felt his intellect to have been dulled by a lifetime of working at jobs that didn't interest him in environments that left him cold.

The door opened and Mike Foley poked his head in to say, 'Cross Keys, round about eight?'

'Sure,' said Gilmore, and Foley disappeared.

He made some attempt at tackling the paperwork that had accumulated during the morning. It proved impossible. Periodically, panic poked fingers into every crevice of his thoughts, stirred them around a little, and left them circling in his mind like the blobs of powdered milk that were floating on tea in his white plastic cup.

He stabbed at the blobs with a white plastic spoon as he read reports, briefs and summaries, but all the while he remembered the shock of turning away from the cordon to find that Driver had been right behind him.

Odd that he had loved Helena yet sometimes had difficulty picturing her face, whereas the mere recollection of Driver's name brought an image sharply to mind. He had changed, aged, shrunk into himself, but it was the same old Driver, and the mere fact of his being there had served as a reminder that, for as long as he was alive, he would always be a danger.

His phone rang. He looked at it. Let it ring. And then he picked it up, his hand shaking, his voice doing the same. 'Gilmore.'

'Ian?'

'Sue,' he said, and the relief was overwhelming.

'You sound strained.'

'You left me,' he said, simply. 'Note on the fridge. Remember?'

Her turn to sound odd. 'I forgot a few things,' she replied.

If she had, he hadn't noticed. Or, rather, he hadn't noticed they were hers rather than the long-forgotten property of the women who had preceded her. Was it that he chose very much the same type of woman, or was it that women naturally gravitated towards collecting the same type of object – a natural-bristle hairbrush, an oatmeal face mask, a colourless lip gloss and those curious, ultra-feminine items of equipment that nestled by his razor?

'Tell me what, and I'll post them.'

Silence.

And then, 'For God's sake, Ian. Didn't I mean *anything* to you? You haven't called me. You haven't even asked *why*!'

He pictured her face and that hurt, pinched look he had grown to know so well. He hadn't wanted to hurt her, and at any other time he might have replied that he was sorry it was over; but he would also have added that it *was* over.

She said something he didn't quite catch, and he didn't bother to ask her to repeat it because, as she spoke, all he could think of was the probability that any minute now the police would turn up to take him in for questioning.

When he made no response, she repeated it. 'I said I think we should talk,' and quite suddenly, he had no patience for her.

'Look,' he said, 'I'm busy, Sue, what do you want?'

'I thought . . .' she began, but he knew what she thought. She thought that by leaving him she might manage to jolt him into making some sort of commitment. It hadn't worked for the women before her, and it wouldn't work now. 'That's it,' he said, and hung up.

For a moment, he experienced a sincere pang of guilt. What he had done was uncalled for, and she hadn't deserved it. He considered phoning her back to apologise but knew that, if he did, he'd end up meeting her for the talk he didn't want about a relationship that was over. So he didn't phone, and the guilt faded to be replaced by worry.

The fact that Driver hadn't been able to break him hadn't reduced his respect for the man. Or his fear of him. During the investigation, never a day had passed without his driving down to Surrey to pick him up and take him back to Oxford for questioning, to sit him in that sparse square room and say, 'Now then. Let's start again shall we?' And then the questions would come. Questions he had answered countless times before: When did you last see Helena? What was she wearing? Where did you go? Did you have sex? Was there a fight?

Did you kill her?

He had simply repeated, as many times as it took, that he hadn't done anything. He didn't know anything. And, no, he had no idea what had happened to Helena. Absolutely none.

It was Joan who had saved his skin. Plain-faced, bespectacled and calm, she stuck to her story, convincing Driver that she had been the last person to see Helena alive and providing him with an alibi cast in stone.

Driver could think of no good reason why Joan would lie on his behalf unless a relationship existed between them, but nobody had ever seen them together; her parents and fellow students had never heard of him and *his* had never heard of *her*; and there was no record of either of them ever having contacted the other at any stage in their lives.

When he looked at it from Driver's point of view, Gilmore had come to the conclusion that, having seen photographs of Helena, and knowing her to be a stunner, Driver had probably been forced to admit that the likelihood of his carrying on a clandestine relationship with some plain, rather dull kid from Warrington was somewhat remote. Whatever the case, he had given up in the end. Not gradually, but quite suddenly.

Ironic, really, thought Gilmore. If he had been interviewed one more time, *just one more time*, he, exhausted to the point of breakdown, would have spilled his guts. He remembered every word of the letter: 'Dad, I am writing this before telling the police, because I wanted you to be the first to know . . .'

He had kept it in his pocket, ready to give to his father when Driver came for him as he had come for him every morning since Helena had been reported missing; but that morning he hadn't come, and the sense of relief had so overwhelmed him that Gilmore did something he hadn't done since the night of the party. He cried. He sat on the couch, his head in his hands, fighting for breath he couldn't find. And his father's face. He would never forget that look, or the way he had held him, rocking him in his arms in a way he hadn't rocked him since he was a child. 'It's OK,' he had said. 'I won't let them hurt you. I swear . . .'

Later, he had destroyed the letter. The moment for confession had passed. He doubted there would ever be another.

At the time, he hadn't understood why Driver had stopped hacking at him, but over the years he had begun to realise that without a body, and without any real proof that anything had happened to Helena, he hadn't had a choice, and the suddenness with which he had dropped the matter suggested to Gilmore that he had done it on the orders of a superior officer who needed him for more urgent matters, matters in which there was at least a shred of evidence to suggest he might get a result. In the case of Helena Warner, there was nothing, and, whilst it was virtually unheard of for an Oxford undergraduate with no apparent problems to go missing without trace, without proof that harm had befallen her, what else could he do?

He looked up. Outside, a thin, miserable sky threw drizzle on the buildings below, and inside Gilmore sat at his desk and, in remembering all this, realised that, if there was one small crumb of consolation to be had, it lay in the fact that his parents were no longer alive.

It seemed to him that his only hope lay in preventing anyone from coming forward with information against him at this late stage. He couldn't imagine they would, but recent events had shaken him, and he wanted to be sure. Trouble was, he had no idea where they might be. He suspected that Joan was living in Warrington on the grounds that she had family there. If so, Foley would probably hack into some computer and pull her current address if he asked him. Same for Wachmann.

It was possible, of course, that Wachmann was living somewhere in Warwickshire, but Gilmore doubted it. The compulsory-purchase order that had driven his parents from Marshfield had enabled them to buy a farm at Thornley Heath. Gilmore had spent a weekend there shortly before Helena disappeared and had met them. His mother had been friendly during his visit, but, following Helena's disappearance, whenever he phoned, she had spoken to him cautiously, almost fearfully. He wasn't sure what she knew, but she knew *something*, and he decided to go to Thornley, not only with the intention of finding out what, but of doing something to ensure she never revealed it.

had happened to [illegible]. [illegible] had a [illegible], and the [illegible] with which he had whipped the [illegible] suggested [illegible] more than he had done it [illegible] a [illegible] [illegible] asked him for [illegible] [illegible] there was at least a shred of evidence to suggest he might get a result. In the case of [illegible], there was nothing, and while it was [illegible] to [illegible] with no [illegible] [illegible] without [illegible] [illegible] [illegible].

He [illegible] with a [illegible] of the [illegible] and [illegible] and in [illegible] small [illegible] in the [illegible] [illegible].

He [illegible] that [illegible] forward with [illegible] at the [illegible] [illegible] [illegible] was he [illegible] suspected that [illegible] was living in [illegible] [illegible] would probably [illegible] [illegible] he [illegible] would be [illegible] [illegible].

It was possible, of course, that Brockmann was doing [illegible] put [illegible]. The [illegible] had [illegible] [illegible] had [illegible] to [illegible] [illegible] [illegible] [illegible] [illegible] [illegible] [illegible] [illegible] [illegible] [illegible] in the [illegible] and he [illegible] to [illegible] [illegible] [illegible] [illegible].

18

Merle Wachmann hadn't yet unpacked. Her clothes were still in suitcases standing by the bed, and they had been there since the afternoon of the previous day because a fourteen-hour flight from Johannesburg had left her too tired to bother with them.

A month ago, she had left the farm in the capable hands of a manager – something her husband would never have allowed had he been alive. But he wasn't alive. She had buried him eight weeks ago, and his death had released her to take a much-needed break.

She had felt guilty about it, almost as if she were betraying his memory, but she had family in Africa, family she hadn't seen for the best part of twenty years.

The day she had left the farm, an ice-cold wind had buffeted the animals into small shivering groups. The last of the green had gone from the grass and it shrivelled close to the earth. Ungrazable. Frozen. Dead.

She doubted Ernst would have referred to it as cold, but then it hadn't bothered him, and over the years she had given up trying to drag him away. He didn't want to leave the farm. Not for a week. Not even for a day. And that was that.

Occasionally, she had left him to it. She had gone to Cheltenham, to London, to Oxford, to anywhere civilised within a day's drive. But always alone, and always bitterly resenting the fact that he hadn't made the effort, if only to repay her for the effort she made every day of their married life.

Twice, in a fit of despair, she had left him altogether, but ultimately she had been dragged back by a shame that was the product of the values that people of her generation held; and each time, this same shame had made her resolve to do better in future, to be a better wife, a better person, more accepting, and more loyal; not only publicly, but in her heart, because she had known when she married him that he was a farmer, and had known also that, after the struggle of farming at Marshfield, Thornley must have seemed like a dream come true.

It hadn't seemed so to her, but then she didn't originate from farming stock and country life didn't suit her temperament, or her skin. In summer, she burned in the sun and the wind. In winter, she burned in the cold and the wind. But, whatever the season, it was always there, a torment that blew through her clothes, her bones, her life. She sometimes felt she had spent her entire marriage trying to shelter from it. But it was omnipotent, all-knowing, and vengeful, and whenever it found her, huddled like the cattle, or dying like the grass, it blew extra hard, just to teach her.

Two months ago, when she had stood by her husband's graveside, it had whipped the words from the vicar's mouth, and although she didn't doubt that he had said the appropriate things – that Ernst Wachmann had been hardworking, a good farmer and a good husband – she and the people standing with her had been obliged to take that on trust because no one had heard him. She had watched his lips forming the words and had caught the odd note from his voice as it battled against the wind, and lost. She knew how it felt.

In the distance, the village surrounding the church looked picturesque. In reality, it had little to offer but a poorly stocked shop, a post office that seemed perpetually closed, and her husband's grave. Socially, it offered the type of event that warranted tea and biscuits in the village hall, and what conversation there was tended to centre around mad-cow disease, set-aside land and hunt saboteurs. She felt she was the only woman in Warwickshire who didn't own a pair of green wellingtons and that if ever she bought a pair she would never escape; that the land would have her forever in life and that, ultimately, she would be buried in it as deeply as Ernst was buried in it now. She was sixty-one. She wanted nine good years. It didn't seem much to ask.

Standing there, at the foot of his grave, she had recalled a time when the freedom his death had enabled her to envisage had seemed so remote, so impossible a thing, that her resulting state of distress had prompted Ernst to call their GP. He had visited her the following day and had asked what she attributed her current state of distress to.

She had gazed past him to a window that looked out onto the flatlands, and replied, 'I should have thought that was obvious.'

'It may be to you, but not to me, so what is it?' he'd said, and she had tried to explain about the dream, the dream in which she clawed at the wallpaper, her hands tearing it off in strips that were no more than inches wide. As she pulled it from the wall, the corpses of birds common to the marsh fell to her feet, birds that were buried alive.

'How does the dream start?'

'I walk into a room,' she said, 'and the wall is patterned with different types of paper. I can't understand why the wallpaper isn't uniform, and I can't understand what causes the small mounds that appear under it, so I strip the paper.'

The doctor stood up. 'I'll prescribe something.'

She dragged her attention away from the window, the flatlands, the river, the reeds. 'And what, precisely, do you intend to prescribe?'

'A tranquilliser, of sorts. Something mild. Something to help you get by.'

He wrote the prescription, paused in the doorway and added, 'I'm not a psychologist, Mrs Wachmann, but I can't help wondering whether you sometimes feel like a small, trapped bird, longing for someone to free you. There could be something in that, don't you think?'

She laughed, so he left it, and by leaving it he also left her to tread, in her dreams, on animals that rose from the bog to drag her down to the marsh.

All in the past, thought Merle. The freedom denied her for so long would soon become a reality. The month in South Africa had clarified her thoughts and she had decided to put the farm on the market and emigrate. South Africa might have its problems, but at least it would be far away from the flatness, the greenness, the coldness and what she felt was the sheer pointlessness of staying where she was.

She walked from an elegant living room to a kitchen that had no such pretensions. Over the years, it had seen farm labourers, feed merchants, vets, agricultural advisers and bank managers, all of them treading the dirt onto stone-flagged floors that she had given up on. Now the kitchen door was closed. All contact by correspondence, please, she had begged, and, taking this as a sign of grief still fresh after eight short weeks and the shock of Ernst's heart attack, people had obliged by keeping their feet off the now shining stones.

She grabbed a paper and took it back to the living room, her heels clicking on the flagging before being silenced by the fitted carpet, and, after shaking it out to catch up on the news she'd missed while on holiday, she sank into a plushly upholstered chair that had been out of bounds to Ernst.

As she read the headlines, it occurred to her that, with luck, there would soon be some other woman sitting in that room. Some other woman who would spend her days looking out onto outbuildings that were modern in design and totally lacking in charm; some other woman to long for a social life that didn't exist in a part of the country that saw Leamington Spa as centre of the universe; some other woman to make plans to jump ship; some other woman to stay, despite it all, because she loved her husband.

The farm had killed him. The work. The wind. The cold. But most of all, the work. The relentless grind of trying to keep one jump ahead of the seasons, the weather and the bank. And Richard. Richard had killed him too. But she didn't allow herself to think about Richard. From the day that he had ceased to play any part in their lives, Ernst had pretended he didn't exist; his name wasn't mentioned, and people who asked whether they had children were told, in manner suggesting that further probing would not be welcome, that their only son was farming in the Transvaal.

She flicked to the second page and came across an article. It was the name Marshfield that first caught her eye, and she read it twice.

At first, she tried to dismiss it. She even turned the page. But then she turned back and read it again. Some days ago, remains had been found in a house submerged by the reservoir, remains that had now been brought to the surface and identified as those of Helena Warner. The police were asking for anyone with information to come forward.

There had been only one house at Marshfield. And it had been their former home. She didn't have to search her memory to confirm the fact. God knows, she had spent years looking out of the windows in the hope that, magically, a town with shopping precincts, cafés and people might have sprung up overnight. But there had only been the reeds, the bog and the birds. No other signs of life. Not what she called life, at any rate.

Minutes later, barely aware of what she was doing, she left the tea and made for the door. Somewhere, en route, she had kicked off her shoes and her feet were cold on the stone-flagged floor. It didn't matter.

Outside, in the porch where Kipper still waited for a master who would never come home again, she had a pair of soft leather boots. They had never seen mud. Not of the kind that divided the farm from the church. She pulled them on and walked out. For once, she wasn't aware of the wind or the fact that the threat of rain would become a reality before she got home. She hadn't taken a coat and already she was bitterly cold. She was walking away from the house – away from the newspaper really, the ink-smudged words appearing before her eyes as if superimposed on her retina.

The dog leaped about her, soiling her skirt with a coat thick with grease licked in against the elements, looking for work. The cattle scattered like billiard balls, moving in all directions as he homed in on them, nipping their heels, barking instructions, and, even if she had wanted to call him back, she wouldn't have known how. Ernst would have whistled, a sound so shrill that even the wind would have parted to let it pass, but she didn't care about the dog, or the cattle, or the ground that was frozen into deep hard ruts. She didn't know she was stumbling, and falling, or that she was crying; and she didn't care that the dog had bounded into the paddock where Ernst's old mare stood sheltering under a tree. She whickered, but Merle Wachmann was oblivious to the sound. She was oblivious to anything other than that she had to contact her son.

19

It was the smell that got to Rigby, the antiseptic smell that somehow failed to conceal the mouselike odour of death.

He was dressed in green overalls, his feet covered in what felt like oversize plastic bags, their grip uncertain on the floor of a lab that was tiled. It was possibly his least favourite place for a pre-lunch rendezvous.

McPherson made a start, the microphone clipped to the front of his gown and catching the words, 'Female. Height five feet six inches. Hair dark brown . . .'

Rigby stared past him to a series of stainless-steel sinks, an attachment for a hosepipe connected to one of the taps. His line of vision followed it to a drainage channel that ran the length of the floor, and he breathed through his mouth in anticipation of the stench that would come once McPherson opened her up.

He heard McPherson say, 'Ligature,' and dragged his attention back to the proceedings in time to see him indicating a thin weal that ran from ear to ear. 'She was strangled from behind.'

'What with?'

McPherson took a piece of Sellotape several inches long, used it to obtain an impression of the weal, and said, 'I'll check this for fibres but at a glance I'd say it was wire as opposed to material or rope.'

He started his preliminary examination, beginning at the head and neck, moving across the chest to the abdomen, the upper and lower limbs, his fingers touching, stroking, feeling, his eyes doing the same.

He needed assistance to turn the body and then he repeated the process, starting once again at the head, noting any unusual mark, paying particular attention to bruising that appeared the length of the spine and attributing it to the body having been dragged into the trough after death had occurred.

His preliminary examination over, he made an incision behind the right ear, cutting cleanly through layers of skin and muscle, curving down to the sternum and groin and back up to the other ear. Once the organs of the chest and neck were exposed, he made a more thorough examination of the neck, slicing through the tissues, feeling for what he wanted.

Rigby tried to picture what her face might have looked like before it became a ball of rotting flesh and was reminded of the way in which the body had seemed to rise as the water drained. It was an illusion, but one that reminded him of a childhood fear: that of swimming in a river or sea, feeling something touch his legs, pushing it away and seeing, slowly – slowly – a body rise to the surface.

McPherson sliced through the breastbone, then used a vice to open the ribcage, the stench that rose from the body making all of them, even him, draw back for a moment.

It was a relief to Rigby to watch the speed with which he worked. He seemed reluctant to speak unless it was absolutely necessary. To Rigby, it seemed miraculous that he could bring himself to speak at all. Speech required breath, breath that Rigby held and then released economically, much like an underwater swimmer.

McPherson made an incision and peeled the scalp from the bone before sawing through the skull and lifting it clean from the brain. He spoke rapidly now, his intakes of breath sharp and shallow. 'The inside of the skull can reveal a pattern of old injuries giving a clue to the victim's lifestyle. In cases involving blunt instruments, skull fractures should match damage to the meninges and to the surface of the brain itself. In this case—'

Rigby decided he'd had enough for one day. He interrupted, 'Are you sure of the cause of death?'
'Yes.'
'We'll be off then.'
McPherson smiled. 'Hunger got the better of you has it?'
Rigby smiled back, weakly. 'You could say that,' he replied.

20

Gilmore ignored the bills and local newspaper lying on the mat, but he stooped to pick up a letter. Its pale blue envelope bulged with the pages within, and he had no need to open it to know it was from Sue.

He took it into the living room, but didn't open it; he left it on the arm of the couch, and looked at it as he drank his coffee in silence.

Normally, some broadcaster's voice would have provided background sound to the breakfast he had grown used to eating alone since Sue walked out, but Marshfield was still in the news and he couldn't face the prospect of its flashing up on screen; so the screen stayed grey, the silence remained, and he found himself trying to visualise the flat that she had fled to.

He only knew it belonged to a friend, that it was in central Oxford, and that, according to her note, she had only the temporary use of it. There had been a subtext to the comment that ultimately she would move out, but didn't know where, and he supposed she was waiting to find out whether the grand gesture of walking out would make him sit up and listen.

He didn't need to be *made* to listen. He'd heard her clearly enough, but every hint she'd made was a hint he had heard before from the women who had come before her and had left before her, having discovered, as she would discover, that a man who lives in the past can hardly be expected to commit to the future. So now she was padding around a flat that didn't feel like home, hoping for words he wouldn't say by way of phone, by way of letter, or by way of apology.

He tried to determine whether he missed her, and couldn't make up his mind. He missed the feel of her body, the way she curled up like a small child and slept with her head on his shoulder, and he missed the softness she'd seemed, somehow, to bring into his life; but he didn't miss those reproachful eyes, or the occasional erudite comment that had managed to bring it home to him that he was resigning himself to a future some might regard as bleak.

Bleak was a word he associated with the past. He couldn't picture it having a place in the future. He couldn't picture himself having a future, and heard the ghost of her voice: 'You're talking rubbish, Ian. Everyone has a future.'

No, thought Gilmore. Not everyone. Some people deny themselves the right to a future by committing acts that even their most loving counterparts would consider unforgivable.

He picked up the letter, and wondered whether to send it back unopened. Despite the weight and feel of it, he couldn't imagine her being verbose in person or on paper. She hadn't been a great talker at the best of times, and that had been one of the things he liked about her. Some of the women he'd lived with had talked him clean out of the house, and when it got too much, he'd taken refuge in the snug of the Cross Keys, Mike Foley sitting opposite. Now, he pictured him sitting in a cubicle at the office, the sides made of plasterboard and giving the impression that he, like his computer, had been installed in an overlarge box and dumped in some spare corner of the office block. It wasn't too far from the truth.

Still holding the letter, he punched a single key on the mobile phone, waited for the number to dial automatically, and got through to him.

'Mike, I can't come in.'

'What's up, mate?'

'I'm sick,' he said. 'Some kind of bug.'

'There's one going round.'

There always was, thought Gilmore, that non-specific provider of the convenient excuse. 'Listen,' he said. 'Could you do me a favour?'

'What?'

'You know about computers . . .'

'It's my job.'

Hacking into other people's systems wasn't part of it though, thought Gilmore, but he wasn't about to say so. 'How easy would it be for you to get an address for me?'

'It'll cost.'

'How much?'

'A pint.'

At any other time, Gilmore might have allowed himself a smile. 'I'm trying to trace a couple of friends of mine. People I knew twenty years ago.'

'How come?'

Gilmore evaded that and added, 'The first is a woman. Joan Poole.' And, as he paused to let Foley make a note, he suddenly found it ironic that he had gone to such lengths to avoid her for so long and was now going to such lengths to get to her before the police did.

'Date of birth?'

'Nineteen fifty-six. That's all I know.'

'Last known address?' said Foley, and Gilmore suffered an almost painful recollection of how he had felt whenever he had received a letter from Joan. Each had evoked in him a desire to recoil, physically, from the pale cream envelopes, their milky backs desecrated by an address that had been printed in large, capital letters.

Most had been written from the bedsit in Southampton, but the last two had been written from her parents' house in Warrington, and, even then, he had been able to visualise the squalor from all that Joan had told him on the night that Helena died. He had stood with his back to her, and was staring out at the darkness that smothered the marsh, and she had been sitting on the mattress, describing a lifestyle that was totally alien to him.

He had almost lost patience at one point, irritated by her conviction that, no matter how great her efforts to escape, she was destined to return to the estate to live a hopeless existence. *It doesn't have to be like that. You can change your destiny, it's up to you.*

'Rosamund Street,' he said. 'Blackwater Estate, Warrington.'

'When did she last live there?'

'Nineteen seventy-five.'

'That it?' said Foley.

'That's it.'

'It's not a lot to go on.'

'No,' said Gilmore. 'I know.'

He waited while Foley hacked into the computer, matching her name and former address to her National Insurance number, discovering she was claiming income support, and obtaining her current address. He gave it to Gilmore, adding, dryly, 'Sorry it took me so long.'

'OK, you're a clever bastard.'

The address caused him a momentary stab of pity. She hadn't even made it out of the road, much less off the estate. 'I hate to think what you know about your colleagues.'

'If you mean do I try to find out what people are earning, where they live, what cars they drive, I can assure you I've got better things to do with my life.'

Gilmore thought of him sitting in a bachelor pad night after night. No woman in his life, his only interests cricket, films, software, and what Gilmore felt to be an almost unhealthy interest in Kim Basinger's private life. 'You're a genius,' he said.

'Keep telling me. Who's next?'

'This one could prove more difficult. Could be he moved to Africa about twenty years ago.'

'Name?' said Foley

'Richard Wachmann,' said Gilmore.

'Date of birth?'

'Fifty-six.'

'Could you be more specific?'

Gilmore scoured his memory for some recollection of Wachmann's having had a birthday while they were living at North Oxford. Nothing came to mind. 'I don't remember,' he said.

'Last known address?'

'Thornley Heath, Warwickshire.'

'When did he last live there?'

'I'm not sure,' admitted Gilmore.

This time, the wait was longer, Foley cursing softly in the background, Gilmore growing bored and increasingly less hopeful as time ticked by. 'Anything?' he said.

'Nothing since seventy-six,' said Foley. 'You'll have to leave it with me.'

'What are the chances?'

'Remote, if he's in Africa, but phone me later.'

'How much later?'

'Try me this afternoon. I'll have a crack at lunchtime.' As an afterthought, he added, 'When will you be in?'

Gilmore wasn't sure. He intended to drive down to Thornley to see Merle Wachmann, and his plans for the following days much depended on what kind of reception he got. 'I might be in tomorrow. I'll give you a ring.'

'Fair enough,' said Mike.

He rang off, put the mobile down, and started to open the letter. The paper would be expensive, he decided, a shade darker or lighter than the envelope, the surface bearing a slightly rippled effect, possibly even a watermark.

He pulled out paper that matched the shade of the envelope to perfection. No ripples. No watermark. Just acres of that gentle, sloping hand.

Do all women write? he wondered. Or is it just that I somehow prevent them from expressing themselves within the relationship? Maybe they feel the need to express themselves only when it's over, if only to enable themselves to move on? But Sue, who had incorporated an extract from some theological text, appeared not to want to move on.

She had used the text to convey what she felt about him,

and the fact that she had inserted so unlikely a thing into what was essentially a love letter struck him as odd. In all the time they had lived together, they had never discussed God. It was as though she knew, intuitively, that it was a subject he shied from, felt himself unable to dwell on, feared even, but she had written that these few words described, better than anything she could write, how she felt, and he read them again.

> *I will never finally let you go. I accept you as you are. You are forgiven. I know all your sufferings. I have always known them. Far beyond your understanding, when you suffer, I suffer. I also know all the little tricks by which you try to hide the ugliness you have made of your life from yourself and others. But you are beautiful . . .*

It reminded him totally of Joan, it being precisely the type of thing he could imagine her to have been capable of inserting into one of her letters. The plain face, the dumpy physique; neither had blinded him to her sensitivity and whilst she lacked the ability to write anything like it herself, having read it somewhere, she would have remembered it, and, in thinking of him, would have sent it, as Sue had done, in the hope that it might somehow change the way he felt about her.

It wouldn't.

On an intellectual level, he could appreciate that the words were beautiful. On an emotional level, they meant nothing. They didn't touch him; and he wished he had returned it, just as he had returned the letters from Joan. Unopened.

He screwed it into a small blue ball, threw it into a corner of the room and watched it expand in the seconds that followed, retaining the same shape, the same creases, but the circumference enlarging so fractionally that it was almost beyond the power of the human eye to judge that it had increased at all.

21

He found no difficulty in locating the side road that led him out of the village, and he followed it until it forked and became the long winding track that served as a drive to the farmhouse.

He slowed to take a good look at it. Twenty years ago, it had been hidden behind a quilt of hedgerows, green and gold. Now, the boundaries that had divided field from field had been obliterated and the house was exposed in a landscape as vast and as flat as Marshfield.

Whether this had been done for reasons that related to current trends in land management, he couldn't say. Many farms were like this, he knew, but he also knew that Wachmann's father had loved Marshfield, that the very bleakness of it had appealed to him, and that it was possible he had tried to recreate that bleakness here. If so, he had succeeded.

The sky hung drab as a dishcloth, heavy and grey, bits of cloud clinging to it like scum from warm greasy water. It seemed to him a typical Thames Valley sky, as if Ernst Wachmann had somehow managed to transfer it along with the cattle, the tools, and the vehicles. But one thing had changed: if his memory served him correctly, the first time he had come here he had experienced the feeling of being surrounded by wildlife, invisible to the eye but there – comfortingly there. Now, there was no such feeling, just the cold ploughed earth, the ironstone house and the prefabricated buildings behind and to the side of it. All that was needed to complete the picture was the tall thin grass, the sprawling shallow river and the slow-flapping birds that nested in the reeds.

He slowed as the track grew increasingly rutted, finally pulling up at the back of the house, and, as he climbed out of the car, Merle Wachmann appeared, her boots thick with mud, the fine woollen skirt caked round the hem, a dog at her heels.

She stopped in her tracks, uncertain, nervous, but the instant he spoke her name, she knew who he was.

'Ian,' she said, but there was no smile. She made for the door to the kitchen, unlocked it, and turned to face him. She had been crying, he thought, the eyes red, the skin slightly blotched.

'I need to speak to you,' he said.

She hesitated. 'I'm expecting someone.'

'I won't stay long.'

Still, she stood there, and he added, 'It's cold, Merle. How about letting me in?'

Reluctantly, she opened the door, kicked off her boots and left them outside before leading the way to the kitchen. He followed her in and was able at a glance to ascertain what it was about it that was so different from the way it had been twenty years ago.

The first time he'd seen it, a waxed-cotton coat had hung dripping from a hook on the back of the door; a dog bowl half filled with meal had stood on a sheet of newspaper next to the Aga; farming magazines were strewn across the table; and soiled crockery from a recently and hastily eaten meal fought for space next to invoices, paperwork and a plate of biscuits.

Now, the kitchen was devoid of the clutter and mess that came of being surrounded by people who spent their lives out of doors. Not only were the surfaces clean, but even the stone-flagged floor had a sheen reminiscent of the patina on antique wood.

Merle, he thought, was still an attractive woman, but the

signs of her age were there in the way that the skin of her neck had lost its elasticity and a network of lines laced the corners of her eyes. She was dressed as if expecting at any moment to be whisked away to lunch, save for the stockinged feet, and, as if noticing that he was studying her, she glanced round the kitchen, locating shoes that had clearly been discarded in haste earlier.

He said: 'I expect you've read the papers.'

'Yes.' It was a simple statement of fact.

'I need to talk to you both,' said Gilmore, a statement of equal simplicity. 'You, and Ernst.'

He had presumed that Ernst would be where he always was: outside, oblivious of the time, the weather and the loneliness of his wife's situation, and when she said, 'He's dead. He died eight weeks ago,' Gilmore was too startled to say anything other than, 'What of?'

'A heart attack.'

It took him a few moments to accustom himself to the idea. 'What about Richard?' he said. 'Where's he?' And, instead of answering him, she replied: 'I could do with a drink.'

He followed her uninvited into a living room that was much as he remembered it, deeply comfortable, the quality of the suite complementing a few well-chosen items. There was a tea tray on the table, and the crockery was some elaborate china affair in white and gold. Tea had been poured but left untouched, the milk having formed a scum on the surface. Recalling the discarded shoes, he thought: She left the house in a hurry. I wonder why.

'Sit down, if you want to,' she said.

He lowered himself into a chair as she went to a cabinet, poured two whiskies, and handed him a glass.

'Marshfield,' she said. 'Why won't it just – go away?' She looked up. Smiled. 'Sometimes I dream we still live there. Something to do with the view from the window. It could almost be Marshfield out there. Don't you think?'

He smiled back. 'It could, as a matter of fact.' As an afterthought, he added, 'What made you stay with him?'

The hand that held the glass tightened momentarily. 'Things were different in my day. Women didn't just walk out.'

No, thought Gilmore, they died instead, sometimes physically; mostly emotionally.

'Merle, I need to contact Richard. It's urgent.'

'Is that what you came for?' she said. 'To find my son?'

There was an edge to her voice, and, treading with caution, Gilmore said, 'We lost touch, after Helena disappeared.'

'I know.'

'So where is he?'

Slowly, thoughtfully, she took the tiniest sip from her glass, the tumbler cumbersome against the small, fine mouth. Gilmore waited for her to think it through, and once she lowered the glass, she said: 'In all the years that we lived in Marshfield, he never once showed the slightest interest in farming. Wouldn't help his father. Hated the place. And then he decided that he hated Oxford too, that what he really wanted to do was farm in the Transvaal.' She tried to gauge whether Gilmore was accepting this before continuing: 'We inherited land there. It was convenient, I suppose. No need to raise capital. It was just sitting there, waiting for someone to take it on.'

Gilmore found it difficult if not impossible to believe. Wachmann, like his mother, had a liking for the finer things in life. Good clothes. Good food. Comfort. 'Merle,' he said, 'the remains that were found at Marshfield are Helena's. I think you know that.'

The instant he said it, it was obvious to him that she knew. 'We lived at the house at weekends,' he added. 'But you knew that too, didn't you?'

'It was none of our business,' she said. 'Once we sold the place, we couldn't control what happened there, though Ernst—' She stopped, and Gilmore was struck by her gentleness, her reluctance to say anything that might cause hurt, her femininity. She was like a fine china doll, her skin weathering towards sunset like cracked porcelain, and she didn't belong here, surrounded by bleakness and mud.

'Ernst?' he said, and hesitantly, she added, 'When he found out you were using the house, he was furious. If I hadn't stopped him, he would have gone down there to tell you to leave.'

It didn't surprise him. The first and only time he had met Ernst Wachmann, Gilmore had suspected that although his capital was now invested in Thornley, his heart was still very much with the wetlands. He had supposed it to be only natural on the grounds that when a man has spent a lifetime tending a particular acreage, nurturing crops from the type of land that would rather drown them than give them life, a bond would develop and it would take more than selling the place to break that bond.

'I need to find Richard,' he said. 'Will you let me have his address?'

'I'm afraid that's impossible. I don't know where he is.'

'But you must know. You've just said yourself that he's farming in the Transvaal.' And then, a little more forcefully, 'Merle – *you must give it to me.*'

'It's out of the question . . . I . . .' She paused to think and he left her to find the words. 'I've known for years that girl was dead.'

'But whatever you know, or think you might know, I deserve a chance to explain.'

She wouldn't look at him. A bad sign, he thought. 'I also came to ask you not to go forward with information. Just let the past be the past. I know it's a lot to ask.'

He watched her carefully, watched natural caution turn to fear as she recognised the isolation, the helplessness of her situation.

'Merle . . .'

She stood up. 'Please,' she said, 'I'd like you to leave.'

Gilmore found the wind, unhampered by natural windbreaks, to be thin, cold and utterly penetrating. He froze in the few strides it took him to walk to the car, and climbed into what felt like a sanctuary of warmth.

He had never felt less like driving anywhere, but he knew he had no choice but to drive down to Warrington straight from Thornley. The prospect of seeing Joan didn't appeal to him at the best of times, but it would have to be done.

As he backed out, he glanced at the window as if half expecting to see Merle Wachmann, and he noticed that the stonework was crumbling in places, that the path to the door was mud and that what served as a kitchen garden was a tangle of weeds. Guttering that had corroded vibrated in the wind, half held by the brackets but threatening to fall, and he found something desolate in the general decay, the isolation, and the way in which everything, including himself, was quietly falling apart.

22

Rigby sat in his office, the veal-coloured walls and air of calm conducive to concentration, and he looked at the report that had come from McPherson. It stated that the victim found at Burford had been strangled from behind. No surprises there, thought Rigby.

His own report was lying on the desk of a superior officer and it stated, quite simply, that they had precious little to go on. The house, which had last been occupied fifteen years ago, had yielded nothing of interest; there were no clothes or personal effects found at the barn, in the house or on the surrounding land, and there wasn't a single pointer to who might have killed her or why. What was more, Oxfordshire was chocker with derelict barns. Farmers refrained from pulling them down because there was always the chance they might get planning permission to convert them into dwellings. The trick was to prop them up, to keep them on their feet, and keep their options open. That meant there were any number of potential hiding places for a body, and despite there currently being no evidence to suggest it, Rigby couldn't help wondering whether there were more where this one came from.

Whatever the case, this was no ordinary murder. An examination of the interior of the barn had revealed a crudely made device to ensure a thin stream of rainwater kept the trough topped up, and the remains had been put there not only in the knowledge that they were unlikely to be found in a hurry, but in the knowledge that with luck, they would decompose slowly.

It wasn't a comforting thought. Given a choice, the majority of killers tended to dispose of their victims in a way that would ensure that they wouldn't be found, or that each passing day destroyed a little more of the evidence as the body decayed. This was a new one on Rigby.

According to McPherson's report, the remains might have been lying in the trough for not less than three and not more than fifteen years. That's helpful, thought Rigby, but he had at least confirmed that they were the remains of a woman in her mid to late twenties, and that her remains had been submerged shortly after death occurred. Chances were she was raped, but he hadn't been able to determine whether this was the case. The body was too old. The evidence saponified. What a word, thought Rigby. What an end to a life. *Saponification.*

He turned to a further report, one in which McPherson had confirmed that the remains found at Marshfield were those of a female in her late teens and that death had resulted from a series of blows that had fractured the base of her skull.

It was accompanied by photographs that had been taken at Marshfield prior to the remains being brought to the surface, and, as he looked through them, he came to the conclusion that, if he hadn't known they had been taken underwater, he wouldn't have known what they represented, for, despite the skill with which the photographer had taken the shots, what they portrayed was a blur.

But there was nothing to blur the shot of what had been hauled up and laid on the embankment. It was crystal clear, close-ups showing him detail he would rather not look at. But he had to look. It was his job.

Hard to imagine that someone might have made love to her once. Whatever it was, this thing, it didn't look human. And yet, even without the benefit of McPherson's report, Rigby would have known that these were the remains of a woman. The bones of the face were fine, the vertebrae bone-china bobbins disappearing into a skull that was small, like that of a child.

He recalled what Vaughan had told him when giving a statement: 'I thought it was a joke. A sick joke.' And he had reached out and pulled the jaw from the face.

No joke.

He dragged his mind away from the thought that there might be some connection between Marshfield and Burford. Both bodies had been found in water, but so what? he asked himself. Marshfield and Burford were thirty miles apart, the murders could be separated by almost as many years, and Helena Warner was bludgeoned to death whereas the victim in the trough had been strangled. No connection, thought Rigby, but the feeling that Driver so often referred to stirred in his gut like a tapeworm, chewing away, giving him no peace.

Rigby wasn't given to gut feelings. He preferred evidence, preferably concrete, and right now there was nothing concrete to suggest the murders were linked, so he dispensed with the idea, attributing it to fantasy born of that primary fear of water, death and rot.

The phone cut into his thoughts and he answered it, one eye still on the photos of Helena Warner. 'Rigby,' he said.

'Driver,' said Dalton.

'Put him through.'

Rigby waited while Dalton arranged the connection, and before Driver could speak, said: 'Forensic pulled Helena Warner's dental records. It's a positive match.'

For a moment, Driver said nothing. Savouring the moment, thought Rigby.

'Can you come in for an hour?'

'When?' replied Driver.

'How about now?'

'Give me twenty minutes.'

There had been, Rigby reflected, a note of satisfaction in his voice, a note that was about to be replaced by one of bitter disappointment.

* * *

Driver was led past an incident room that had changed out of all recognition since his retirement. Everywhere he looked, he caught sight of a computer. All very different from his day. Faster, he supposed. More efficient in many ways, and the mountains of paper that went with the job, that had *always* gone with the job, had been pinned or weighted into submission, compressed into obliging stacks in the in-trays and out-trays that stood on the desks around him.

One long wall was taken up by cabinets, all of them fire-proof, heavy and immovable. A place for everything, thought Driver, including Dalton, who was accessing a computer whilst drinking coffee from a polystyrene cup.

Some things, thought Driver, hadn't changed for the better. He remembered those cups, the coffee pulled from a machine, the way it tasted of plastic and something resembling baby formula that passed for powdered cream.

'Coffee?' said Rigby, opening the door to his office.

'I'd have to be desperate,' said Driver.

Rigby merely smiled. 'Sit down,' he invited, and Driver looked round the office, its veal-coloured walls, the pot plants, the venetian blinds. It was opulent by comparison with what he'd been used to and he said, 'You're doing all right for yourself.'

'Spend half my life here,' said Rigby. 'Like to make it a home from home.'

Driver, who felt he had spent a good deal more than half his life on the floor below, merely said, 'Wasn't like this in my day.'

Rigby could imagine. He said, 'There are a couple of points on file I want to clarify. We talked them through briefly the other night, and I've read the file now, but I just want to make sure I've got it straight.'

'Fire away,' said Driver.

'Right then,' said Rigby. 'Richard Wachmann was born and bred at Marshfield. A compulsory-purchase order forced his parents to sell the place to what was then the Thames Valley water authority, and, on the weekend that the party took place, his former home was about to be submerged by a reservoir.'

'Right,' said Driver.

'So he invited about twenty people to a "goodbye, house" party at his former home. At the time, he was sharing a house in North Oxford with Ian Gilmore, so naturally he invited Gilmore to the party, and Gilmore brought his girlfriend, Helena Warner.'

'It was a bit more complex than that,' said Driver. 'Gilmore and Helena had been living at Marshfield at weekends.'

'But they didn't live together at the house in North Oxford.'

'No,' said Driver.

'Why not?'

'No idea,' said Driver, but, even as he said it, he could remember the half-smile that had been on Joan's face when he had asked her why Gilmore and Helena didn't live together. 'Ask him,' she had said.

Driver had done so, but had failed to elicit any meaningful or useful response.

Rigby said, 'Joan was a former schoolfriend of Helena's, and Helena invited her to the party.

'She was studying in Southampton at the time,' said Driver. 'She travelled to Oxford by train, arrived Friday, went to the party on Saturday, and took the train back on Sunday.'

'And Helena waved her off,' said Rigby.

'According to Joan she did. I doubt it, personally.'

'Assuming it's true, she would have been the last person to see Helena alive.'

'Assuming it's true, yes.'

'But you don't believe her.'

'No. Helena Warner never left Marshfield, I'm pretty sure of that.'

'Why should Joan lie?'

'She was covering for Gilmore.'

'Why?'

'Wish I knew,' said Driver. 'At one stage, I was convinced they must have known one another prior to the party, but everything I tried in order to prove it came up blank. It looks as though she and Gilmore never set eyes on one another before that weekend. I couldn't understand it.'

'Fear?'

'I don't think so. Fear's the obvious option, but I'd opt for infatuation.'

'Doesn't make sense,' said Rigby. 'If Gilmore killed Helena, and she knew it, she was hardly likely to fall for him.'

'Sexual attraction breaks all the rules,' replied Driver. 'It may not make sense, but it's still my guess. Wachmann, on the other hand, was a different matter. He was frightened of Gilmore. That's why he covered for him.'

'What reason could he have had for being afraid of Gilmore?'

'Who can say? Maybe Gilmore convinced him he could implicate him. Maybe he threatened him with violence, or maybe he just had a hold on him for something he'd done that had nothing whatsoever to do with Marshfield. It could have been anything.'

'But either way, he and Joan covered for Gilmore,' said Rigby. 'Think they're likely to change their story now?'

'Ask them,' said Driver. 'Find out.'

This was the difficult bit, thought Rigby. He said, 'We'll certainly make a few enquiries.'

Picking up on his tone, Driver said, 'A few enquiries? What's that supposed to mean?'

Steeling himself, Rigby added, 'It means it's by no means certain we'll throw all our resources at it.'

'What are you—'

'Let me finish. Twenty years ago, you failed to bring a prosecution even though the case was fresh—'

'I didn't have a body,' said Driver.

'Come on, Bill, we can't crack Gilmore's story on the grounds that we now have a body. You know as well as I do that even a mediocre barrister will claim that Helena could have left Marshfield with the others in the early hours of Sunday morning and returned there anytime during the three days it took for the water to submerge the house. Anybody could have murdered her. Unless we can persuade either Poole or Wachmann to change their story and admit that she never left Marshfield, we don't have a hope.'

'So you reinterview them, try to persuade them to stop covering for Gilmore.'

'Why should they change their story? They stuck to it rigidly twenty years ago.'

'You're not even going to try?'

'Like I said, we'll make a few enquiries, but – no, I doubt it'll come to much.' There was no response from Driver. 'I know you're disappointed.'

'Twenty years is a long time,' said Driver. 'They might be prepared to come clean if it's been haunting them all this time.'

'You know that's not likely, and we can't afford to throw resources at cases we know are unlikely to result in a prosecution.'

'Is that what it comes down to, resources? *What about justice?*'

This was turning out harder than Rigby had imagined. Somehow, he had pictured Driver taking the news badly, but quietly, and then resigning himself to it.

'Bill,' he said, 'you were a good copper – I daresay you could teach me a thing or two, but the fact remains, we have no fresh evidence.'

'What's the body if it isn't fresh evidence?'

'It isn't enough,' said Rigby. 'I'm sorry, Bill, but it simply isn't enough.' Driver went totally quiet. 'I know how you feel,' added Rigby.

Driver obviously doubted it, thought Rigby, adding, 'Listen, Bill, you've probably read about the remains found in a barn in Burford.'

'Show me someone who hasn't,' said Driver. 'Two murder victims found locally a matter of days apart. The local rag thinks it's Christmas.'

'I'm handling it.'

'I didn't know that. What have you got?'

'Nothing,' said Rigby. 'Nothing to go on, and it's an old murder, Bill. You know what that means. Chances are, I'll end up winding it down for lack of information.'

'Bit early to be saying that.'

'Maybe, but I can see it happening unless I get lucky.'

'What are you saying?'

'I'm saying there's an element of luck involved in solving any murder case, and I'm also saying that sometimes you have to face facts and let go.'

'I don't have a problem letting go,' said Driver.

'So why can't you do it with regard to Helena Warner?'

'Buggered if I know,' admitted Driver. 'I just can't.'

'Sometimes you don't have a choice,' said Rigby. 'Sometimes those choices are made on your behalf.'

'You're making one now. Is that it?'

'I didn't say that.'

'But you're not prepared to do anything substantial.'

'I didn't say that, either. All I'm saying is, we don't have a shred against Gilmore.'

'We've got a body.'

'It isn't enough,' said Rigby. 'I'm sorry, Bill, but right now I can't justify doing anything other than making a few enquiries.'

Driver stood up abruptly. 'Anything else?'

'Bill . . .' said Rigby.

'Right then. I'll be off.'

Rigby watched him go. Couldn't stop him, and wouldn't have known what to say even if he could. Some you won, and some you lost. Driver had been onto a loser with Marshfield from day one, and it looked as though he had never come to terms with that. Maybe the time had arrived for him to come to terms with it now.

23

Driver walked out of the station and headed for his car. His initial disappointment had been replaced, if not with resignation, at least with the realisation that Rigby had a point. Twenty years ago, Poole and Wachmann had stood by Gilmore for reasons he couldn't fathom, but, whatever those reasons were, they must have been good in order to have persuaded them to stick out their necks for a man they knew to be guilty of murder. *And they did know*. Driver was certain of that.

He also knew Rigby was right when he said the discovery of the remains didn't constitute fresh evidence. The fact remained that Helena might have left Marshfield only to return there at some point before the house was submerged, but he doubted it. According to the water company, it had been anticipated that the water would rise by one inch per hour, but water was unpredictable. Rain many miles away could cause a sudden rise of several feet, and Marshfield had been unsafe in the days following the party. An intelligent girl like Helena would have known that. He doubted she would have taken the risk. But what if she had? What if, for reasons that hadn't yet come to light, she had gone back, and had been murdered by someone who hadn't even come under suspicion at the time? It was unlikely, but the fact remained that *it was possible*, and, notwithstanding the discovery of her remains, no jury would bring in a guilty verdict on Gilmore unless Joan or Richard provided further evidence by changing their story. Again, Rigby was right in his assumption that they were unlikely to do so at this late stage, but what about Wachmann's mother?

Driver recalled an impression rather than an accurate image of her: the delicate scent, the pale skin, the almost ethereal qualities that her son had inherited.

Fine art.

Driver had seen his work and had regretted, not for the first time, that his own appreciation of art was so limited. He didn't doubt that Wachmann's work was good, but only because he could at least tell what it was. A row of houses. A church. A woman eating a pear. None of that cubic nonsense where you didn't know whether what you were looking at was one face or two. Driver couldn't cope with the abstract. He was better on the straightforward stuff, and the only way to get down to brass tacks was to do some straightforward investigating, which brought him back to Merle Wachmann.

Twenty years ago, he had initially thought her naturally reserved, but, after meeting her for a second time, he had come to the conclusion she was merely unnaturally afraid. She knew something, and he had been unable to win her confidence, so he had failed to discover what. Perhaps, now that a number of years had passed, he might succeed where once he had failed. He didn't know, but there was only one way to find out: he would go back to Thornley to question her again. With luck, she might provide a word, a passing glance, some minor gesture that he could take to Rigby with a plea that the investigation be reopened, despite the difficulties inherent in solving a murder so old, so well concealed.

It had been so long since he last set foot on the farm that he had forgotten what it was like, but the driveway soon reminded him. The hatchback bottomed out on the humps of earth that rose between ruts dug by tractor tyres, and as he neared the house he viewed it through rain that was driven from the windscreen by wipers that were giving up the struggle.

His attention was taken by outbuildings, great slabs of

prefabricated grey that blended with the ironstone sky. They dwarfed the house and older buildings which huddled in their shadow, subservient and miserable. It was desolate, and remarkably like Marshfield, as though the hand that had moulded this farm had brought the soul of the reservoir to abide on the flat, still land. And in the midst of it all was Merle Wachmann, the most delicate-looking of women. It couldn't be much of a life, thought Driver, when all was said and done.

He wondered whether Richard had kept in touch with Gilmore and Joan or whether all three of them had agreed never to contact one another again. You never knew: Driver, who had witnessed the fragmentation of marriages, businesses and entire families, knew that accomplices in murder reacted in different ways. Some wanted to cling to the others for security. Some couldn't bear the others in close proximity. He wondered what had been the case with Gilmore, Wachmann and Poole.

He climbed stiffly from the car, hurried through the downpour to the back of the house, and knocked on the door. The steady sound of rain being driven against the grey stone walls added to the air of desolation, and he caught his breath in a wind so thin, so cold, he could barely stand to suck it into his lungs.

There was no reply and, more from the cold than impatience, he looked through the kitchen window.

From here it was possible to see a sleek, almost lustrous sheen to the stones and the large oak table, its surface devoid of clutter, and then he sensed someone behind him and he turned to see a man he initially took to be Richard's father. His waxed-cotton coat was of the undecorative variety, the elbows worn, the pockets bulging and torn, but this man was in his forties, and Ernst had been forty twenty years ago. He didn't speak; he merely stood in the driving rain, perhaps not oblivious, but certainly accustomed to it, and he waited for Driver to explain what he was doing there.

Not for the first time, Driver realised there were certain

advantages to being old. He looked what he was, a man in his late sixties, respectably dressed, and unlikely to be a thief. He found himself shouting to be heard above the rain.

'I was hoping to see Mrs Wachmann.'

He moved towards the door, raising his voice but not shouting as Driver had done. 'She should be in.'

Driver waited while he knocked, but the man got no reply.

Merle Wachmann wasn't the type of farmer's wife to be found anywhere in the buildings, thought Driver, especially in weather like this. He'd been unlucky. 'You work for her?' he said.

'Barker,' he replied. 'I manage the place.'

He turned and began to walk away, Driver calling after him, 'Mind if I look round, make sure she's not here?'

He didn't turn to speak, but Driver caught the words, 'See if her car's in the barn.'

He followed him, each drop of rain like the sting of an insect, a barrage of sharp, thin barbs hammering on the skin of his face. His eye was drawn to water gushing from a broken gutter. It rattled into a barrel, the metal bands rusting, the rotting wood disintegrating at the rim, and the stone of the barn it leaned against was totally out of keeping with its prefabricated neighbour.

As they entered, Driver caught sight of a rear wing protruding from behind machinery, a dust sheet over the roof, a yellowish cream, the edges ragged.

Barker had gone on ahead, walking past the car and into the depths of the barn, calling back to Driver. 'That was Ernst's car. Hers should be—'

There was nothing, just the sound of the rain, the smell of damp. Driver called out, 'What is it?'

Barker reappeared. There was something about him. Driver couldn't quite place it. His voice was quiet now, the rain that bounced in the doorway almost drowning his words as he said, 'Stay back.'

'What?'

'Don't argue,' said Barker, but Driver had seen that look before, and he pushed past him.

He came to a halt in the barn, looked up at the long wooden beam that ran its length, and, for what seemed a long time, he felt light, as though he could float if he put his mind to it.

From behind him, Barker merely said, 'Her husband died two months ago. I didn't realise . . .'

The years suddenly fell from Driver and he was back at St Aldate's, the officer in front of him pushing him back from the door to a cell. Then, as now, he had ignored the warning, determined to look for himself, and he had regretted it later. The sight that had greeted him had left a lasting impression, one that had served as a constant reminder of the depths of despair to which some people could plunge if left alone to dwell on a future they considered hopeless. It had made him ensure that Gilmore was never left unobserved when held for questioning, and he remembered saying, 'He's calm, Mr Gilmore. Too calm.'

Gilmore's father had replied, 'He's innocent. Why shouldn't he be calm?' And Driver had struggled to explain what he meant. He had seen that calmness in other people. A dangerous calm, and he had said, 'Don't let him out of your sight.'

Point taken: Gilmore's father had given the merest indication that he understood what was being said to him, but nevertheless, he had repeated the words, 'He's innocent', and Driver had refrained from listing his reasons for doubting it.

'I'll call the police,' he said.

24

The barn was now sharply defined in the harsh glare of arc lights that had been positioned at various points to illuminate it like a stage. The walls were suggestive of props that had been hastily painted by helpers at an amateur theatrical company; the cracks were too black and too deep; the stone appeared to have been constructed of polystyrene blocks.

The wind had dropped and the rain was no longer driving into the ground from an angle, but it fell steadily, heavily, so that those who were not in the barn were working in an area that was already ankle deep in mud, and shadows flitted into and around the buildings, men moving silently as if the dead could hear.

It was dark, the sweeping blackness that came in late afternoon seeming to have fallen quite suddenly – the dimming of a switch by an unseen hand, thought Driver. He felt impotent, a bystander who would have been removed from the scene altogether if not for his previous status as a DCI. As it was, he stood in the passage with a man he took, correctly, to be half his age, a man who had descended on the farm with quiet authority, bringing a multitude of people in his wake, a pathologist, Buchannan, among them.

He had introduced himself as Detective Superintendent Hillier, Warwickshire Police, and initially, he had been suspicious of Driver: 'Who are you? What are you doing here? When was the last time you saw Merle Wachmann alive?' It reminded him of the way in which he had questioned Gilmore: '*Did you kill her?*'

They stood together and watched as Buchannan directed the men who brought the body down, two of them supporting it, another slipping the noose from the neck but not cutting it.

In the rafters above, cobwebs that were dense with dust hung like linen rags, one of them catching in her hair and becoming a veil, and the men struggled to lower her with some semblance of dignity, finding her heavy in death, the limbs beginning to stiffen.

Driver reproached himself for the thought that he might be staring through the window of a department store to watch a plaster mannequin being manipulated into position. It wasn't how he wanted to remember Merle Wachmann, but he knew from experience that from now on, whenever he thought of her, he would think of the peculiar cast that spotlights had thrown on the once alabaster skin. Now it was grey, like porcelain stripped of enamel, the fingers pale at the tips as though dipped in a fine white powder.

She was placed on the concrete floor, the men straightening her clothing as if she were still alive, an instinctive, caring act that Driver found oddly touching. 'Why do they do it?' someone said, and Driver felt that in this case he could probably provide an answer of sorts, but he refrained from giving it, choosing instead to watch as Buchannan began the preliminary examination, his hands like those of a corpse in the waxlike gloves.

In the silence accorded Buchannan, Driver could hear rats scratching above. He looked up and caught sight of a trap so old, and placed so high on the rafters, he suddenly had a vision of Ernst Wachmann perched on a ladder and cursing under his breath. Rats were suspicious. Streetwise. Athletic. Too clever by far for Ernst, and they had thrived on a farm devoid of cats – of what Driver would have called cats, at any rate.

The last time he'd been at Thornley, Merle had been in the kitchen, a seal-point Siamese wailing at her feet. 'Valuable cat,' Driver had said. 'Don't you ever worry that it might wander off?'

'I keep my cats in,' she'd replied. 'I don't let them out of my sight.'

Buchannan stood up and peeled the gloves from his hands.

'Suicide?' said Hillier.

'Looks like it. The post-mortem will confirm it, but I can't find anything to suggest otherwise.'

Driver looked at the impression left by the rope. It gave the body the appearance of a doll with a removable head. One quick twist, and it would come off, that was what it looked like.

'How long has she been dead?'

'Hours. Three at the most.'

Would it have made any difference, thought Driver, if I'd arrived earlier? Probably not, and if she'd done it after I'd questioned her I would have spent the rest of my life feeling in some way responsible.

Outside, the rain started up again. It hammered on the roof, the wind that drove it finding Driver's bones.

'Better get back to the house,' said Hillier. 'See if they've managed to turn up a note.'

They made their way to the house, walking through mud that had held scant regard for the fine leather footwear Merle had been in the habit of wearing. Hillier said, 'You mentioned earlier that you came to speak to her in connection with an investigation you were involved in twenty years ago.'

'The disappearance of Helena Warner,' Driver confirmed. 'I think she knew Helena was murdered. I also think she knew that Gilmore killed her.'

'Then why didn't she come forward?'

'That's what I came to find out.'

They entered the house via the front door, and, as they walked into the hall, Driver's recollection of a conversation with Merle supplied him with a picture of what it had looked like when she and her husband moved in, the flagstones encrusted with mud, the stairway covered with a carpet that was threadbare.

At the foot of the stairs, a mirror that had lost much of its backing of silver had hung on the wall like a cool green pool. 'I threw it out,' she'd said. 'All of it. Cleaned it. Painted it. This was *my* part of the farm.'

Now the floor was carpeted, the ivory walls decorated with prints. The banister flanking the stairs had been stripped of paint, the varnish light, the hardwood close-grained and rich in colour. It was almost a cry from the heart, thought Driver. She hadn't belonged there; but, once she had resigned herself to the probability that she would never escape, she had done what she could to surround herself with comfort.

He followed Hillier to the door of the kitchen and watched the scenes-of-crime officers opening cupboards and closing them again, dusting for prints, finding plenty, most of them probably belonging to people who had totally innocent reasons for being there at some point in the preceding days and weeks.

Addressing one of them, Hillier said, 'Anything?' and the man replied, 'No suicide note, if that's what you mean.' He indicated two cut-crystal tumblers, now sealed in polythene, standing on the kitchen table. 'But she had a visitor. Those were found in the sitting room. We lifted prints.'

Driver felt a dull thud behind the breastbone. 'Check them against Gilmore's. If I was so keen to talk to her, maybe he was too.'

'I take it his prints are on record?' said Hillier.

Driver smiled to himself. During the original investigation, he had taken prints from Wachmann, Poole, Gilmore and everyone at the party. 'Fax them through to Rigby,' he said.

'From what you've told me, Gilmore doesn't strike me as being stupid enough to leave prints.'

No, thought Driver, and, even if he *had* paid Merle a visit, he couldn't be held responsible for the fact that she had brought her own miserable existence to an end.

Hillier broke into his thoughts: 'What made you think she knew Helena Warner was murdered?'

Driver found himself hard pushed to reply. If he were honest, he would have to admit he didn't know. He said, 'There was something wrong between Richard and his parents. I'm not sure what. It had something to do with Helena's disappearance, though, I know that much.'

'What happened to Wachmann after the investigation was wound down?'

'He dropped out of university at the same time as Gilmore, never went back at the start of his second year.'

'Then what?'

'I lost track,' said Driver. 'I know he lived at home for a couple of months, but that's about all I know.'

The scenes-of-crime man looked up and said, 'There's nothing in the house to indicate the Wachmanns had a son.'

'You sure?' said Driver.

'No photographs, letters, birth certificates. Nothing, but according to the farm manager Merle Wachmann returned from a holiday in South Africa yesterday.'

'Then let's check the possibility that Richard might be there,' said Driver. 'Liaise with Rigby, let him know what you come up with.'

'I take it he knew you intended to pay Merle Wachmann a visit?' said Hillier, and when Driver didn't respond he added, 'Then I take it he won't be amused?'

Driver didn't know Rigby well enough to be able to hazard a guess, but he knew what his own reaction would have been to learn that someone had been poking his nose into a murder investigation he was handling. 'Break it to him gently,' he said, and Hillier smiled to himself.

'I'll do my best,' he replied.

Fuller broke into his thoughts. 'What made you think she knew Helen's mother was murdered?'

Driver heard himself [illegible] a reply. If he were honest, he would have to admit he didn't know. He said, 'There's something wrong with the [illegible] and the [illegible]. I'm not sure what. It had something to do with Helen's disappearance, though, I [illegible] that much.'

'What happened to Washburn after the [illegible] went down?'

'He doesn't [illegible] at the same time as Gilmore, never went back at the start of his second year.'

'Then where?'

'[illegible],' said Driver. 'I know he lived at home for a couple of months, but that's about all I know.'

The [illegible] man looked up and said, 'There's nothing in the house to indicate the Washburns had a son.'

'You sure?' said Driver.

'No photographs, letters, birthday cards. Nothing, but according to the farm manager Mark Washburn returned from a holiday in [illegible] yesterday.'

'They [illegible] the possibility that Richard might be there,' said Driver. '[illegible]. Let him know what you come up with.'

'I take it the news was [illegible] to pay Mark Washburn a visit,' said Fuller, and when Driver didn't respond he added, 'Then I take it he won't be amused?'

Driver didn't know [illegible] well enough to be able to hazard a guess, but he knew what his own reaction would have been to learn that someone had been poking his nose into a murder [illegible], [illegible] himself.

'I'll do the talking,' he replied.

25

It wasn't often that Dalton saw Rigby reduced to quiet rage, but the news that Driver had been down to Thornley did the trick.

Deciding that discretion might be the better part of valour, Dalton took himself off to the incident room to fax Hillier with information relating to Marshfield. That done, he got stuck into a computer that, to all intents and purposes, appeared to be identical to many that were available for policing the country. There was just one difference: most of the men who had ever tried to coax anything out of it agreed that it was female. What's more, this little sweetie was a redhead. One false move, and she could go off on one, no trouble, but, whereas she tended to lose it with most people, she appeared to have taken a shine to Dalton.

Over the years, with a variety of cases, she had spilled information into his lap as if showering him with small signs of approval, and Dalton sincerely hoped he had done nothing of late to offend her. He treated her like a little goddess, making small, idolatrous offerings by keeping her keyboard dust-free and covering it with a plastic sheet on cold winter nights, and she conveyed her appreciation by divulging information.

Rigby had told him to get hold of current addresses for Wachmann and Poole, and tracing Joan proved easy enough: the tax office confirmed that, according to her National

Insurance number, she now lived a mere few hundred yards from her former home.

He checked the information twice over, and, having satisfied himself that he'd found the right Joan Poole, he turned his attention to finding Wachmann, quickly discovering that he appeared not to have held down a job, driven a car, claimed income support, or left the country once in the past twenty years.

He decided that his best option would be to tackle the problem of tracing him via medical records because he did at least know that Wachmann had once been registered with a general practice in Marshfield. It was therefore Dalton's guess that, when he started his first term at Worcester College, his medical records would have been transferred to a practice in Oxford.

The computer broke into his thoughts, a slight burring from the monitor attracting his attention and the words 'phone the surgery at Marshfield' forming in his mind.

He got the number from directory enquiries, dialled it, and said, 'DI Dalton, Thames Valley Police. I'm making an enquiry in connection with medical records relating to a patient who was registered with your practice twenty years ago.'

The voice that replied was middle-aged and efficient. 'We don't divulge—'

'I know,' said Dalton. 'I'm not asking you to, but these particular records were transferred, and we need to know where to. That can't be confidential, surely?'

'Well,' said the voice, uncertainly.

'Come on,' said Dalton. 'It can't be a state secret.'

'What was the name?'

'Richard Wachmann.'

'Oh yes. Richard.'

The computer clicked and whirred in a way that equipment as sophisticated as that installed at Thames Valley had no right to click and whir.

Cautiously now, Dalton asked, 'The name seems to ring a bell?'

'It does. I've worked here donkey's years. Knew the whole family. I remember his records being collected.'

'What do you mean, collected?'

'His parents took them. They had a written authority. I remember the doctor asking me to put them in an envelope, ready for collection.'

Dalton's mind went into overdrive. There had to have been thousands of patients registered with the surgery over the past twenty years and the idea that a receptionist would recall something like that was near impossible for him to believe. 'How come you remember?'

'I thought it was odd at the time. People don't usually collect their own medical records, and they certainly don't collect records that don't belong to them. Mr and Mrs Wachmann's own records were transferred to a practice in Thornley by the usual method, but they called in to collect their son's records personally.'

So they weren't transferred when Wachmann went up to Oxford. They were collected a year later, after Helena Warner was reported missing, thought Dalton. He said, 'I didn't realise it was possible for people to collect medical records.'

'Oh yes, it's possible. Anyone can collect their own medical records, and they can also collect records relating to other people provided they have written authority.'

'Which Wachmann's parents had?'

'Yes. And what with everyone knowing Richard was being questioned by the police about the student who disappeared, it stuck in my mind.'

Dalton paused for thought, one eye on the computer, which was blinking now, the screen rolling, an idiosyncrasy that infuriated his colleagues but didn't bother Dalton. *Ask her whether she's any idea what his parents did with the records.*

'Any idea where the records went?' said Dalton.

'I had a phone call,' said the voice, 'weeks after they were collected.' Good girl, thought Dalton. Keep it coming. 'Somebody wanted a word with the doctor for background information. I put them through.'

'You wouldn't happen to remember who?' said Dalton.

'Now let me see . . .'

Please, thought Dalton. *Please* don't let me down. Not now . . .

'Churchill House,' said the voice.

Dalton let out breath he hadn't realised he was holding. 'What's that?'

'A mental hospital. Private,' said the voice. 'Somewhere in central Oxford, I think.'

Dalton could have kissed her. He ended the call, pulled out the local telephone directory, found the number for Churchill House, and dialled it.

'DI Dalton, Thames Valley Police,' he said.

'How can I help you?'

This voice was different, younger, sultry, the accent more educated. 'I believe Churchill House admitted a patient in 1975, a Mr Richard Wachmann. You wouldn't just check your records and tell me if I'm right, would you?'

'I don't need to,' she replied. 'Richard's still a patient.'

The computer chattered softly in the background. Dalton threw it the kind of glance he usually reserved for seriously attractive women and said, 'Let me get this right: you're saying he's at Churchill House?'

'He's one of Dr Thurston's patients.'

'Thurston?'

'Consultant psychiatrist,' said the voice.

'We need to speak to him,' said Dalton. 'When would be convenient?'

He waited while she checked with Thurston and then confirmed that they could see him now if they came straight over.

Dalton checked his watch. It was 3.15 p.m. He didn't know what Rigby's plans were, but he reckoned he could probably spare an hour to speak to Thurston. If not, he'd just have to phone them back and make another appointment.

He ended the call, and patted the monitor affectionately. The screen stopped rolling. 'Thanks, sweetheart,' he said.

He left the incident room, dived up two flights of stairs and entered Rigby's office 'I've got a fix on Joan Poole.' He put a note of the address on Rigby's desk.

Rigby, still white with rage, merely said, 'Warrington?'

'I also got a fix on Wachmann.'

Rigby indicated a chair and Dalton sat as he added, 'He's at Churchill House.'

Rigby knew it, a former stately home on the outskirts of the city, the buildings so similar in design to many of the colleges that tourists sometimes mistook it for one and tried to find the entrance.

'Thurston can see us now if we get down there,' said Dalton.

'Thurston?'

'Consultant psychiatrist responsible for his treatment. I guessed you'd want to see him before questioning Wachmann.'

'We might as well know what we're letting ourselves in for,' said Rigby, coldly.

'What about Poole?'

'I can't be in two places at once. Besides, when Driver gets back from Thornley, I want a word with him.'

'He meant no harm.'

'He was out of order.'

'He still thinks of this as his case.'

Rigby stood up. 'He shouldn't have been there.'

'No,' said Dalton, humouring him. 'Well, we'd better let the lads know where we are in case somebody needs to contact us, and then we'll go, shall we?'

They made their way to the incident room, Rigby briefing men who had been assembled to form the team that would now work on the investigation before turning on his heel and walking out, Dalton following him down the corridor towards the lift.

As he strode alongside him, Dalton wondered how best to phrase what was going through his mind. In the end, he decided to be blunt and leave it at that. 'Wachmann's mother has just been found dead, sir. If we get to speak to him, I suggest—'

Rigby pressed the button for the lift, turned to him and said, 'I don't need any suggestions on that score from you.'

The lift arrived and they got in, Dalton pressing the button for the ground floor. 'No sir,' he said.

26

The journey from Warwick to Warrington had taken three hours. Gilmore arrived late in the afternoon, and, once he reached the estate, he searched to find Joan's flat.

Darkness was closing in, the streetlights already flickering into life, and he found that the estate consisted largely of houses that were semi-detached, each of them standing back from a small square of garden.

Some were lawned. Others were fronted by patches of dirt. There were no garages and on each side of the road, cars sat half on, half off, the pavement, crushed together nose to tail.

He found a row of shops at the bottom of Rosamund Road, parked the car in a side road, and doubled back. The flat was above a shop, and once he'd checked the address he walked round the back to a yard. Much of it had been swallowed by an extension, and there were two doors set almost opposite each other, a matter of yards between them. One quite obviously belonged to the extension, and Gilmore focused his attention on the other.

There was no bell, just a door knocker, and beneath it a letterbox minus the flap. He peered through and saw a flight of stairs covered in lino and encrusted with grime. From that alone, he could visualise what the flat above might be like.

As he straightened, the door to the extension opened, and a man he judged to be in his mid to late fifties said, 'Who are you looking for?'

The accent was local, the vowels flattened, the question

abrupt and to the point. A sign above the shop bore the lettering. 'A. A. Turnbull' and Gilmore guessed this was him. 'You Mr Turnbull?'

'What's it to you?'

'I'm looking for Joan.'

'She's not in.'

'I'm an old friend of hers.'

'Well like I said, she's not in. Want me to give her a message?'

'No,' said Gilmore.

He turned from the door and sensed Turnbull staring after him as he walked down the passage. He wondered whether, if Turnbull described him to Joan, she'd know who'd been looking for her. Probably not, thought Gilmore. Twenty years was a long time and he'd changed; she'd know him on sight, but not from a mere description – the description of the man was a far cry from what he'd looked like at nineteen.

He made for the car and drove off the estate, stopping in a layby and using his mobile to contact Foley. He was where he had thought he would be, at home.

'Any luck with Wachmann?'

Foley sounded tense. 'Where are you?'

'Why?'

There was no reply, and Gilmore knew instantly that, at some point in the day, the police had been to the office, looking for him. 'It's OK,' he said. 'You don't have to tell me.'

'What's going on?'

'Long story,' said Gilmore, and then he cut the call.

27

Dalton had expected that Churchill House would comprise a sprawl of annexes tacked onto and around a building that was in some way depressing, and he was unprepared for what greeted him as he drove through the gates of what proved to be a minor stately home.

He followed as Rigby was guided into a room on an upper floor, then looked out of a stone-mullioned window to gardens that were reminiscent of the deer park at Magdalen. Places like Churchill House didn't come cheap, thought Dalton. He, for one, didn't doubt that the fees were astronomical.

He turned as Thurston entered the room, a room that had more in common with a sitting room, the furnishings soft, the decor soothing, and guessed him to be in his fifties, the suit austere, his manner smooth. Like Rigby, he showed his identification, then he melted into the background as Rigby said, 'Good of you to see us at short notice.' He indicated the room and added, 'This where you treat your patients?'

'Some of them.'

'It's very comfortable.'

'Comfort is relaxing,' said Thurston. 'Relaxed patients tend to respond to treatment rather better.'

Rigby wondered what kind of surroundings National Health patients were treated in. He doubted they enjoyed the undivided ministrations of a psychiatrist in an environment that was . . . He looked around him and struggled to find an appropriate description, the word 'sumptuous' coming to mind. Churchill House was doing all right, he decided, and so, by the look of it, was Thurston.

They sank into armchairs that were, as Thurston had said, relaxing – *deeply* so. I could get used to this, thought Rigby. Stiff whisky. Good book. No worries. He said, 'One of your patients, Richard Wachmann.'

'What about him?' said Thurston.

'We'd like to question him.'

Thurston merely nodded. 'What about?'

'His mother committed suicide this morning.'

Nice one, thought Dalton. Wachmann being here would have given it a certain polish, but you can't have everything.

'I'm sorry,' said Rigby. 'It's been a difficult day. I could have put that better.'

Thurston smiled. 'We do a good line in stress counselling if ever you feel the need.'

'We've got an in-house shrink,' said Rigby, smiling back. He lightened up a little, getting into his stride. 'His mother's suicide may have been connected to the fact that we recently found the remains of a woman Richard knew at Oxford some years ago. Helena Warner.'

The name clearly meant something to Thurston. 'I don't think I'd be betraying any confidences if I revealed that Richard and I have discussed her disappearance during therapy.'

'We've got a prime suspect,' said Rigby. 'Somebody Richard shared a house with at the time she disappeared.' He had intended the comment to make it clear that Wachmann was out of the frame and Thurston appeared to absorb that. 'We've got nothing concrete on him, and we were counting on Richard to withdraw an alibi he gave him when he was first held for questioning.'

'No court is going to convict a man of murder on the strength of a statement made by a long-term psychiatric patient.'

'I realise, but Richard might give us something we can

build on, and I thought it might be wise to talk to you before questioning him. When was he admitted?'

'December seventy-five.'

A matter of months after the party, thought Rigby. 'And how long have you been responsible for his treatment?'

'Several years,' replied Thurston. His former psychiatrist, Dr Levinson, retired in eighty-seven.'

'What was the reason for his admission?'

'Depression.'

'Genuine?'

'I'd say so,' said Thurston.

'He's been here nineteen years,' said Rigby. 'That must be quite some depression?'

'Unfortunately, it tends to recur.'

'And when it recurs, what then?'

'We treat him and it wears off. Then it returns. It's a cycle.'

'What causes it?'

'Difficult to say. Levinson initially labelled him manic depressive, largely, I think, because so many of his symptoms fitted the bill.'

Rigby, who was only vaguely aware what the symptoms of manic depression were, said, 'What are the symptoms?'

'To put it in the simplest terms, normal to high spirits interspersed with bouts of debilitating depression. But, as I say, Richard was misdiagnosed, so there's little point dwelling on that.'

'So what's his problem?'

'I'm not sure.'

It seemed an odd admission for a psychiatrist to make and Rigby pressed him on it. 'You must have some idea?'

'Richard tends to avoid sensitive issues.'

'You mean he doesn't co-operate with therapy?'

'You could say that, yes.'

Tentatively, Rigby made a suggestion: 'Have you ever tried pointing out that his condition is likely to remain much the same unless he starts to co-operate with treatment?'

'I suspect he doesn't want treatment. Treatment equals the possibility of some improvement in his condition, which equals the possibility that he might be asked to re-take his place in society. In the past, whenever we've suggested that perhaps he should try to become independent of Churchill House, his depression has recurred.'

'Why?'

'This is his home. He feels safe here. Any suggestion that he should leave results in an insecurity that triggers his depression.'

Rigby picked up on the fact that there might recently have been some question of whether Richard should stay at Churchill House. 'Is he about to be forced to move?'

'Prior to their respective deaths, his parents indicated they would shortly be unable to continue paying the fees to keep him here.'

'And what did that mean to him in real terms?'

'It meant he would have to enter some sort of sheltered accommodation before taking responsibility for his own welfare. Either that or he would find himself moved to an institution run by the National Health.'

'I take it neither option appealed?'

'Richard has a studio here. He isn't keen to lose it, and nor is he keen to find himself working out of a bedsit paid for by social services.'

I can imagine, thought Rigby. He said, 'A studio?'

'He's an artist. The coach house was converted for his use. You can see it from here.'

Thurston stood up, Rigby and Dalton doing likewise and following him to the window. Darkness was drawing in fast, but in the distance, they could see the tiled roof of a stable block, the coach house rising above it, a clock tower set over an arch, a weathercock depicting a fox.

'Who paid for the conversion?'

'A patron. Cora Bowerman.'

Thurston walked back to the chair, and reseated himself, Rigby and Dalton doing likewise. Rigby said, 'It was generous of her to go to the expense of converting a coach house into a studio. Fond of him, is she?'

Catching on his tone, Thurston replied, 'She's in her seventies, and, anyway, Richard isn't the only one to have benefited from her generosity of late. She recently donated a property to us and paid for extensive alterations so that it could be used as a halfway house.'

'For people like Richard?' suggested Rigby, and again, his tone wasn't lost on Thurston who replied, 'I think you'll find that Cora's motivation for making philanthropic gestures arises from the fact that her father prevented her from marrying a pilot who died in the Second World War. She recently commissioned Richard to sculpt a statue of him.'

'You're obviously fairly well acquainted with her past.'

'The fact that she was to inherit considerable wealth motivated her father to view her penniless lover as a gold-digger. Consequently, she associates wealth with pain. She's trying to give her pain away. Richard is merely one of the beneficiaries of her attempt to rid herself of what she sees as the root cause of all her anguish.'

Fascinating though he found Cora's motivations to be, Rigby was more interested in what motivated Wachmann, and he returned to something that had been said earlier. 'You said a minute ago that Richard's parents had indicated they couldn't afford to keep him here much longer.'

'I'm afraid that was the case, yes.'

'Were they happy with the proposed move to this halfway house?'

Thurston hesitated. 'I'm not sure I can answer that.'

'In other words, no,' said Rigby, succinctly. 'What was the problem?'

'I really don't think—'

'We're investigating a murder, Dr Thurston, albeit one that happened twenty years ago. What was the problem?'

Reluctantly, Thurston replied, 'They wanted him moved to an institution run by the National Health.'

Dalton looked up, sharply. 'Why?'

'They didn't want to have to take responsibility for his everyday care.'

For a moment, nobody spoke, then Rigby said, 'Why didn't his parents want him?'

'I don't know.'

'Did they ever visit him?'

'No.' It came out flat, inviting no further comment.

Ignoring, the tone, Rigby said, 'We had a job finding him.'

'Why?'

'His parents appeared to have wiped him out of their lives. No photos, no letters, nothing, and nothing to indicate he'd ever held a job or claimed income support.'

'So how did you manage to trace him?'

'We eventually discovered that his parents collected his medical records personally. They brought them here when Richard was admitted.'

'Ah yes,' said Thurston. 'I seem to recall that Levinson made a note on file.'

He was clearly prepared to leave it at that, but Rigby had other ideas.

'I thought medical records were handled with the utmost confidentiality,' he said.

'Anyone can get hold of medical records provided they relate to themselves or provided they have the written consent of the person to whom they relate.'

'So his parents must have had that consent?'

'I assume so. They couldn't have obtained them otherwise.'

'Don't you find it odd that his parents should have gone to the trouble of collecting the records personally?'

'A little, yes.'

'Only a little?'

Thurston made no reply, and Rigby added, 'Perhaps they didn't want anyone to know their son was in a mental institution.' He looked up and met Thurston's eye. 'Were they ashamed of him?'

'Having a child admitted to a mental hospital is something the majority of people wouldn't care to have known, and Marshfield was a small village, I believe. It's probable that the nurses and secretaries working for the local GP were themselves local, and the Wachmanns might have feared gossip. They certainly didn't ask their local GP to refer Richard. It was done privately, and very quietly.'

That was an explanation, of sorts, and Rigby settled for it, feeling, in any case, that the matter of the medical records had drawn him away from the purpose of his conversation with Thurston. 'And you've really no idea what lies at the root of his depression?'

'Not really, no,' replied Thurston, his candour disarming.

'Nevertheless, you were prepared to institutionalise him for as long as he and his parents wished him to stay here, provided his parents could afford to pay the fees?'

There was an edge to Thurston's voice as he replied, 'Perhaps you should ask patients, and relatives of patients, how their lives are affected under the current rules governing care in the community.'

Rigby decided there was no point alienating Thurston. He softened a little, and said, 'How could the Wachmanns afford such astronomical fees for so many years?'

'I believe Richard's father inherited land from near relatives. It was sold, and the money was put into trust.'

'And now?' said Rigby.

'The house is mortgaged twice over. They ran out of resources.'

That's useful to have, thought Rigby. 'In other words, Richard was suddenly no better off than anyone else being forced back into the community.'

'I'm afraid not, no.'

'Not very pretty, is it?'

'No,' said Thurston, 'but life in general is anything but pretty, as I'm sure you'd be the first to agree.'

Rigby couldn't argue with that. 'And now, with both his parents dead, where does that leave him?'

'I'm not sure,' said Thurston, cautiously. 'Richard will inherit the farm, but, as I said, it's heavily mortgaged. I doubt there's any equity as such.'

'So who'll foot the bill when he moves into the halfway house?'

'Chaggfords?' said Thurston. 'Social Security.'

Rigby made a mental note of the name. 'What if he needs medical care?'

'He'll have to register with a doctor. It's up to his local GP after that.'

'He's been your patient for nineteen years,' said Rigby. 'Can you really just wash your hands of him once the money runs out?'

Thurston made no reply, and Rigby added, 'What was the real reason for his parents' reluctance to visit him?'

'I've really no idea.'

'Did you ask them?'

'No.'

'Why not?'

Thurston stood up and went to the window. He stood with his back to Rigby as he said, 'Having a child admitted to a mental hospital is traumatic, Mr Rigby. It's something the majority of people wouldn't care to have known, and a surprising number cope with it by blocking it from their mind as best they can. Richard's parents dealt with it by preventing their son's problem from impinging on their lives. Selfish, I know, but a very human response to a problem the majority of us would find difficult to cope with.' He turned to face him. 'Wouldn't you agree?'

Rigby tried to put himself in their position. 'I wouldn't turn my back on any child of mine.'

'They didn't turn theirs. They did their best. They found the money to keep him here instead of relying on what the state had to offer. It was something.'

Maybe, thought Rigby. 'Would you like me to break the news to him?'

'Of his mother's death?'

'Yes,' said Rigby.

Perhaps mindful of the way in which Rigby had come straight out with it moments earlier, Thurston replied, 'I think he might take it better if he hears it from me.'

Rigby smiled. 'I'm not usually so insensitive. Like I said, it's been a difficult day.'

'Even so,' said Thurston.

'We'd still like to see him.'

'Tomorrow,' said Thurston.

In the circumstances, Rigby didn't see how he could argue. He could hardly plough into Wachmann with the Warner investigation moments after the man had been informed that his mother had committed suicide. 'Tomorrow then,' he agreed, but it wasn't without reluctance.

'After the unveiling.'

'The what?'

'The statue that Cora commissioned. It's being unveiled tomorrow afternoon. I suggest you allow me to give him a light sedative; then allow me to stay with him while he's questioned.'

Nodding agreement, Rigby stood up. 'Where is it being unveiled?'

'Chaggfords,' said Thurston. He reached into the pocket of a suit that might have been cut by industrial diamonds and pulled out a notepad. It was minute, leather-bound, and the pencil was capped with gold.

Rigby watched as he wrote an address, then tore out the page and handed it to him, saying, 'Tread lightly. His state of mind is fragile at the best of times.'

Rigby made for the door, Dalton in tow. 'What time is the ceremony?'

'One o'clock,' replied Thurston.

'I'll look forward to seeing you there.'

"Yes," said Rigby.

Fernando was delighted at the way in which Rigby had come straight out with it moments earlier. [illegible] "I think he might take it better if he hears it from me."

Rigby smiled. "I'm not unduly [illegible]. Like I said, it's been a difficult day."

"Even so," said Thurston.

"We'd still like to see him."

"Tomorrow," said Thurston.

In the circumstances, Rigby didn't see how he could argue. He could hardly plough into Wardour with the Wright investigation [illegible] after the man had been informed that his mother had committed suicide. "Tomorrow, then," he agreed, but it wasn't without reluctance.

"After the [illegible]."

"The what?"

"The [illegible] that [illegible] commissioned [illegible]. I suggest you allow me to give him a light sedative, then allow me to stay with him while he's questioned."

"Pending agreement." Rigby stood up. "Where is it being [illegible]?"

"Headlands," said Thurston. He reached into the pocket [illegible] and pulled out a notepad. It was [illegible], and the pencil was capped with gold.

Rigby watched as he wrote an address, then tore off the page and handed it to him, saying, "[illegible]. His state of mind is [illegible]."

Rigby [illegible]. "What time [illegible]?"

"Ten o'clock," replied Thurston.

"I'll look forward to seeing you there."

28

It was the last day of November. Joan didn't have to look at a calendar to know that. She sensed it almost physically, and felt herself recoiling from the prospect of submitting to the act required of her when each month came to an end.

She stood at the foot of the flight of stairs that led to her flat and climbed silently despite the food that slapped against her legs in flimsy plastic bags.

It was a waste of time, and she knew it. No sooner had she entered the flat than Turnbull knocked on the door at the foot of the stairs. She ignored the knock, and moments later heard him use his key.

She leaned against the wall, the door to her flat still open. Turnbull mounted the stairs, his footsteps grating on the dirt-encrusted Lino as if he were walking on cinders. And then he was there, not bothering to smile, his face only inches from her own.

'You got the rent, Joan?'

She made no reply. None was necessary, and, as she went through the motions of touching him where he liked to be touched, she thought, not for the first time, that it was as though something within her had died, something that ought to have enabled her to feel repelled by Turnbull. She was reminded of the way in which Helena had stood with her back to the wall of the outhouse, only now it was she who stood with her back to the cold plaster wall, the damp seeping through her clothing, her jeans pulled down to her knees, Turnbull fumbling to penetrate her, the brief stab of pain, his slightly apologetic expression. 'You don't mind, Joan. You don't mind . . .'

She didn't know whether she minded or not. She didn't care, that was more to the point. She didn't care because she didn't feel, but she couldn't help wondering what it was that had caused Helena to cry out like one of those slow-flapping birds that had risen from the marsh. Why had the ability to experience such ecstasy been denied her, even with Gilmore? Too late now, thought Joan. I'll never feel it now. Not with anyone, or *for* anyone, least of all for myself.

As always, it was a brief, clumsy act, the pain of Turnbull's fingers where he gripped the tops of her arms, his stinking breath, that slightly dazed expression he had when he came.

And then it was over. The fingers relaxed, and he pulled away, his back to the opposite wall, the hallway narrow, dark and reeking slightly of mould.

He hitched his trousers and fastened a series of minute buttons at the fly. Those buttons amused her. There were five of them, none of them matching, and all of them more trouble than they were worth, his fingers like the sausages he served, pink, fat, speckled. They disgusted her almost more than the pathetic flaccid dick that he was tucking out of sight.

'Bloke was here today, asking for you.'

'What kind of bloke?'

'Late thirties. Well dressed.'

She owed so much money, it could have been anyone. 'Did he give a name?'

'No. Said he was a friend. Said you were expecting him.'

'I wasn't.'

'Didn't think so.'

Debt collector, thought Joan.

She fastened her jeans and zipped them, the movement almost masculine in its abruptness. 'That's it then, for a month,' said Turnbull, and she almost laughed at the petulance in his tone.

'You'll have to wait and see what Santa brings,' she said.

Maybe he didn't hear, or maybe he just picked up on how deeply she wished him dead. Either way, he didn't reply. He merely turned on his heel and left the flat.

She ran a bath, climbed in, and submerged herself, the water covering her face. At times like these, she imagined herself to be Helena Warner, calmly waiting for divers to discover her remains. She had known they would come, that one day someone would come, and that when they did, she would rise to the surface, a living, breathing demon, come to take revenge.

And then she was out of her body, or so it seemed, floating above the bath and looking down at the corpse of a woman who seemed a total stranger, the eyes staring, the mouth open, the rush of bubbles that burst through the water exploding into screams.

29

It was gone eight by the time Driver got home, the phone ringing as he stepped through the door and walked into the hall.

He lifted the receiver knowing it would be Rigby. The words 'poking around in police business' rang in his ears, Rigby barely allowing him to get a word in edgeways.

'I get the message,' said Driver.

'Do you? I hope so, because I won't have it.'

Driver let him get on with it. He didn't really blame him when all was said and done. Moments later, Rigby calmed down a fraction – but, his voice still tense, he added, 'Buchannan's done the post-mortem.'

Driver wasn't surprised. Buchannan had said he intended to do it immediately, and, once the body had been removed, what remained of his afternoon had been spent at the station in Warwick where one of Hillier's underlings had taken a statement from him. As far as he knew, Buchannan would merely confirm what they already knew to be the case, that Merle Wachmann had committed suicide, and he was more interested in hearing about whose prints had been on the glass. 'Did one of your lads manage to fax a copy of Gilmore's prints through to Warwick?'

'She was murdered,' said Rigby.

For a minute, Driver thought he hadn't heard him right. '*Murdered?*'

'Bruising across the abdomen, ribcage, shoulders, wrists and skull. There was skin under the fingernails – not hers. She put up a hell of a fight, Bill.'

It took a few seconds for the implications to sink in. 'Are you saying—'

'And the prints on the glass,' said Rigby. 'They were Gilmore's.'

Rigby had no choice now, thought Driver, no choice but to reopen the investigation. The thought should have pleased him, but as he cast his mind back to what would comprise his last memory of Merle Wachmann, he wished there could have been some other way of getting the case reopened.

Twenty minutes later, Rigby and Dalton were sitting in Driver's living room, Rigby giving a repeat performance of everything he'd said on the phone.

'What did you think you were playing at?'

'Like I said, I was trying to find out what she wouldn't tell me twenty years ago.'

'You were out of order, Bill.'

'So you said on the phone.'

Rigby gave him the kind of look that Driver reserved for villains. It wasn't meant, and Driver merely smiled, Rigby giving up when he realised he wasn't about to get an apology or anything even remotely resembling one. 'Fill me in,' he said.

Driver briefed him, Rigby interrupting occasionally to tell him something passed on to him by Hillier.

Finally Rigby said, 'Gilmore phoned his office this morning, reported in sick. We know he went to Thornely. Not only were his prints on the glass but the farm manager saw a car of the same make as the car he drives.'

'Stupid of him,' said Driver. 'Where is he now?'

'You tell me. We're watching the house. We'll know when he returns.'

'Airports?' said Driver.

'Covered,' said Rigby. 'Everything's covered.' His voice aching with self-reproach, he added, 'We'll find him. Believe me.'

Driver recognised the signs of a man kicking himself for not listening when he was told days ago that perhaps it might be an idea to bring the former prime suspect in for questioning. They caught each other's eye and Driver looked away, embarrassed on his behalf. 'Where's Wachmann?'

'He's spent the past twenty years in Churchill House.'

Driver knew it. He'd passed it often enough. 'He seemed sane enough to me when I questioned him twenty years ago.'

'He's sane enough now,' said Rigby, 'but deeply depressed, apparently.'

'Where's Joan?'

'Warrington,' said Dalton. 'We'll get ourselves down there first thing.'

'No,' said Driver.

'No?'

'We go now.'

'What's the rush?'

'He's right,' said Rigby. 'Merle Wachmann was murdered. We don't know for certain at this stage that she was murdered by Gilmore, but if she was, chances are he did it because he was worried that the discovery of Helena Warner's remains might make her come forward with information.'

'Why should she do that now?'

'I've no idea,' said Driver. 'Maybe she always had her suspicions, but wasn't willing to voice them because a body hadn't been found. Don't forget, it was because I was convinced she knew something that I went down there today.'

'I haven't forgotten,' said Rigby.

'But you take my point?' said Driver.

Dalton thought it through, but couldn't see it. 'She stuck her neck out to protect him twenty years ago. Why would he think her a threat?'

'Maybe he doesn't,' said Rigby.

'And maybe he does,' said Driver. 'Who can say what's going through his mind?'

Rigby said, 'What time is it now?' and Dalton checked his watch.

'Just gone nine,' he said.

'We'll get there by midnight, if you put your foot down,' said Driver.

'We?' said Rigby, darkly.

'*We*,' repeated Driver.

30

The book was increasing in volume but veering wildly from the original plot. It flickered onto the screen of Joan's computer, defying her to get it back on track, and eventually she gave up on it altogether.

She switched the computer off, turned the TV on, and picked her way through a living room littered with coffee cups, ashtrays, and the clothes she had stepped out of before her bath. Somehow, the bath invariably failed to wash away the stench of Turnbull. She smelled him still, on her skin, in her hair, and seeping through her pores. It made her sick, sometimes physically.

She dumped her clothes in the washer and made a sandwich, taking it through to the sitting room, pulling the curtains, and sitting on the couch to watch the end of an Australian soap. It was pushed off screen by the early-evening news, Merle Wachmann's connection with Marshfield having ensured that her murder featured prominently. The police were appealing for anyone with knowledge of Gilmore's whereabouts to contact them.

So quick, thought Joan. So bloody efficient. They didn't hang around.

She was too shocked to react at first. She listened to the news as if none of it had anything to do with her, and then a picture of Merle Wachmann came up on screen. Joan had never met her, but she came to the conclusion that, even if she hadn't known this was Richard's mother, she might have guessed. The evidence was there in the curve of the particularly fine mouth, the arch of the brow, and the delicate structure of the face.

For some moments, she wasn't sure how this changed things, or if it changed them at all. For years, she had justified her decision to protect Gilmore on the grounds that Helena had driven him to kill her, but what possible reason could he have had for killing Richard's mother – unless, of course, he had deemed her some kind of threat?

She stood up and went to the window. The small sad tree that was all that was left of a row that had existed during her childhood cowered under drops of rain that were heavy, regular, and perpendicular. They came straight down, half an inch apart, streaking past like slivers of glass to shatter on the ground.

What was it Turnbull had said? That someone had called at the flat?

The room seemed smaller and darker. She didn't know why. It was cold and she moved away from the window, bent down to switch the bar fire on and was angry with herself for the sudden stab of fear that she felt to be unreasonable. For twenty years, she had kept what she knew to herself and Gilmore had no reason, no reason whatsoever, to think her a threat.

But what if he did?

Stop it. *Stop it!* It wasn't Gilmore. It *couldn't* have been Gilmore.

She left the flat and walked through the passage to the road. The lights from within the shop lit the pavement, and she walked in to find Turnbull serving a customer. She pushed in and interrupted him. 'The man who was here earlier, asking for me . . .'

'What about him?'

'What did he look like?'

'Told you. Late thirties. Well dressed.'

She leaned her hands on the counter. 'Anything else?'

'No.'

'It's important.'

He stopped what he was doing. 'What's wrong?'

'He might have been a friend of mind, from years ago.'

Turnbull thought back and could recall nothing of interest. 'He wasn't local.'

'How do you know?'

'Southern accent.'

That could mean anything. 'Kent, Sussex, Gloucester – what kind of southern accent?'

'I'm not an expert.'

'Try.'

The queue was beginning to grow, people getting impatient.

'Surrey,' said Turnbull. 'I could be wrong . . .'

She doubted it.

'I'm going away for a while.'

'What you telling me for?'

'I'll sort the rent.'

He grinned. 'By post?'

'I'll sort it. Don't start looking around for a new tenant.'

'I wouldn't do that, Joan. Not to you.'

The sarcasm wasn't lost on her. 'Got a pen?'

There was one tied to the till by a piece of string. He passed her a scrap of paper and she wrote an address. 'This is my sister's address. Will you forward any mail?'

'How long you planning on being away?'

How long will it take for the police to get their hands on Gilmore? she wondered. 'I don't know, but like I said, I'll see the rent gets paid.'

'See that you do,' said Turnbull.

She left the shop and returned to the flat, turning the television off and crumpling onto the sofa. If Gilmore had murdered Merle Wachmann and had then driven straight down to Warrington looking for her, chances were he hadn't called in for a chat. He would probably also be looking for Richard, but he wouldn't find him easily, Joan knew that.

Over the years, she'd kept in touch with him, writing maybe four times a year, Richard replying in the extravagant hand that artists so often had, and always he answered the same, tired questions. No, he hadn't heard from Gilmore. No, he didn't know where he was, and yes, he would let Joan know if Gilmore got in touch.

Maybe Richard had lied. For all she knew, he and Gilmore might have kept in touch, in which case, Gilmore would know that Richard had spent the best part of twenty years in Churchill House. He would also know that Richard was moving to a halfway house, his last letter having given the address in the knowledge that Joan would want to continue to write.

She stood up and walked into the back bedroom, the long disused mattress lying flat on the floor, the edges curling with damp, the smell of rotting flock filling the room so that not even she could ignore it.

A small chest of drawers stood by one of the walls and she opened the topmost drawer, pulled his last letter from a pile, and read it quickly: 'I'm moving in on the first of December, the day the statue is unveiled . . .'

That was tomorrow, thought Joan, so, if Gilmore had traced him to Churchill House, he wouldn't find him there. But it wouldn't take him long to find out where he'd gone.

She put the letter back and returned to the living room. If Gilmore had got it into his head that she and Richard were a threat, her only sensible option was to go to the police. Not a uniformed copper, but a DCI, someone like Driver, a man of considerable experience, *a man who would know what to do.*

Her phone stood by the computer, the grey plastic casing in keeping with the drabness of the room. She rarely used it these days, the frequency of rejections having made her lose the motivation so crucial in soliciting commissions from various magazines. She picked up the receiver and, seconds later, replaced it, held back by the knowledge that in the eyes of the police her involvement in Helena's death and her twenty-year silence wouldn't be expunged by the fact that eventually, ultimately, she had gone forward with information. The police would give her a hard time. There wouldn't be much tea and sympathy. When they knew the degree to which she was involved, they would hold her for questioning, some of which might well be brutal.

You had met him a matter of hours before, and yet you had sex with him?

She could imagine the smirk on the face of the man who would say that. He would look her up and down and try to imagine what she might have looked like twenty years ago, and, with the best will in the world, he wouldn't be able to imagine her to have been sexually attractive.

Why did you keep quiet all these years?

Because I loved him.

You hardly knew him.

They would be right, thought Joan. In hindsight, she realised that she hadn't known the first thing about him; that what Helena had conveyed in her correspondence was no substitute for the knowledge that comes from being in a relationship with someone. She had no way of guessing what Gilmore might think or do. She only knew that she couldn't sit there and wait to find out. She had to get out while she still had a chance, and *stay* out, until he was caught.

31

She moved away from the window, switched off the lights, and left the flat abruptly. The rain had grown heavier in the past few minutes, each drop like the jab of a finger against her face. The road seemed deserted now, a combination of foul weather and the darkness having driven people into their homes.

She walked with her head bowed, her hands thrust into the pockets of the duffel. If Gilmore came for her now, if he were to pull up in a car and pull her inside, no one would see. There was nothing she could do about that other than hope that she made it to Cathy's without running into him.

Her sister would call the police, find her a solicitor, *be there* for her. She didn't know what made her think it, or even if she believed it, but she had to believe it; she couldn't do this alone. She would want to know what was stopping Joan from telling the police herself, and she would try to explain that the police might not look kindly upon an admission that it had not been so much infatuation as hatred that had made her protect Gilmore. *I hated Helena Warner.* It was something she had never once admitted, not even to herself, but she did so now. *I wanted her dead.*

At the top of the road, she turned left for the Ship Canal and the swing-bridge loomed before her. As a child, she had thought the mass of arches huge, but now it seemed like a toy, the mechanism that operated it hidden from view under the water. She stared down at the thin film of oil that lay on its surface, the lights from the bridge reflected there as if it were a mirror. It occurred to her that, if she were to jump, that would be it. The banks were sheer. No ladder, no steps, and no quarter given to those who experienced a sudden change of heart.

She walked on, the rain soaking through her duffel, and in fewer than twenty minutes she found herself on the estate Cathy had lived on since marrying.

The house, like many others, was tucked into a crescent: a small, three-bedroomed affair, a step up from the council estate on the other side of the bridge, but not much of a step when you looked more closely.

To Joan, it represented everything she had once so assiduously tried to avoid settling for, and she found it ironic that not only had she been denied the opportunity to refuse it, but what she had in its place was even less desirable. And it wasn't just the lack of money, the lack of room, the lack of hope: it was the loneliness. Cathy at least had a husband, and he might be worlds apart from the type of man she wanted for herself, but, over the years, he had provided for Cathy and the children, and at least he was there, reassuringly there. There was a lot to be said for that.

The front garden was a patch of lawn bordered by a wall. There was no gate. She had never noticed before, but she noticed now, and wished there had been one to close behind her, a symbolic gesture to mark the fact that she was about to close something on the secret she had harboured for the past twenty years.

Cathy would be in the kitchen. Joan didn't have to see her to know that, just as, when she walked to the back of the house, she didn't have to hear the splash of water gurgling down the drainpipe to know that she had just washed the dishes from dinner.

She opened the kitchen door, walked in, and wasn't sure what happened next. One minute, she was stumbling into the kitchen; the next, Cathy was holding her up, keeping her on her feet, peeling her out of the dripping coat and guiding her to a chair. 'Don't cry,' she said. 'Whatever it is, we can sort it out.'

She slumped into a chair by the kitchen table. Not this, thought Joan. You can't sort this out.

'What is it?' said Cathy, and Joan was suddenly painfully aware that, by divulging what had happened at Marshfield, she would be committing an act of betrayal; there could be no going back, and she knew well enough that, once Cathy realised the seriousness of what had been revealed to her, she would go to the police. *I will never betray you.* Were such promises still to be kept under circumstances such as these? She didn't know. She needed to think. Perhaps she had no grounds for the bitterness that had crept up on her over the years. After all, he couldn't have made love to her without feeling *something* for her, surely?

Don't be ridiculous, Joan, she admonished herself. He felt nothing; nothing but anguish and regret.

She looked round the kitchen, the floral design of the tiles unbelievably kitsch, the oily smell of fish lingering. For years, she had looked down on all this, but it was light and clean, and in daylight it looked out onto a garden with patio furniture, a lawn and a fence that blotted out all sight of the neighbouring properties. And, if it was boring and mundane, well at least it was safe and paid for, and, little though it was, it was more than she would ever call her own.

It suddenly occurred to her that she hadn't known what she expected to arise from Helena's death, but that, for reasons that were inexplicable even to herself, she had somehow believed that, as a result of it, her own life would change for the better. She hadn't known then what she knew now, that something that came from within herself, something that dictated that everything she did – from what she had chosen to do with her life to the way she had carried out those choices – would always go wrong.

She had given up, she supposed. Given up before she had even got going, because the competition, symbolised in the shape of Helena Warner, had been so strong she had believed from the start that she couldn't compete. The world was too clever, too beautiful, too sexual – and she was none of those things.

Cathy left her to her thoughts, walking away from the table, picking up cups from the draining board, wiping them, putting them down; finding things to do, thought Joan, giving her a chance to speak in her own good time. That time had been twenty years in the coming, but it had arrived; and, now that it was upon her, she wasn't sure how to begin. 'Have you seen the news?'

'I was making dinner. Paul watched it before he went on night shift. Why?'

'A farmer's wife was found hanging in a barn this afternoon.'

'What about it?'

'They're treating her death as murder. Imagine,' said Joan.

'Imagine what?'

'Imagine the killer, putting a noose round her neck, and winching her up to a beam.'

'*Joan!*'

'No – *think* about it. I mean *really*. Think what it must have felt like to die like that . . .'

'What's brought this on?'

'She and her husband used to . . .'

'Used to what?'

Why was it hard to reveal even the most mundane aspects of what she was trying to say? '. . . Used to farm at Marshfield.'

The cup that Cathy was holding clattered into the sink. 'Marshfield?'

'She was Richard's mother.'

Cathy moved towards her with what, to Joan, seemed unnatural slowness, as if she were wading through water.

'Don't do that,' said Joan.

'Do what?'

'Wade towards me . . .'

She broke down, allowing the tears she had wanted to cry when Gilmore returned the letters.

'. . . *That's what she does in my dreams . . .*

* * *

Cathy Walker stood at the kitchen window, Joan at the table behind her. It was pitch black out there, and the garden was lost to her. Pity that, thought Joan. A view of the garden might have been some consolation to her sister, some semblance of normality in a world gone mad. 'I have to tell the police, you realise that?' said Cathy.

Joan had arrived in the hope that she would take that attitude, but, now that it came to it, she found herself saying, 'Not yet. I need to think.'

'What about?'

She couldn't explain, but what she had suffered was a vision of Gilmore being given a life sentence. Their eyes would meet across a courtroom, and it would be as though he were saying, 'You promised you'd never tell.'

'I can't do it to him.'

'Don't be ridiculous. He *murdered* her.'

'She deserved it,' said Joan

'Nobody deserves that.'

She was rocking now, rocking in the chair. 'I'll never forget her cries . . .'

'Joan . . . *calm down*.'

'And there was no one to help her. No one. And I stood there. And I watched . . .' She began to push against the back of the chair as if trying to topple it over. 'It wouldn't go in. I pushed with my back against the door of the wardrobe, but it wouldn't close and I didn't know why. I looked down, and then I saw her hand . . .'

Cathy dived towards her, grabbed her by the shoulders. '*That's enough!*'

'It was warm. It was still warm. Such a warm person, Helena. Everyone said so. Even in death, she was warm. And I opened the door, and, I pushed the hand inside, and I turned the brass knob.' She smiled. '"There," I said to myself. "There. *She's gone.*"'

[illegible] would be done at the same [illegible]

[illegible] and the garden was [illegible]

[illegible]

[illegible] the police [illegible]

[illegible]

"What about?"

[illegible]

[illegible]

[illegible]

32

The shop was still open, but there were no lights in the flat above. Gilmore stood outside for a moment, then walked straight into the shop.

Turnbull recognised him the minute he walked in. 'You've missed her,' he said.

'Any idea when she'll be back?'

'She's gone to stay with her sister.'

Gilmore absorbed the news and hoped his frustration didn't show. 'I don't suppose you know where she lives?'

Turnbull reached down behind the counter and pulled out the scrap of paper Joan had written on. He copied the address, handed it to Gilmore, and said, 'She was asking after you.'

'Like I said, I'm a friend.'

'Thelwall. Over the bridge. Turn left.'

'Thanks,' said Gilmore.

He left the shop and climbed into the car, aware that if the police were to turn up, and if Turnbull were to tell them someone else had been looking for her, they would realise he had been there.

It didn't matter. From the moment that Helena Warner's remains had been found, he had known it would be a mere matter of time before the police pulled him in for questioning. His only hope of avoiding what might happen as a result lay in finding Joan and Richard and ensuring they didn't go forward with information, and he didn't have time to fuck around playing hide and seek. He had to find them before the police did, and the risk with regard to Turnbull was therefore calculated.

Even so, this Rigby guy would no doubt play it for all it was worth – his initial experience of the police had taught him that much. Twenty years ago, and notwithstanding the fact that it was a two-hour drive from Oxford, Driver had turned up on the doorstep of his parents' home, never missing a day, never apologising for what surely must have constituted harassment, and never doubting his guilt. So polite. So sarcastic, the slightly mocking 'Sorry to keep bothering you, Ian'. An insult. He had known he was breaking him down, and he had enjoyed every minute. Gilmore had seen it in the glimmer of amusement that accompanied Driver's 'We just need you down at the station.'

He drove towards Thelwall, crossing the bridge, and pulling up at a bus queue, winding down the window, and calling across the passenger seat to the first person he saw. 'I'm looking for Belmont Crescent.'

He listened as directions were given, wound up the window, and pulled away. My God, thought Gilmore. So easy. How much easier would it be for the police to find him? Even now they were probably aware that he hadn't been at the office, and that he wasn't at home either. Let them draw what conclusions they like, thought Gilmore. It's what they can prove that counts.

He turned into Belmont Crescent and picked out the house from the number displayed on the gate. He pulled up, and used his mobile, dialling the number that Turnbull had written beneath Cathy Walker's address.

As the phone was answered, it occurred to him that, after all these years, he might not know her voice, and he was hesitant as he said, 'Joan?'

'I'll get her,' said Cathy.

He heard them talking in the background and seconds later Joan came to the phone.

'Joan,' he said. 'It's Ian.'

She hung up.

* * *

'Who was it?' said Cathy.

'Gilmore,' said Joan.

Cathy grabbed the receiver from her hand.

'What are you doing?'

'Calling the police.'

'Don't.'

'Joan . . .'

'I need to think. Just give me a minute. I need to think things through.'

'You may not have *time* to think things through.'

'Just give me a minute,' said Joan. 'Then I'll call.'

'Joan . . .'

She put her hands to her face. He had found her, and by staying in the house she was putting Cathy in danger as well as herself.

'I have to leave.'

Cathy began to dial.

'What are you doing?'

'Like I said, I'm calling the police.'

'Don't.'

Exasperated, desperate, Cathy was screaming now. '*For God's sake!*'

Joan grabbed the phone from her hand. 'I hid the body. That makes me an accessory . . .'

'You did it because you loved him.'

Joan dropped the receiver down, and, quietly now, replied, 'No. I did it because I hated Helena Warner.'

She opened the front door and walked out, Cathy plunging after her.

'Where are you going?'

'Get inside,' said Joan. 'Lock the doors.'

'Joan!'

She was gone.

Cathy ran down the path and, for one brief second, considered running after her, but even if she caught her, she wouldn't be able to drag her back into the house or keep her there. She ran back inside, lifted the phone, and dialled the emergency services.

'Emergency, which—'
'Police,' screamed Cathy.

As Gilmore saw Joan leave the house, he realised that he would have known her anywhere. She had changed, of course, but not out of all recognition. She looked thinner that was all, and a great deal older, as though she had ten or more years on him. She can't have had much of a life, thought Gilmore, but then I can't say I've been having a ball, come to think of it.

She passed the car and he watched her through the rearview mirror, seeing which direction she took when she reached the end of the crescent. She was heading towards the main road, and, having just driven down it, he knew the canal flanked it on one side and that the houses opposite were detached, well spaced and secluded. It couldn't be better, thought Gilmore.

He started the engine, reversed in a driveway, and drove after her, slowing as she came into view, watching as she crossed the road to walk alongside the rails.

The canal was to her left, and he could see the locks now, the gates wide enough to allow for an ocean-going liner. They were well lit, the water glittering blackly thirty feet below.

Cars sped past, indicating, pulling out to overtake him as he crawled along behind her. All it would take was for Joan to turn and see him. But she didn't turn. She just kept walking.

It was *perfect*.

Joan sensed, rather than heard, the car draw up beside her, and as she started to run she heard a car door slam. Then it was just the sound of her rasping breath, the locks flashing past to her left, the feel of his hand on her arm and Gilmore wheeling her round, sending her crashing into the rails, knocking the breath from her lungs.

He lifted her to her feet as if she were a rag, half dragging, half carrying her to the car, Joan lashing out, Gilmore avoiding the blows, hauling her into the passenger seat, locking the door, and moving across to sit behind the wheel.

'Shut up!'

She wasn't aware she'd been screaming, but, once she stopped, the silence was deathly. He'd picked his moment well, thought Joan. There was no one around, not even a car, and nobody had seen him.

He pushed her forward and bound her hands with rope. No wonder, thought Joan, that women are abducted. Christ, it was easy. So easy.

He didn't attempt to calm her, or answer when she garbled something not even she could catch. He pulled away from the pavement, the tyres burning rubber.

She tried again, and this time the words made some kind of sense.

'Where are you taking me?'

'Marshfield.'

33

The estate that Joan had lived on had changed so little in the past twenty years that even in darkness Driver navigated for Rigby with relative ease. These were the same dismal houses with the same unkempt gardens and broken-down cars fronting them, and it occurred to him, not for the first time, that real evil, unlike the romanticised fantasy of evil, was merely gloomy, monotonous and boring. He recalled one of his senior officers once saying that the majority of murders were not committed with malice, but with indifference, by people who lived in the type of environment that deadened the soul. This was just such a place, for these were the roads of his childhood, different roads perhaps, but essentially the same.

Rigby pulled up at the flat, and, after leaving the car, he, Driver and Dalton stood in front of the shop. The lights were out. The shutters were up. They went round the back and found it equally quiet.

There was nothing to choose between the door that led to Joan's flat and the door to the extension. They knocked on them both, waking Turnbull and showing their IDs when he came to the door.

'We're looking for Joan Poole.'

Turnbull didn't pay their IDs that much attention. 'She's out.'

'Where?'

'How should I know?'

'When did she go out?'

'It's gone midnight for fuck's sake.'

'When?' insisted Rigby.

'Eight. Maybe half past.'

'Did she say when she'd be back?'

'Why should she tell me? She's my tenant.'

'Let us into the flat.'

'You got a warrant?'

'No.'

'That's that then,' said Turnbull.

Trying a different tack, Driver said, 'Listen, she could be in trouble,' and his tone and choice of words succeeded where Rigby's slightly more abrasive style had failed. Turnbull, who seemed anxious to get back to his bed, said, 'What kind of trouble?'

'Someone's looking for her, someone who wouldn't do her any favours if he found her. You get my drift?'

Turnbull was chewing it over. Driver left him to it, and after a moment's thought, Turnbull said, 'So why do you want to see inside the flat?'

'Not really sure,' admitted Driver. 'You can be present. Keep an eye on us. Won't take a minute.'

Turnbull gave in, a combination of tiredness and total disinterest resulting in his saying, 'Wait there a minute.' He disappeared into the hall, grabbed a coat, and put it on over boxer shorts and the T-shirt he slept in, then stepped out into the yard, reaching in his pocket for the key to the flat.

Moments later, they stood in the doorway, Turnbull behind them, awkward, uncertain.

Rigby flicked a lightswitch. 'When was the last time you saw her?'

'About half eight, and you're not the only ones looking for her.'

It was a bit of a conversation stopper.

'What?'

'Bloke was here earlier. Came back about nine. Said he was looking for Joan. She'd already gone.'

'Describe him,' said Driver, but, even as Turnbull had a stab at it, he knew it was Gilmore.

'Have you any idea where she went?'

'She left an address,' he admitted.

Quietly now, Rigby said, 'Why didn't you say so up front.'

'I didn't know . . . I wasn't sure whether Joan was in some kind of trouble with the police . . . she wouldn't have thanked me . . .'

Driver could imagine. 'Go and get it,' he said. Turnbull disappeared down the stairs to do just that while Driver, Rigby and Dalton walked into what clearly served as a sitting room. In size and shape, it was larger and shabbier than the flat Joan had occupied in Southampton. That had been more of a bedsit, a galley kitchen leading off from a room strewn with possessions. This at least had a bedroom, but it appeared that Joan preferred to sleep on the couch, judging by the bedclothes and pillow still lying on it.

A cup and a soiled plate rested on a floor that was littered with items of clothing, the carpet beneath it threadbare, the underfelt showing in places.

'What a way to live,' said Rigby. Like Driver, he'd seen worse, but it was the staleness that was the hardest thing to stand. The air was thick with the smell of damp, unwashed clothes, and it wasn't a recent staleness. Over the years, similar smells had lodged themselves into the furnishings to rot slowly, filter into the air, and catch at the back of the throat.

'I'll check the other rooms,' said Dalton, disappearing, and, once he and Driver were alone, Rigby said, 'God Almighty.'

Driver touched the rim of a plate with the toe of his shoe. The food was congealed as if baked into the enamel, a glutinous pasta, the sauce smelling of fish.

Dalton returned. 'Nothing seems out of order,' he said.

'No sign of a struggle?' said Rigby.

'Just mess,' replied Dalton. 'Mattress on the floor in the other room. Damp. Don't blame her for sleeping in here.'

Turnbull returned with Cathy Walker's address. Rigby took

it, handed him a card, and said, 'If she turns up, don't tell her we called, just call us.'

'You said she's in trouble.'

'Danger,' said Driver. 'Big difference.'

'What sort of danger? I don't want any problems.'

They left him to lock up the flat and returned to the car. Driver, lowered himself into the passenger seat, picked up the map and found the quickest route to Cathy Walker's. 'Follow the road that runs parallel to the Ship Canal. I'll tell you when to turn.'

'I don't like the look of this,' said Rigby.

Driver thought of the speed with which Gilmore had got himself down from Warwick. 'Neither do I.'

34

Rigby turned into Belmont Crescent and pulled up outside the Walkers' to find a patrol car outside.

Minutes later, he knocked on the door and it was opened by a uniformed man.

Rigby showed his ID.

'That was quick.'

'Meaning?' said Rigby.

'What did they do, fly you down?'

'What are you talking about?'

The uniform showed them into the living room where Cathy Walker turned from the window, her husband standing up as they walked in.

Driver had met him before. He and Cathy were courting when he'd first interviewed Joan.

Paul Walker recognised him, but indicated the men from the patrol. 'They got me at work. Told me to come home.'

'What's happened?' said Rigby.

'I called the police,' said Cathy. She gave the uniforms a look they shrank away from. 'It took them about an hour to get here.'

'It didn't sound much like an emergency, love.'

'My sister—'

'All right,' said Rigby. He looked to the uniform for further explanation.

'Once we realised what she was trying to tell us, we contacted Thames Valley. They said you were already down here. They've been trying to contact you, but you weren't in the car.'

No, thought Rigby. We were in Joan's flat in all probability.

'Gilmore phoned,' said Cathy. 'Joan panicked and left.'

'When?'

'About two hours ago.'

'Why?'

'She said it wasn't safe for her to stay.'

'Have you any idea where she might have gone?'

'No.'

'Did she tell you what was going on?'

'She told me she thought Gilmore had murdered Merle Wachmann.'

That makes two of us, thought Driver.

Rigby said, 'She knows the area, right?'

'She's lived here all her life.'

'Are there any friends she might have gone to, or a favourite place, maybe?'

'I can't think of anyone, or anywhere,' said Cathy. 'Not off hand.'

'Have you got a picture of her?'

She had to think for a minute. 'The only one I can think of is one that was taken at our wedding. It wouldn't be much good. That was eighteen years ago.'

It was better than nothing, and Rigby said, 'Is it handy?'

Cathy stood up and walked across the room to a wall unit, opened a bottom cupboard, pulled out a photograph album and searched through it. She found what she was looking for, handed the album to Rigby and said, 'That's Joan. She was my maid of honour.'

Dalton peered over his shoulder at a plump face half hidden by large round glasses. Despite the obvious effort that had been put into it for the occasion, her hair hung straight and limp, slightly dull, the pale ash-coloured dress doing nothing for the sallow complexion. Joan Poole's no beauty, thought Dalton, that's for sure.

'Can we take this?' said Rigby. 'It'll give us something to distribute if we need to circulate a picture.'

'What use can it be? It was taken years ago.'

'We can still use it, create an impression of what she might look like now.'

Driver said, 'Did she tell you what happened at Marshfield?'

'You *know* she did.'

She didn't say anything further, and Driver added, 'Come on, Cathy . . .'

'*He murdered Helena Warner.*'

It wasn't exactly news to Driver, but to hear it stated was nevertheless gratifying. 'And Joan covered for him, right?'

'She hid the body.'

Driver had suspected she was covering for Gilmore, but he hadn't realised she was quite so deeply involved.

'Did you know this at the time of the original investigation?'

'No. That's what she came to tell me.'

'Why now?' said Driver 'Why after all these years?'

'Once she read that Gilmore had murdered Merle Wachmann—'

'We don't know that he did,' said Rigby, interrupting.

'Go on,' said Driver.

'. . . She thought that maybe he now saw her and Richard as some kind of threat.'

She's probably right, thought Driver.

'She can't stand the cold,' said Cathy.

It was an odd comment, thought Driver, one that would have been easy to pass off as being born of sisterly concern, but he picked up on it. 'Cold?'

She moved away from the window, slumped into one of the chairs. 'She can't look after herself, not properly.'

He walked across the room and crouched down by her chair, taking her hands in his, looking up at her. 'What do you mean?'

Cathy Walker looked vaguely surprised. 'I thought you knew – you seem to know so much about her.'

Driver said nothing, just waited, and she added, 'Joan is anorexic. Has been for years. She weighs less than six stone.'

Dalton caught a glance from Rigby who said, 'If she doesn't come back, it doesn't mean Gilmore's managed to find her. It could simply mean she's lying ill somewhere.'

Driver let go of Cathy Walker's hand, stood up, and thought it more likely that Joan Poole would be lying *dead* somewhere. But he didn't say so.

35

Rigby told the uniforms to stay with the Walkers pending further instructions from their own superior officers, then he, Driver and Dalton left the house.

Once they were back in the car, Dalton said, 'So where do we go from here?'

'Might as well head back to Oxford, interview Wachmann in the morning, arrange for him to be moved somewhere a little more secure than Chaggfords, and hope we find Gilmore before he finds Wachmann.'

He put the car in gear and pulled away, heading towards the motorway, none of them stating the obvious: that Joan Poole, assuming she was still alive, was as good as dead if Gilmore managed to find her.

'What are the chances that Hillier might find Gilmore before we do?' said Driver.

'About fifty-fifty.'

'And if he does?'

'Nothing I can do about it. If it happens, it happens, but I can't say I relish the thought of having to drive to Warwickshire every time we want to interview him.'

Driver was aware that in circumstances such as these, with two separate forces wanting the same man for questioning, possession was nine-tenths of the law.

Rigby said, 'And *when* we find him, it might be an idea to have back-up handy before we attempt an arrest.'

Driver didn't comment, and Rigby added, 'What do you think?'

Driver thought back to the many occasions on which he'd knocked at the door to Gilmore's home. His father had usually answered, Gilmore standing behind him, looking even younger than his nineteen years. He had known the boy, but he didn't know the man. The boy had been a killer, there was little doubt of that, but he hadn't been stupid, and, whilst he knew from experience that killers could sometimes grow a little arrogant, a little careless, he wouldn't have had Gilmore down as the type.

It was the first mistake he had ever known him to make. In all the weeks of questioning, he had been word perfect, his every step covered by alibis provided by Wachmann and Joan. Now, he'd taken a day off work, he'd gone down to Warwickshire, he'd murdered Merle Wachmann, to and he'd left his prints all over a glass. It wasn't his style, and it worried Driver.

'Gilmore claimed he last saw Helena the morning after the party,' said Rigby.

'What about it?'

'So what were his movements that day?'

'He claimed that he and Wachmann woke late and that Joan and Helena turned up at the house mid-afternoon.'

'Then what?'

'They had lunch, then Gilmore drove to Surrey to collect the tickets.'

'Why was it necessary for Gilmore to concoct an alibi that would cover him for Sunday afternoon?'

'He wasn't covering himself for Sunday afternoon. He was covering himself from Sunday evening to Monday morning so that when it was discovered that Helena was missing there was no chance of anyone assuming that they met up after she left Joan at the station.'

It sounded probable, thought Rigby. 'If Gilmore went to such lengths to cover himself, Wachmann must have done the same?'

'He claimed to have spent Sunday night with a second-year student. There's a statement on file.'

'How come they made no plans to cover themselves for the following days?'

'They probably expected people to notice almost immediately that Helena wasn't around.'

'But that didn't happen.'

'No. She wasn't missed until Wednesday, and only then because she'd missed two tutorials. The water didn't reach the house until Wednesday, so, if she had been reported missing on Monday, I would have had it searched as a matter of procedure and we would have found her. As it was, by the time I went to Marshfield, the house was no longer visible.'

'So Gilmore was lucky.'

'Very.'

'You didn't send divers down?'

'I didn't think it was worth it. Nobody in their right mind was going to hide a body in a house when there was a vast expanse of marsh to bury it on.'

Rigby seemed to think it wiser not to comment, and, picking up on that, Driver added, 'Look . . . I made a mistake.'

'We all make those,' said Rigby. 'It was a fair assumption. And if she *had* been buried on the marsh, once it was submerged, then, as you say, the likelihood of finding her body was remote.'

'So, three months down the road,' said Driver, 'with no body, and unable to crack Gilmore's story, I was left with no option but to drop the case.'

Three months, thought Driver. He had been an experienced DCI and he had begged his chief superintendent to allow him more time and resources, but word came back that it would prove a waste of time, and that had been that. He might have been convinced that Helena Warner was dead and that her remains were buried on the marsh, but that vast expanse of water had convinced his superior officers that he would never be able to prove it.

Rigby was lost in thought, and Driver, who could almost guess what was on his mind, smiled when he said, 'Why a wardrobe?'

It was question Driver had asked himself more times than he cared to remember.

'Who knows,' he replied. 'They weren't stupid, so there had to have been a reason.'

'It must have been a good one.'

'Bloody good,' said Driver.

36

She remembered the road to Marshfield as soon as he turned off the ringroad. Oxford lay several miles to the south, but Gilmore headed east and then dipped towards the village. There was no new town development choking the old like a cancer: just a row of shops, a small church, a post office. Everything in darkness. Another world, thought Joan. She had no idea what the time was. Long gone midnight. That was all she knew.

The hardcore road to the reservoir sank beneath the tyres and Gilmore slowed. It was too black to see much, but she knew what it looked like out there. She had seen footage showing the divers bringing the remains to the surface, and, despite the fact that she couldn't see beyond what the headlights picked out, she could picture it.

He stopped the car, and they sat in silence, the water so close she couldn't see the embankment.

'I won't beg,' she said.

'I don't want you to.'

He had never seen her like this, vulnerable, defeated, and he struggled to find a way of saying what he knew she wanted to hear, what she'd *always* wanted to hear. It would cost him so little to say it, and it would mean so much to her. 'I wasn't in love with you. I didn't even know you, but it wasn't meaningless.'

He thought he heard the echo of a laugh, a soft and mocking thing as Joan looked up, her face only inches from his own. It was perhaps the most unattractive face he had ever seen. 'You stuck your neck out for me, and I was grateful.'

'You were grateful, but now you're going to kill me.'

'If not for you, Driver would have taken me apart.'

She stared straight ahead, her eyes fixed on the water.

'I'm sorry,' said Gilmore, 'sorry it's ended like this.'

The minutes ticked by, and still he made no move.

'Do it,' she said, quietly. 'Get it over with.'

Christ, thought Gilmore. I've never felt so lonely. 'It isn't that simple,' he said.

Somehow he hadn't visualised that it would be like this, but then he didn't really know what he'd imagined. He'd had some vague idea that he'd find it easy, that, having done it before, he would be able to do it again; but killing Joan was different: she'd done everything in her power to protect him and he couldn't depend on some sudden outburst of rage to provide the trigger.

At least his father wasn't alive to be devastated, or to hold out a promise he wouldn't, in any case, have been able to keep. *I won't let them hurt you.* If the police got hold of him, they would hurt him plenty, and Gilmore knew it. But it wasn't physical hurt he feared: it was the mental anguish of being made to answer questions he had answered so often before: 'Tell me again, Ian, what time did you leave the house to get to Marshfield?'

He and Wachmann had gone in separate cars, Wachmann in the Volvo Estate passed onto him by his parents, the boot filled with beer, spirits, mixers and food. His own car was smaller, the back seat crammed to capacity along with the boot, and when they were ready to make a move he had expected Helena to get in beside him. Instead, Joan had taken the opportunity to jump into the passenger seat and he and Helena had exchanged glances. 'It's OK,' said Helena. 'I'll go with Richard.'

He hadn't wanted Joan's company, but it wasn't until much later that he realised this was largely because, prior to introducing them, Helena had ensured he would see her in an unfavourable light. They had been driving to the station to pick her up, and he had said, 'What's she like?'

'You be the judge,' Helena had said, and the way she had said it, the curl to the lips, had ensured that, from the moment he met Joan, he would become dismissive of her in a way that was both polite and total.

Wachmann drove on ahead, and, as he followed in the hatchback, Joan had said, 'I expect you think I got into your car because I'm too stupid to realise you would have preferred me to go with Richard.' And the comment was so accurate that he hadn't known how to respond. 'But it was the only opportunity I was likely to get to speak to you alone, so I didn't have much choice.'

Even then, a warning bell was sounding. The way she had followed him around in the house hadn't been lost on him, but he thought she was just going to tell him how she felt and he could have handled that. He wouldn't have hurt her. He would merely have lied through his teeth to save her feelings and, even as she spoke, an appropriate response was forming in his mind. *I'm sorry Joan, I find you attractive, but I'm in love with Helena. If ever we split, I'll let you know.*

'Do you and Helena have what some people might refer to as an *open* relationship?'

The stock response evaporated. 'How do you mean?'

'I mean do you turn a blind eye if either of you wants to have sex with somebody else?'

'What are you getting at?'

The mocking tone, the note of surprise in her voice: 'Don't tell me you don't know?' He could see her smiling on the periphery of his vision.

'I think you'd better shut up,' he said.

She pulled from her bag a bundle of letters, drew one out at random, and started to read it aloud: '"I begged him to make love to me, but all he could think of was Ian and how he might feel."'

She was joking, thought Gilmore. She had to be joking.

'Or this,' said Joan, choosing another: '"Ian was in the next room, a mere wall away, and likely to walk in on us at any moment . . ."'

It was, he reflected, an almost incoherent torrent of venom, her spittle on the windscreen, her fingers surprisingly strong on his arm as though by exerting some physical pressure she could impress it upon him that what she was saying was true.

He had pulled into a side road and had ordered her out of the car, but she had merely insisted he should listen and had justified herself by saying, 'She's screwing you around.'

She wouldn't get out of the car. That had been the worst thing. He had begged, demanded, and finally threatened, but she sat there like a great fat spider. Repulsive. Determined. Immovable.

Short of opening the passenger door and hauling her out, he had felt himself to be helpless. She had him trapped, and she knew it, and, as the minutes ticked by, she continued to give him the benefit of excerpts from the letters.

He had felt, at one point, like killing her. 'Why?' he said. 'Why are you doing this?'

It had been a beautiful afternoon, the warmth like milk on the skin, the sky a Wedgwood blue. And yet he remembered this only in hindsight. At the time, the only thing that registered with him was the greasy transparency of her moonlike face as she replied, 'I should have thought that was obvious. I love you.'

It had been a relief, in a way, a relief to know she was mad and that he could therefore disregard what she had told him.

He climbed back into the car, pulled away, and was profoundly grateful to discover she appeared to be of the opinion that she'd said enough. Consequently, the last few miles were driven in total, blissful, silence, but once they reached the house he felt drained, as though he had taken a severe emotional beating, which, in retrospect, he supposed he had.

He climbed out of the car and walked away from it, passing Wachmann, who called out as he was unloading the Volvo. 'What took you so long?'

Ignoring him, he walked round the house to the back. The

outbuildings were empty now, the silo devoid of grain, the last of the farm machinery having been moved to Thornley some weeks before and leaving the place deserted.

A post-and-rail fence divided what passed for a garden from the paddock where Ernst Wachmann had kept a mare. Weeks before, he had seen the mare loaded into a trailer, a foal at foot, one man loading the foal before the mare so that she'd walk up the ramp without protest. Now the paddock was empty, and already the grass had grown thick and lush for lack of grazing. It was the time of year when the pasture, like the corn and like the reeds on the land below, grew rapidly, and in the few short months since the Wachmanns left the farm had already shaken off almost every sign of its ever having been cultivated.

He walked to the trees and looked down at the water edging towards the house. He was aware of the stillness, the silence, the smell of the hot damp earth, and he knew then what it was that had kept Richard's father anchored to the flatlands: Marshfield was as close to paradise as any man had a right to get, and it soothed him so that, if not for the fact that he had no choice but to go back to the house, he might not have given another thought to the things Joan Poole had said.

He made his way from the trees and across the marsh, birds rising from the long damp grass like ghosts flapping silently on the periphery of his vision, and, as he entered the kitchen, Wachmann looked up from the food he was eating illicitly and said, 'Helena's upstairs.'

He checked his watch. It was seven. People would soon start arriving. He bounded up to the bedroom, and, as he walked in, Helena turned away from the wardrobe. 'Where did you get to?'

Hell and back, thought Gilmore. 'I went for a walk.'

She pulled clothes out of a rucksack along with a travelling iron, and, after switching it on and standing it on the windowsill to heat, she said, 'Something the matter?'

He was tempted to tell her, but decided to wait. If he were to tell her now, there was nothing either of them could do about Joan until after the party, and he didn't want the party ruined for Helena. It would be better to wait until they could confront Joan and then take her straight to the station.

He watched as she slipped a sweatshirt over her head and black denim jeans down her long slender legs. They were the only clothes she was wearing, those and the pumps that she kicked off her feet and left by the door to the wardrobe. And then she stood in front of him, confident that what he was looking at was enough to please even the most critical man, and said, 'Come here.'

Despite himself, despite the gnawing doubts, the anger, the confusion, he made love to her, and later, when they lay quietly together, he said, 'I'd die for you, do you know that?'

Ironic, really.

She pulled away from him. He remembered that later. It was something about the way she did it, as though she had found his sincerity embarrassing, and he listened to her footsteps recede as she walked to the only functioning bathroom.

While she washed, he ironed the clothes that she'd pulled from the rucksack, the sound of running water a backdrop to what he was thinking; for, despite his best efforts, he found it impossible not to think about what Joan had said. Certain pieces of the jigsaw were falling into place. Lies he'd persuaded himself that Helena would never tell; the look on the face of a friend when he asked after Helena; the half-smile that followed Gilmore's reply of 'She's fine'. It was like a poison that seeped through all reason.

He switched off the iron as she returned, and after handing her the clothes he watched her dress in a wrapover skirt and black silk blouse that she knotted at the waist. She ran her hand through her hair, confident of how she must look, and untroubled by the lack of a mirror. 'We ought to go down,' she said.

'I need to wash.'

She waited for him and, when he came back to the room, he dressed in the clothes he'd worn earlier, and they went down, oblivious of what was to come.

Driver knew nothing of this. The story Gilmore had given

him was a far cry from the truth, and he had never deviated from it, never left anything even resembling a loose end that Driver could pull at in order to unravel the lie.

But things were different now. Twenty years ago, Driver had *suspected* that Helena had never left Marshfield. Now that the remains had been found, Rigby *knew* she hadn't.

He was running out of time.

37

Joan was afraid. Deeply, quietly afraid. Just sitting there, waiting, knowing he would kill her. She knew now what it meant when people spoke of having seen a condemned man walk to his death calmly. It wasn't calmness, it was disbelief, an almost dreamlike state.

She realised now that he'd got the address from Turnbull. She hadn't thought to tell him not to say where she was if anybody asked. She hadn't been thinking straight. Not that it would have made much difference: if nothing else, her stint with the *Evening News* had taught her that information was rather more easily come by than most people realised.

She wondered what was going through Gilmore's mind. This tense silence reminded her of the silence they had shared on the day of the party. Once they had arrived at the house, he had left her in the car and had walked to the trees. He had stayed there for more than an hour, looking down on the house below, and she didn't doubt that his memory of it would probably reflect the fact that in early evening the sun had struck it at an angle, setting the brick ablaze with a depth of colour probably denied it at other times of the day.

Her memories were somewhat different in that, whenever she thought of the house, it was forever couched in darkness, notwithstanding the fact that it had been early evening and quite light when they had arrived.

Perhaps her perception of this perpetual darkness was born of the fact that a vast proportion of the house had been closed off, the doors locked, the rooms minus light bulbs, and cold. Bitterly cold.

Gilmore had left her to extract herself from the car. He hadn't spoken a word after she'd lapsed into silence and she had entered the house to find that Wachmann had restored the electricity some weeks before. An emergency generator that his father had intended as a back-up in the event of a power failure was throbbing in the outhouse, vibrating against the brick, lighting a fraction of the house and providing the power that had enabled Gilmore to set up his sound equipment.

The floor in the hall had been wooden, her footsteps deadened by the dampness of what might once have been a highly polished feature, and she had experienced the uncomfortable feeling that the cellars would resemble a dungeon, the walls dripping with moisture, people hanging from chains. But it was a farmhouse, no more, no less. Functional, and totally devoid of architectural interest.

A downstairs room had been furnished with items scavenged from junk shops, and over a bottle-green sofa Helena had thrown a mock-Turkish blanket in russet and gold, a simple act that had transformed the room; but that was Helena all over – touching, transforming, and . . . Her heart misgave her as the word 'disfiguring' leaped to mind.

She had been shamed into turning on her heel and walking into the kitchen, where she had helped Helena with the food, and Helena had said, 'So what do you think of Ian?'

'I think he's too good for you.'

Helena had stopped what she was doing, the butter knife in her hand, a drop of the soft golden substance dripping gently from the blade. 'You shouldn't behave as you do,' said Joan. 'He loves you.'

Helena had thought that was funny. Her gentle laugh, the whiteness, the evenness, of her teeth, the dark glossy hair cut short and soft and shining in the light from the window. She has no idea, thought Joan, no idea at all of the anguish she causes others. Either that or she doesn't care. 'Does he know?' she said. 'Does he know you . . .' She wondered how best to phrase it. Somehow, the words 'sleep around' sounded old fashioned. Helena would probably laugh if she used them.

Helena unwittingly saved her the agony of having to pick an alternative phrase by saying, 'If he did, he'd kill me,' and Joan thought how apt that comment had been. How literal. Killing Helena Warner had been an instinctive thing; Gilmore's attempt at saving himself from a life steeped in misery, a life loving someone like her.

In a just world, her death would have marked the end of his misery, but the world wasn't just, as her body had surfaced to prove, washed by the water until only the bones remained, pebbly smooth and devoid of that beautiful skin.

She supposed that, in the event of Gilmore's having found her out, Helena would have expected him to forgive her with the further expectation that their relationship would continue much as it had before. That would have taken a degree of presumption Joan didn't possess, but then Joan had never in her life been beautiful, and men like Gilmore didn't fall in love with women like her. She had known it even in the car when she had thrown all pride to the wind and had told him she loved him on the grounds that she might never again find the opportunity or the courage to do so. The fact that he had responded by telling her she was mad had been a small price to pay for the pleasure, a bittersweet memory, perhaps, but at least it was a memory, of sorts. She had never, before or since, told any man that she loved him, but she would go to the grave knowing that at least she had said it once, and meant it, even if at the time her saying it at all had resulted from loneliness and the pathetic hope that she might one day, somehow, be able to teach him to love her in return.

She had stood at the kitchen window and had watched him walking down from the trees. The early-evening sun would ultimately go down behind them, but now it hung low, soft and full, the colour and texture of a mango, dripping its juice on the wetlands. She had wanted that memory of him to last forever, and had impressed upon herself the way in which he walked, unhurried, lost in thought, unmindful of the birds that rose casually into the air at the sound of his approach.

He used the front door, and Wachmann had called out from the kitchen to let him know that Helena was upstairs; and then she had heard his foot on the stair, quick and light as he took them two at a time.

People began to arrive, men mostly; some of them bringing girlfriends, most of them bringing wine.

There had been little for Joan to do other than to melt into the background and observe, and, on the few occasions that people had attempted to draw her into conversation, she had dulled their interest by describing herself as an acquaintance that Helena had brought to help with the catering. It wasn't entirely untrue. She might just as truthfully have said she was Helena's portable backdrop, something that by the very nature of itself enabled her to shine the brighter by comparison.

She found herself looking at Wachmann and trying to imagine him painting those butterfly thighs. He didn't look the type. Too sensitive. Too quiet. She had attempted, at one point, to get him to talk about it, and he was polite enough, but that was as far as it went, as far as it would ever go. She knew the signs. They were signs she read every day of her life from men she bumped into at college, on buses, in shops.

He had been looking past her even as they spoke, and, when Joan turned her head a fraction to see what had caught his attention, she saw that it was Helena, and that they were exchanging the sort of look Joan doubted she would ever exchange with a man: the provocative, lascivious look that had prompted her to watch them, keep them in view, and anticipate their moves.

Hours later, her patience had been rewarded. The instant they slipped from the house, she noticed, and she followed them, knowing instinctively that, if she lost sight of them, they might slip into any one of a dozen outbuildings and be lost to her.

The moon was a mere quarter full, but the very darkness was incandescent, and as black as it was, and as hidden as they were, she could see them as clearly as if she were looking through some third eye.

Helena stood with her back to the outhouse, the sound of the generator humming through the bricks, and Joan fled then, fled, not only from the imminence of their lovemaking and the certainty that it would be a visual reminder of everything she would never be or achieve, but from the threat of a lost opportunity.

She found Ian pulling extra glasses out of a box and shook his arm.

'What is it?' he said, and his voice held a trace of mistrust mingled with irritation.

'You'd better come,' she said.

Her tone of voice made him pay heed in a way that the ranting whine of her earlier efforts had failed, and he followed her, followed her back to the outhouse to where Helena, beautiful in her ecstasy, had cried out like one of those slow-flapping birds that had risen from the marsh.

The triumph of that moment would stay with her forever, greater than the satisfaction of turning that brass knob and feeling the body heavy against the door, falling out as she pushed it in until only the hand remained, the fingers slender, the flesh like wax, and Gilmore's *'Christ, oh Christ . . .'*

the room, she could see them [illegible]. [illegible] looking through a red-rimmed eye.

[illegible] stood [illegible] for [illegible] the cupboard, the sound of the [illegible] through the [illegible], and [illegible] [illegible] from the [illegible] [illegible] [illegible] would be a [illegible] [illegible] [illegible] or [illegible], but [illegible] [illegible].

[illegible] pulling [illegible] off, [illegible] about his arm.

"What if it's [illegible]," [illegible] held [illegible] [illegible].

"[illegible]," [illegible] said.

[illegible] put [illegible] that all [illegible] had [illegible], and he followed [illegible] back to the [illegible] [illegible] [illegible] and [illegible] one [illegible] from the marsh.

The [illegible] of the [illegible] would [illegible] of [illegible] and [illegible] the [illegible] against the door, [illegible] out of [illegible], and [illegible] [illegible] and [illegible].

38

There had been no sleep for either of them, just cold, hunger and the total blackness that swallowed Marshfield whole. She remembered that blackness. It had been a long time coming on the night of the party, but once it came it was absolute, blocking out the buildings, the land, and the relentless insidious way in which the water had crept to the door.

Now the light was creeping across the water, lighting the opposite bank, the trees, the hills.

'It's time,' said Gilmore. He pushed her forward, untied her hands, then eased himself out of the car. She followed him down to the water, stiff with cold, aching with fear, and stood by his side on the bank. She stared at the point where she knew the house must be, imagined she could see the faint outline of the small, brick building that housed the generator, and he said, 'Over the years, I've thought of how you led me from the house.'

'You had a right to know.'

'You weren't thinking of me. You were lashing out at her.'

She considered her options and found that, even with her hands free, she didn't have any. Even if she caught him off guard, she had no weapon, and, as he had already proved, he was stronger than she. The likelihood of her overpowering him was remote. She looked around, the light growing stronger by the minute and revealing things that only moments before had been cloaked in darkness.

There was nowhere she could run to. The trees were thin and offered no place to hide. The road to the village was steep, long and devoid of cover. He wasn't stupid, thought Joan. He had known that by bringing her here he was as good as locking her in a wardrobe. He said, 'Why did you accept the invitation to the party?'

'The need to win,' said Joan. 'The need to hang around long enough to get one over on her, just once.'

'And how did you plan to do that?'

'By showing you the letters.'

'But that's not all you did.'

'No,' said Joan. 'Turning the knob on that wardrobe was an unexpected bonus.'

'I saw your face as you did it. I'll never forget that look.'

'You wore it too.'

'Not me . . .'

'Just for a moment, when you caught her with Richard and lashed out, you wore a look on the outside that I'd been wearing on the inside for longer than I could remember.'

'Is that what made you protect me?'

'No. I covered for you because you'd done something I'd wanted to do for years.'

She wondered how different things might be now if she hadn't covered for him, and if, on the night of the party, she hadn't taken control. She had pushed him into the car, Wachmann following in his own car, and as she drove she had invented the story they told to the police. Keep it simple, she told herself. The simpler, the better. No elaborate digressions, nothing unusual, just simple.

They had hardly spoken while they were in the car, but once they got back to North Oxford, she stood in the living room, Richard on the couch, Gilmore slumped in a chair, and she had taken them through the story, ensuring they knew it by heart.

Richard had got it in an instant, but Gilmore had been too shocked to take it in. She had persevered, shaking it into him as best she could, impressing the details upon him.

'Are you listening, Ian. Are you? Good. Now repeat what I just told you.'

She could remember, still, the way he stumbled through it, his voice a monotone.

'Richard threw the party. It broke up at roughly two a.m. I drove you and Helena back to Oxford and dropped you off at Somerville. Richard drove home in his own car. There was nobody with him. He got back to the house the same time as I did. He saw me drop you both off.'

'What did we talk about during the journey?'

'Nothing,' said Gilmore. 'You and Helena had crashed out. Helena in the passenger seat. You in the back.'

'Good,' said Joan.

Once he'd grasped it, she told him that, a few days previously, Helena had bought some tickets to a concert at the Free Trade Hall.

'They were meant to be a surprise', said Joan. 'They'll come in useful now, because when the police question you you're going to claim you bought them and left them at home by mistake.'

'Why?'

'Because tomorrow you're going to Surrey. You're going to tell the police you went to get the tickets, stayed overnight, and drove back to Oxford on Monday.'

'Why?'

Irritated, she said, 'Why what?'

'Why do you want me to have an alibi for Sunday night and Monday morning?'

'Because I'm going to claim that Helena waved me off at the station on Sunday night. Got it?'

'No,' said Gilmore, stupefied by shock.

'*Jesus Christ!*' She turned to Wachmann in despair, but he merely shook his head as if he too had given up on any hope that Gilmore would ever get it. 'I want the police to believe I was the last person to see her alive.'

He broke down. She couldn't bear it.

She gave up, aware that he was in no fit state to cope with

any more pressure. She would have to hope he'd got the basic story, but only time would tell. He might crack under questioning, but she wouldn't. She had known it even then.

As if sensing that she and Wachmann had given up, he pulled himself together a fraction. 'These tickets,' he said. 'They're in Helena's room.'

'So?'

'So how will you get them? The room will be locked.'

'I know,' said Joan, 'but her room is on the ground floor. We left the window open. If I climb the wall tonight . . .'

'Someone might see you breaking in.'

'I don't have a choice. The tickets are important.'

'The police will want to know why I didn't just ask one of my parents to post them.'

'So you tell them you didn't want them poking around in your room.'

'I still don't see why you want me to drive to Surrey . . .'

She rounded on him, repeating what she'd told him only seconds before: 'I want the police to believe I was the last person to see Helena alive. *I thought you'd got that!*' And, as she snapped the words, she realised her tension was born of jealousy. He was mourning Helena's death, and he would always mourn it; not because he had killed her, but because he had loved her.

She hated him for that.

She stood in front of him now, rubbing the weals on her wrists, feeling the blood pumping painfully into her fingers, and was aware when he stepped back silently to stand behind her. She expected the feel of a rope around her neck or the stab from a blade, but neither came, and it seemed to her that she stood like that for a lifetime.

No wind, no cloud in the blanket of grey that hung overhead, just a piercing cold that numbed the skin and the water reflecting the trees.

Now, thought Joan. *Do it now.*

She thought of Turnbull, the flat, the years ahead. What was there to live for? Endless rejections for features that never sold, for a book that would never be published; just dirt and chaos and misery, and paying the rent in a way that took a piece of her life every time.

'Get out of here, Joan.'

For some moments, she did nothing, and when she turned round, he sank to his heels, reaching down to touch the ground where the launch had come to shore. He could see it still, the plastic sheet, the way it had fallen open, and despite the horror of it, he had wanted to touch this remnant of the woman he had loved.

She crouched beside him. 'What is it?'

'I loved her,' he said.

How odd, thought Joan, that even now, after all these years, and despite the fact that she's dead, to hear him say he loved her still has the power to hurt me.

She straightened and made for the car, climbed in behind the wheel, and he followed, climbing into the passenger seat, relinquishing control. Some things, thought Joan, don't change.

'Why didn't you kill me?'

'Maybe I just haven't got the guts.'

'Maybe you're just not a killer,' said Joan, softly.

She backed away from the bank, the water receding, the coots taking flight.

'Where are we going?' said Gilmore.

'To Richard,' said Joan.

39

Cora dressed with care, choosing a tailor-made suit, the fine woollen cloth a deep green, the silk blouse ivory.

At her shoulder, she pinned a brooch, the centrepiece a large Cape Yellow, its sunburst of diamonds scattering shards of light on the walls and floor.

'How do I look?' she said, and she sensed the ghosts of the kitchen staff around her, one of them brushing a speck from her shoulder, another tucking a strand of hair into the tortoiseshell comb.

You're leaving us, Miss Cora . . . but where will you go?

To a bungalow, Alice.

But why do a thing like that when you've got all this?

It isn't worth having. It never was.

A distant sound, one that was still unfamiliar to her, broke into her thoughts, and she climbed the stairs to answer the door. There had once been a time, not so long ago, when the doorbell was answered by her companion, and she was still unused to responding to the shrill, sharp ring that had replaced the slightly less penetrating sound of a bell that had been in use in her father's day.

She left the room and felt her way down passages she had run through as a child, and at the foot of the stairwell she paused a moment.

The window before her was small and arched, its stained glass depicting the family crest as if to remind the servants who their employers were. One of the builders had asked if he could have it, and Cora didn't doubt that he intended to sell it despite his protestations to the contrary. It would end up in a restaurant in Hong Kong, or perhaps in a house in America.

Let it go, thought Cora. Sooner or later, the heat, or some drunk, would fracture the hand-blown glass, and, in trying to get it repaired, the new owner would discover that it was unrepairable; that they don't make glass like that any more; and that the colour, as well as the quality, would prove impossible to match. And that was just the trouble, thought Cora. The colour and quality had gone out of everyone's life. The entire world was proving unrepairable, and those who cared enough to make some attempt at rectifying the damage had been reduced to patching it up as best they could.

Odd images remained like a stubborn stain: the way in which she had stood at the foot of these stairs to bar her father's way as he thrust the child into Alice's arms.

'*Keep it out of my sight!*'

She had never seen the child again, but the fragment of fabric that came from his gown was with her still. She kept it on her person like a knife; held it to her cheek, could smell him still. Or was that merely fancy?

The doorbell rang again, and she opened it to find herself being addressed by people she didn't know. It was nothing new.

'We're looking for Richard Wachmann,' said the woman.

Cora felt for the fragment of cloth, still warm from its contact with skin the texture of silk.

'You'd better come in,' she said.

She led them down to the cellar and found Richard where she knew he would be, inscribing the concrete support that stood beneath the plinth.

'I'll leave you to it,' she said, and they stood in the doorway, Wachmann aware they were there, not knowing who they were, not caring particularly.

Gilmore had lost count of the times he had watched him

work, the smell of paint pervading the house, his obsession with the light; but he somehow couldn't see him as some kind of stone mason. 'What are you doing?' he said, and Wachmann, a chisel in one hand, a mallet in the other, recognised his voice, but didn't turn round.

'Hello, Ian.'

'Mind if I take a look?'

He carried on working, putting the finishing touches to an inscription that wasn't intended for public display. 'Give me a minute.'

He hadn't changed, thought Joan. Not even ghosts from the past could pull him away from his work.

'Done,' he said, standing back.

She read it.

The dead demand a double vision. A furthered zone.
Ghostly decision of apportionment. For the dead can claim
The lover's senses, the mortgaged heart.

'Carson McCullers,' said Gilmore.

'You have a good memory.'

'What's its significance?' said Joan.

'Helena's favourite poem,' said Wachmann, adding, 'I take it you've come for the unveiling?'

'No,' said Joan. 'We've come because Ian needs help.'

'Help?' He put the chisel down. 'He seems to make a habit of needing our help.'

'Richard,' she said softly, 'I don't know whether you know, but Helena has been found.'

She searched his face for some sign that he understood the implications of what she was saying, but Wachmann merely pushed past her. 'I've got to get cleaned up.'

He led them up a flight of stairs that led to the kitchen and rinsed his hands under an old-fashioned tap, the chrome flaking, the draining board wooden and rotting.

The grey, powdery dust that had come from the concrete

upport washed off in an instant, and, when he dried his hands on a rag, Gilmore saw they were clean.

If only it were so simple, thought Gilmore, to wash blood away.

40

Rigby, Driver and Dalton stepped across the threshold to find themselves in what had been the entrance hall of the house. All that remained of its former elegance was the way in which the banisters of a stairwell swept in a graceful curve to upper rooms, its former proportions having been lost to the recent alterations.

As Cora led them into the house, Driver tapped a wall. Much as he suspected, it was studding, a lath-and-plaster job. The plain, mass-produced doors that led from it were each numbered. He guessed that a similar arrangement had been constructed on the upper floors and that, at the back of the house, there would be further units, each much like another, the walls magnolia, the kitchens avocado. In a house of this type and size, a house that was not of sufficient architectural interest to warrant an order protecting it from what he saw as a form of vandalism, he supposed that the sitting room alone would probably have become two units. It seemed something of a crime to him, but then he wasn't an expert; all he had to go on was his gut reaction to what he saw as a form of desecration.

Cora walked ahead and they followed her down the passage to wide, arched doors. They framed a hall that had clearly been left untouched, and Driver said, 'The rest of the house has been converted to units. Why not this?'

'I wanted it left as it is,' Cora replied. 'The statue had to stand in a suitable setting.'

Rigby stood in the doorway and was able to visualise what it might have looked likę with the banqueting table running its length. The sweeping velvet curtains he could imagine to have been at the windows were long gone, and the windows looked out onto a wilderness: a skip dumped haphazardly in the centre, a half-felled tree, the fragments of a statue half ıidden in the grass.

Along one panelled wall, a table had been laid with a white inen cloth, linen serviettes, silver cutlery and lead-crystal gobets. The elegance of the tableware seemed out of keeping with he quiche and sausage rolls provided by a catering company. Provision had been made for fifty or more, but there were ewer than fifteen present, the murmur of their voices audible, heir conversation lost on him.

At the far end, the statue stood screened from view. Impos-ible to hazard a guess at what it might look like, but one hing was for sure, thought Driver: whatever it was, it was ig.

He turned his attention to those present. Most seemed istinguished in some way, their clothes expensive, their man-er confident, and yet they also seemed diminished by the legance of the Jacobean splendour that surrounded them. ike small, worried animals, they huddled together in front f a fireplace, resting their glasses on the mantelpiece, their ords disappearing up the chimney to a wide grey sky.

He recognised Thurston, who saw Cora and made his way owards her, ignoring Rigby and Dalton, but affording Driver brief look of mild curiosity. 'Cora,' he said, 'you remember Dr Mulholland, and this is his wife, Annette . . .' And then he ıw Wachmann.

He took the opportunity to study him unobserved. He adn't changed, thought Driver; he'd give him that. Gilmore ooked his age, but Wachmann could be taken for late twenties t a push, the hair still dark, the skin round the eyes unlined. Ie backed off, then positioned himself so that he was standing ehind him in much the way he had stood behind Gilmore t Marshfield, and Wachmann turned instinctively. Their eyes met, but there was no sign of the shock that had registered on Gilmore's face. 'Remember me?'

If Wachmann had been about to respond, he didn't get the chance. From within a group of people, Gilmore and Joan appeared, and, if Gilmore had been stunned to see Driver at Marshfield, it was nothing to what he felt now.

In that brief moment, he looked back through the years and realised that Helena's death had cost him everything he had ever felt worthy of owning – not just his happiness or the chance of a normal life, but his belief in himself as a good and decent person. He almost broke down then, but all he had left was his dignity, and he was fucked if he was going to lose that.

'Hello Ian,' said Driver, and it was exactly as he had imagined it would be, right down to the way in which Driver then added, 'It's been a long time.'

It was over.

41

In an instant, Rigby and Dalton were striding towards them, but before they could say or do anything constructive, Thurston tapped a glass, 'Ladies and gentlemen . . .'

They had no option but to give him their attention, and throughout the speech that followed Driver kept Gilmore in view.

As Thurston got into his stride, Cora began to lose interest. The truth was, she didn't much care for his speech, his gratitude, or his hypocrisy. She cared only about fulfilling the promise she had made to James, one in which she had sworn to demolish the statue of her father and replace it with a monument to him. The worst of it was, she knew now that the past fifty years had been a waste. Much that was said about people who ended their lives as a result of losing the partner they loved was nonsense. Better to get it over with and join the loved one as quickly as possible. What had been the point in dragging on, year after year, waiting to be reunited with her only reason for living?

You're leaving us, Miss Cora. But where will you go?

To James.

You lied to me, Miss Cora.

It's forgivable, Alice. I lied to myself. We all do that at times.

The speech over, Thurston turned a fraction to indicate the screen, his action prompting people to the left and right of him to wheel it away from the statue, and, when it was exposed, it seemed, to Cora, that time itself stood still. She had heard the phrase so often in her life and yet, before that moment, she had never quite known what it meant.

The photographer broke the spell, the snick and whir of his camera echoing through the hall. Initially, he focused his attention on the statue, and then he turned his lens on the sea of faces that were staring up at it, frozen in shock.

Cora imagined a voice. It was so familiar, and yet, she couldn't quite place it for a moment. Then it came to her that the voice was not the product of some ghostly visitation but the recollection of something her mother had said when she found her in the coldroom: 'Oh Cora . . . what have you done?'

Somebody spoke and, by doing so, snapped her back to the present. 'What is it?' they said.

Cora had no more idea than they, but she hazarded a guess. 'I think it's some sort of body,' she said. 'Some sort of body, in stone.'

42

In seeing what Wachmann had portrayed, Gilmore's worst nightmares took on flesh and smiled down at him. It depicted what the body had looked like some days after death occurred. There had been no obvious signs of decomposition for Wachmann to record, but what he had captured was death. *Helena's* death.

His eyes travelled from the neck to the breasts, across the hard, flat belly and down to the lips of a vagina that had been carved into an insect, the clitoris its body, the vulva a pair of wings intricately carved. Wachmann had caught the essence of her to perfection. She had been like some giant butterfly, a beautiful, poisonous thing that sucked people in and drowned them in their own inadequacies. He wanted to run, to escape as he had longed to escape the day he had turned and seen Driver at Marshfield, but now, as then, he realised there *was* no escape. It was an image he would carry for the rest of his life, something to be slotted into his memory alongside his last glimpse of Helena and the horror of the moment.

Joan staggered back, raising her arm, pointing a finger directly at the face but saying nothing, and in those few moments Driver took stock of how a combination of passing years and lack of care had worn her down.

Joan, who had never been anything to shout about, looked as though she had plunged into middle age with something approaching gratitude. Everything about her spoke of her no longer feeling any need to make any kind of effort with her appearance. Her drawn-back hair needed washing, and the skin around the eyes was deeply creased, the thick-lensed glasses emphasising lines that might have been there from birth. Her clothes, which were similar to those she had worn when he'd questioned her years ago, hung tent-like on what was now an emaciated frame, and he saw again her squalid room, the slap of tyres through rain.

She was struggling to maintain her composure, and the hand lowered gradually, the fingers curling. She looked at Driver. How long, thought Joan, how long has he waited for this? How sweet it must be. She cast her mind back to the day she had advised him to give up, the day when he had dropped all pretence at gentility and had made it clear that, by mocking him, she was making a grave mistake. This was his day, the day Driver had waited for, knowing it would come.

She stood before him, old before her time, and whatever she might have done, thought Driver, she didn't deserve what had become of her. He watched the threat of tears spill over, and, despite what he knew she was going through, found himself saying, 'You shouldn't have covered for him.'

She looked up, her face already swollen. 'I thought I loved him,' she said. 'But he could have been anyone – it was what he represented that mattered to me.'

'I know,' said Driver, and as the implications of what he was looking at began to register, he found himself wondering how many times he had stood on the embankment to wonder what the remains would look like now. As a result of his experience in such matters, he had believed himself to have a pretty good idea, but not in his wildest imaginings could he have come up with anything quite so horrific as this.

'Good, isn't it?' said Wachmann.

Good, thought Driver. It wasn't a word he would have chosen, but then he wasn't quite sure what words would adequately describe it. The way in which the skin had somehow relaxed on the bones; the suggestion of discoloration; the fractional drop to the jaw revealing teeth that were slightly parted. He studied the face and found it hard to imagine it as the face of a person who had actually existed. It was too unbelievably beautiful for a start. There was a suggestion of arrogance about it, perhaps even cruelty, and he found himself wondering whether that was what art actually was, the ability to portray something of the soul. 'Why did you do it?' he said.

'I'm not really sure,' replied Wachmann. 'Ask Thurston. He's the expert.'

Somebody laughed, and Driver turned to see the elegant woman Thurston had introduced as Annette, her eyes wide with shock. Her husband led her to a chair, sat her down. He turned his attention to Cora, but, ironically, she seemed less perturbed by the statue than most of those present.

Thurston, outraged, his voice magnified by the proportions of the hall, said, 'I'll see that it's removed.'

'Oh, *leave* it,' said Cora. 'What does it matter?'

It was a crushing blow, but that was all. She was neither horrified nor outraged – merely deeply disappointed. Without realising it, she had allowed herself to look forward to touching those familiar contours as if the statue were James come back to her from the dead. Instead, there was some dreadful thing on the plinth, and that, almost certainly, had come back from the dead.

She glanced at Wachmann, who returned her look with something approaching amusement. 'I'm sorry,' he said. 'I meant to sculpt James, but I found myself sculpting her. I can't explain it.'

'Did you know her?'

He caught the curiosity in her voice but felt, as he always felt with Cora, unthreatened by it. 'Not terribly well,' he admitted.

43

Gilmore, suspecting he looked more composed than he felt, watched as Rigby sat opposite with Driver to his left and Dalton remaining by the door. This was going to be like an action replay of the interviews with Driver, thought Gilmore, and he had a suspicion that this was one of the interview rooms he'd been questioned in before. If not, then it was as near as made no difference. The walls were the same old cream and the table dividing him from Rigby and Driver was bolted into the floor. Even the strip light that flickered overhead seemed the same, as if the past twenty years had never happened.

He had been nineteen the first time he saw this room. Nineteen, frightened, and feeling acutely alone. It was only later that he realised how careful Driver had been. At the station, he had never allowed him to be left unobserved, not even for a moment, and at home, at Driver's suggestion, his father had embarked on a number of ploys in order to keep him in constant view, one of them being a total redecoration of the house. Gilmore had watched him painting over walls that had previously been papered so that his bedroom was the only room left habitable. 'You won't mind, Ian, if I kip on the floor in your room for a couple of weeks?' And every time he had gone for a walk, his father had grabbed a coat. 'Think I'll come. The air will do me good.'

Rigby inserted a tape into the deck, gave the date, time, location, name and rank of the officers present, and asked whether he would like a solicitor present.

'No,' replied Gilmore, and Rigby spoke for the benefit of the tape to record the fact that he had declined the services of a solicitor.

'Not very wise, Ian.'

Gilmore glanced at Driver, but made no reply. He didn't intend to speak unless it was absolutely necessary. Besides, the only solicitor he could think of was the man his father had chosen to represent him twenty years ago. He had stood up to Driver, threatening to slap an injunction on him if he didn't stop harassing his client, and Gilmore had respected him. More than that, he had been profoundly grateful to him, but he had also suspected that, like Driver, the solicitor had thought him guilty, although he hadn't pressed him to admit it. He had merely explained, carefully, cautiously, that, if Gilmore were to admit to him privately that he *was* in fact guilty, he could no longer represent him as being *not* guilty, and Gilmore had taken the hint. 'I'm not guilty,' he said, and quietly, his solicitor had replied, 'Then I give you my word that I will do everything I can to help you.'

He had kept his word, but he had also kept his distance, detaching himself on a personal level, and inadvertently making it obvious that he thought him guilty as hell.

Rigby placed a file on the desk between them and opened it. 'Recognise this?'

'Yes.'

'Thought you might. It's the file relating to Helena Warner's disappearance.' He produced another file, Dalton having handed it to him. 'Recognise this?'

'No,' said Gilmore.

'It's the file relating to the discovery of Helena Warner's remains.'

He placed it on top of the older, thicker file, folded his hands on top of it and said, 'In 1975, you were questioned in relation to Helena Warner's disappearance.' Gilmore sat impassively. 'Do you admit that you knew Helena Warner and that when she disappeared you were questioned in connection with her disappearance by Detective Chief Inspector Driver of Thames Valley Police?'

'Yes,' replied Gilmore.

'According to a statement you made to DCI Driver at the time of Helena Warner's disappearance, you claimed that Helena left Marshfield with you, in your car. Joan Poole and Richard Wachmann backed up that story.'

Gilmore made no comment. Rigby hadn't asked for one, and when he remained silent Rigby added, 'Clearly, that was untrue. Helena Warner never left Marshfield.'

Rigby wasn't surprised when Gilmore responded by saying, 'The fact that her remains have been found at Marshfield proves nothing. She left the party with us, and she could have gone back to Marshfield any time between the early hours of Sunday morning and the following Wednesday.'

It was much the reply that Driver had expected him to make and he allowed himself a smile, a smile that wasn't lost on Gilmore, who returned it with what Driver took to be a look of pure insolence.

Rigby was aware that there was little he could ask him that he hadn't already been asked before, many times, by Driver, and that Gilmore had all the answers. They were answers he had probably spent twenty years turning over in his mind, answers he had improved upon, perfected perhaps, made totally watertight. He therefore changed tack and came at him with something he hoped would shake him a little.

'According to a statement on file, you once admitted to having met Merle Wachmann.'

Gilmore wondered where this was leading. 'What of it?' he said.

'When did you meet her?'

'Shortly after the Wachmanns moved from Marshfield to Thornley.'

'How did you come to meet her?'

'Richard invited me for the weekend.'

'When was this?'

'May 1975.'

'And did you, at any time, meet Merle Wachmann again after that?'

'No.'

'So you are saying that the only time you ever met Merle Wachmann was in May 1975.'

'That's what I'm saying,' said Gilmore.

'Are you sure about that?'

Gilmore tensed. He didn't like the tone that had crept into Rigby's voice. It sounded a warning bell. He made no reply, and Rigby added: 'Your fingerprints were lifted from a glass found in the sitting room at Thornley. You were there the day she was murdered, Ian. We can prove it.'

You stupid, stupid bastard, thought Gilmore.

He allowed his thoughts to drift back to Thornley and recalled how Merle Wachmann had appeared as if out of nowhere, he eyes bloodshot, her skirt spattered with mud. She was standing with her back to an outhouse, the door wide, her frame blocking his view of the generator it housed. It was similar to the building Joan had led him to on the night of the party at Marshfield, right down to the way in which damp had crumbled the plaster to expose the brick, and, as he heard the hum of the generator, he saw a vision of Helena standing with her back to the wall, Wachmann making love to her.

When they were a matter of yards away, Joan had gripped his arm, unbelievably strong, her eyes magnified by the thick-lensed glasses: '*Now do you believe me?*'

No, he hadn't believed her. Not even the evidence of his own eyes could persuade him of something he didn't want to be true, and then the anger had come – cold, complete, and bringing with it an almost supernatural strength.

He had gone for Wachmann like an animal, ploughing into him, hitting him with a strength he hardly knew he possessed, and when Wachmann turned and ran he had lashed out at Helena, an anguished, unpremeditated act, but no less unforgivable for that. He had sent her crashing back against the wall, had heard the crack of her skull against the brick, had seen her sink to the ground. And after that . . . nothing.

Wachmann was gone. He didn't know how he knew that;

he just knew it. There were just him, and Joan, and Helena on the ground.

She was alive then. He knew that much at least. She had her hands to her head and she was moaning. Not crying, just holding her head and moaning.

'Come on,' said Joan. 'Let's go.'

'We can't just leave her.'

'There are plenty of people to look after her. If you're that concerned, you can always make an announcement in the kitchen for someone to go to her. God knows, there are plenty of men in there who owe her a favour . . .'

Strangely, he had wanted, instinctively, to leap to her defence but he hadn't seen how he could under the circumstances.

She had taken him back to the house, letting him in through the front and guiding him straight up the stairs to a bedroom beyond the room he had shared with Helena.

Wachmann had made up a bed there, a mattress, a duvet, a clock radio, and blankets at the windows.

He couldn't remember sitting on the mattress but he recalled that Joan had rocked him in her arms in much the way that his father was to rock him weeks later, and she had listened to him as he went through the first few hours of what would be years of grief. It was over between them. He could never take Helena back. But it didn't stop him from feeling the loss. He loved her. Could Joan understand that? Christ. Why couldn't something like this take that feeling away?

She understood. Of course she understood. In those few hours, she had seemed to him to be the warmest, the most supportive woman he had ever come across. The plain face, the dowdy clothes and the thick-lensed glasses seemed suddenly not to be there, as though they had been replaced by a warmth he could sink into, wrap round himself and suckle from for the rest of his life. And he had made love to her, or, rather, he had acquiesced when she had made love to him. His had been the action of one who had hoped that the woman he loved might stumble in on them to be hurt as he had been hurt, and yet he had somehow found himself capable of channelling his rage into a sexual act that had made Joan cry out with a pain that was all his own.

He was aware that she was sexually inexperienced, but he was aware of nothing else about her in the physical sense. He was neither attracted to nor repulsed by her. He was indifferent. She didn't exist, other than as a comforter, a confidante, and a vehicle for betrayal. 'What would you do if she found us like this?'

His rage had poured out of him, and, when he had done with it, he had smelled her hair, so strange a smell after Helena's perfume, not offensive, just different, the texture of her skin less smooth, her body alien territory, and he had pulled himself away.

'Where are you going?'

'I've got to see her.'

'Don't go . . . don't leave me . . .'

The kitchen door was open, the night air cold, and he stumbled through darkness towards the small still form. 'Helena,' he said, and he squatted down beside her.

Liquid had dripped down the side of her face. Oil, he thought, oil from the generator, although, even as he thought it, he knew it to be wrong. The machinery was inside, behind a closed door, and yet he had allowed himself to believe it was oil. He touched it, then stood up, turning his hand this way and that, and finding that already it was drying as if his skin were absorbing it – Helena seeping in through his pores, flesh of his flesh, blood of his blood, and then came the frantic wiping that wouldn't remove it from his hands. Her blood would be there forever. He had known it even then.

'She's dead,' said Joan, so matter-of-fact, and it wasn't until that moment that he realised she had followed him. He looked down and saw what Joan had seen from the start: that the lips were slightly parted, the eyes open, dull, and staring at the moon. 'She can't be. Christ, she *can't* be!'

'I'll find Richard,' said Joan, and she left him, left him alone with his amateurish attempts at resuscitation. He had fallen to his knees beside her, had torn at the black silk blouse and had rested his head on her breasts in the hope of finding them warm, yielding, and the heart beating strongly. But there was nothing, and when he had put his lips to hers he had found that her mouth was a cave of blood.

He leaped back then, disgusted, beside himself with fear. Somebody must have heard him shouting. Christ, they couldn't just leave him there . . .

Eventually, he had collapsed against the wall, silent now, and that was how Joan had found him, pinning himself to the brick and knowing that, without it, he wouldn't be able to stand. 'Come on,' she had said quietly. 'We need to sort this out,' and she'd led him, as if he were a child, back to the house.

with [illegible] open-mouthed attempt at [illegible]. He had taken to [illegible] [illegible] [illegible] [illegible] [illegible] and [illegible] his head on [illegible] in the hope of finding them [illegible] and [illegible] [illegible] [illegible] and when he [illegible] his [illegible] he had found that the [illegible] was a [illegible] of [illegible].

He knocked [illegible] [illegible], beside himself with [illegible]. Somebody must have [illegible] of Clara [illegible] couldn't [illegible] him alone.

Eventually, he [illegible] collapsed against the wall, [illegible] and that was how [illegible] found him, [illegible] [illegible] the [illegible] knowing that, without it, he wouldn't be able to [illegible]. 'Come on,' she had said [illegible]. 'We [illegible] out,' and she'd [illegible] him [illegible] [illegible] [illegible] [illegible].

44

Hillier, who had ordered the search of all property belonging to the Wachmann family, stood in a barn that was situated a good half mile from the house. It measured twenty by forty, and was of a type that was used to store hay for winter cattle.

The large double doors that provided its main entrance were bolted closed, a smaller door cut into one of the larger doors having provided day-to-day access. It stood open, a thin oblong of light providing their only means of seeing what was stored inside the barn.

The copper beside him looked nervous, anxious to be out of there.

'You all right?' said Hillier.

'Yeah, I just didn't know what it was. What any of them were, come to that.'

Hillier tried to imagine what it must have felt like to enter the barn and find what he had found.

They trod across an earthen floor that absorbed the sound of their footfalls, and he made for the object that had sent his detective sergeant crashing out of there. He stopped in front of a coffin-shaped object that lay on the ground covered by a sheet. 'I came back,' said the detective sergeant. 'Covered it up. Don't know why. Just didn't want anyone walking in and seeing it unprepared.'

Hillier bent down and took a corner of the sheet, peeling it back to reveal what lay beneath it. That it was a coffin of sorts hardly came as a surprise, but it was unlike any he'd come across before.

Its contents seemed frozen in time, preserved for posterity. He had seen similar objects in catacombs, but none had been like this. He reached out, and touched the face. 'When did you find it?'

'About half an hour ago.'

'Anyone else seen it?'

'No.'

Hillier picked up the sheet and the two men covered it again, Hillier straightening as he said, 'I'd better contact Rigby.'

'Why should he be interested?'

'Thames Valley found something similar a week or so back. He's handling it.' He took a last glance round. 'Let's get out of here.'

The junior officer needed no further invitation, and after they'd left the barn Hillier stood ankle deep in mud and took a good look at it. From here, it looked innocent enough, a barn like any other. Not the kind of place where one could expect to encounter horror, but then years on the job had taught him that horror wasn't choosy. It manifested in the most unlikely of places, and in various guises.

The farm was on the market. Somehow he couldn't imagine a rush of buyers. Not when people discovered what had been found in a barn on its land. 'Rigby,' he repeated. 'We'd better get him down here.'

45

There was no question of interviewing Wachmann without a solicitor and Thurston present. The solicitor was easy to organise. Thurston wasn't. 'I've got a hospital to run, patients to see. I can't get down to the station until after six p.m.'

Rigby, keeping the tone of frustration out of his voice as best he could, had been unable to do anything about it. He replaced the receiver, turned to Dalton and Driver and said, 'I've met psychopaths with a better attitude than him.'

Driver smiled, though there was little to smile about. Gilmore had proved immovable. He hadn't admitted to murdering Helena Warner or Merle Wachmann, and he had insisted he'd had no intention of harming Joan.

Joan was as bad. She had sat in the interview room exercising a right to silence she no longer had – not if she knew what was good for her. Driver, who had tried pointing out that her silence would look bad in court, had been met with a blank stare. He was tired. He gave up. And then the call had come in from Hillier, and a short time later he found himself subjected to the driveway at Thornley for the second time in three days.

This time, it was Rigby's saloon that took the punishment, the suspension better than that of Driver's hatchback, but nevertheless doing little to save their backs.

'You'd have thought they'd have laid hardcore down,' said Rigby.

'Not Ernst,' said Driver. 'He thought luxuries were a waste of good money.'

'His wife didn't think so,' said Rigby.

'No,' said Driver. 'She hankered after a bit of softness in her life.'

'You have to feel for her, looking at this.' Rigby viewed the farm though a fine cold drizzle. It was preferable to the downpour Driver's hatchback had struggled through, but it seemed, somehow, to find its way into the car to penetrate their clothing and remind them of what it had been to stand on the embankment and wait for the divers to surface with Helena Warner's remains.

Hillier was already there, sitting in a police Range Rover, one of his men beside him. He climbed out when the saloon pulled up, and Rigby and Driver got out. They nodded an acknowledgement and Driver looked at the barn where Merle Wachmann's body had been found hanging.

The entrance was surrounded by a glittering blackness, police activity having churned the ground that led to it into a quagmire. Bouquets had been placed at the door, the flowers already dead. He stooped to read one of the cards, the name meaning nothing to him but the sentiment familiar enough. The name on each of the cards would have meant something to Merle. They were put there by locals, people she rarely saw, people who lived in the village and beyond, perhaps women in a similar situation to her own, women who had married farmers only to discover they had chained themselves to a life of mud and loneliness.

'In here?' he said.

'No,' said Hillier. 'Over there.' He pointed across the fields and then indicated the Range Rover. 'We'd better go in mine.'

Rigby and Driver climbed into the back and soon realised why they needed it. The barn they were heading for was way across the fields, the ground giving way beneath them, Hillier putting the vehicle into four-wheel drive.

It was small, old, and tucked away behind hedging that Ernst had uncharacteristically left unfelled. Driver soon saw why. Part of the hedge was supporting one wall of the barn.

Hillier pulled up and they climbed out, the detective sergeant opening the wicket door. As Driver and Rigby followed Hillier into the barn, Hillier said, 'Once we knew we were dealing with murder, I organised a thorough search of the outlying buildings, and we found this.'

Driver looked in the direction Hillier was indicating. The walls of the barn were a mixture of stone and cob, whitewashed in places. There was no electricity. Just a pale, inadequate light from the open door.

It was as though they had stepped into some kind of funeral parlour, thought Driver. Statues stood everywhere, figures like angels draped with cloths that hid their faces from view. Rows of canvases were stacked against the walls, some of them standing on the earthen floor, others standing on pallets, none of them framed, and Driver caught sight of a painting, a picture of butterflies painted on the inner thighs of a woman. It was the type of thing that, once seen, would not be forgotten easily, and he remembered it well enough. He had first seen it at the house in North Oxford. 'What's this?' he had said.

'A painting,' Wachmann had replied.

'Don't get clever with me.'

Turning to Rigby and Hillier, he said, 'This is down to Wachmann.'

'How do you know?'

'I recognise his work. Some of it, at any rate.' He indicated the painting of butterfly thighs, as he'd called it, and added, 'The statues are a new one on me, but Wachmann definitely painted that.'

'That's quite something,' said Hillier.

I'm getting old, thought Driver. It does nothing for me. But then, he reflected, he hadn't found it arousing the first time he saw it, and that had been twenty years ago. There had been something about it. He couldn't quite put his finger on what it was, but it left him cold.

He recalled squeezing himself into the room in North Oxford where Wachmann had worked and slept. It had been tidy from necessity, canvases striving for survival in the midst of personal possessions that were few, but of high quality. Like his mother, Wachmann had taste, thought Driver. That taste had driven him to produce the finest work with the finest materials available, and much, if not all of it, appeared to be stored here.

'Why should he keep his work here?'

'There's a lot of it,' said Driver. 'Maybe he can't sell it, and doesn't want to destroy it.'

It sounded reasonable, thought Rigby. Hillier said, 'You said on the phone that you'd found him.'

'We're waiting for his psychiatrist to grace us with his presence so we can interview him.'

'I'll want a word after you.'

Rigby didn't doubt it. He whipped a cloth from one of the statues. It revealed the figure of a woman, but there was nothing remarkable about it. 'OK,' he said, 'so he stores his work down here, but I don't see why you had to get us down here to show us. A fax would have done.'

'I wouldn't be too sure about that,' said Hillier. 'You're dealing with a case in Burford.'

'What about it?'

Hillier reached for the sheet that concealed the coffin. He peeled it away, and what he revealed sent a shockwave through Rigby and Driver. It subsided almost instantly, as they realised that the figure lying in it was carved from stone.

Rigby moved closer, reached down and touched the coffin. Like the trough found at Burford, it tapered towards the feet, but it was the figure lying in it that was of interest to Rigby. It was so well carved, it looked like a calcified corpse.

He touched it as though taking some kind of reading, a personal history, a dialogue, and as he studied it further he realised just how accurate it was. It depicted the features as being bloated, the lips peeling back from the teeth. It was too accurate for comfort, and he stood up.

'Well?' said Driver.

'It's a replica of what we found in the Saxon coffin at Burford.'

'Saxon?'

'So I am reliably informed by Thames Valley's answer to the Met's Antiques Squad,' said Rigby, drily. 'And who are we to argue?'

Who indeed? thought Driver. 'Saxon, then,' he conceded.

When he had watched McPherson drain the trough, Rigby had been more interested in how the victim had come to be there than in the trough itself. Even so, it had struck him as something that would arouse interest if auctioned. It was in near perfect condition, and McPherson, peeling the gloves from his hands had said, 'Wouldn't mind that in my garden.'

Personally, Rigby wouldn't have had it within fifty miles of his own garden, but he could imagine McPherson planting it out, replacing its cargo of dead flesh with a living burst of colour; not giving its former contents so much as a passing thought other than to remind himself of the events that had put him in possession of it.

'Reckon you'll get an ID on the victim at Burford?' said Hillier.

'Maybe,' said Rigby. And maybe not, he thought. As revealed by a piece in *The Times* that appeared in March 1992, Scotland Yard's Missing Persons Index was so inaccurate it was advised that the whole thing should be obliterated and restarted from scratch with a check on every name still listed as missing. Chances were, he'd find a match, but it would take time.

He brushed imaginary dirt from his hands as Driver pulled a portfolio out from a stack, laid it on the ground, and untied the tapes that held it closed.

The sketches it revealed appeared to be anatomical studies, the flesh stripped from the muscle, the muscle stripped from the bone. Nothing to alarm in that similar sketches had been made by artists over the centuries, but, as he flicked through them, the sketches became increasingly obscene, some sexual, others merely horrific.

The last sketch of all was of Gilmore, and Driver cast his mind back to the day he had said, 'Not gay, I take it?'

Wachmann had brushed the comment aside, but the sketch of Gilmore now gave him pause.

'Who is it?' said Rigby.

'Gilmore,' said Driver.

Rigby pulled a cloth from a statue that reminded him of a postcard. It had been sent to him from some far-flung corner of Europe, a card purchased in one of the better-known museums. The figure it depicted had been found frozen in a glacier, the skin brown, pierced, tattooed. The statue was milk-white, a fine, translucent marble; but the effect was the same.

Driver returned the sketch to the folder and walked towards the statue, his footfalls silent, the damp cool earth absorbing all sound, all dust, all light. He came to a stop in front of it and Rigby said, 'I hate to say it, but it's incredible. All that talent . . .'

Bugger talent, thought Driver. He turned away.

There were several cardboard boxes by the door, each of them small, each of them held together with masking tape. He pulled one from the pile, ripped the tape that held the lid, and opened it.

'Anything of interest?' said Rigby.

'Magazines,' said Driver. He thumbed through them. They were of a similar type to the magazines found at the house in North Oxford, and he recalled saying to Wachmann, 'Go on, take a look. They're Gilmore's, right?'

He put them down, walked towards the door, and paused there a moment.

'You OK?' said Rigby.

Driver didn't know. Gilmore was a killer. He murdered Helena Warner. The likelihood of his sharing a house with someone who also just happened to be a killer seemed highly unlikely. 'I can't get a grip on all this. I need to think.'

They left the barn, walking out of the gloom and into the comparative brightness of a December afternoon.

'I'll arrange to have it all moved and stored,' said Hillier. 'OK by you?'

'No problem,' said Rigby.

They drove to the house in silence, Rigby and Driver climbing out of the Range Rover and making for the saloon.

As they climbed into the car, Driver looked back at the scene. He saw the barn against a backdrop of cold, ploughed earth and a slate-grey sky. The stone, the house, the surrounding land, all were in tones as muted as those he had seen when he'd first gone to Marshfield, and the only splash of colour came from the bouquets of flowers that were dying by the door.

He thought of what her life had been. Not much of a life, he thought again. A high price to pay for a simple mistake. Love, marriage, and a lifetime's incarceration in places like Marshfield and Thornley. Whoever had killed her had done her a favour in a way. He pushed the thought from his mind as Rigby fired the engine.

'What do you think?' said Rigby.

'I don't know,' said Driver. 'Right now, I honestly don't know what to think.'

'That makes two of us,' said Rigby, 'but when we get back, we make a start on Wachmann.'

'Always assuming Thurston has graced us with his presence.'

'I'll arrest him if that's what it takes to get him into the interview room with Wachmann.'

Right now, Driver didn't doubt it.

46

It was dark by the time they got back to Thames Valley. Driver stood in the interview room that Gilmore had sat in hours before. Gilmore was now in the cells three floors below.

He stared out of a meshed window, which gave him a view of the High Street. There was nothing particularly picturesque about it, but he found something consoling in the sense of continuity it gave him. Same bridge. Same afternoon traffic. Same thirty-foot drop to the pavement. He turned back, glanced at Rigby, Wachmann, Wachmann's solicitor and Thurston.

Rigby opened the file and pulled a statement, one that Driver recognised as having been taken from Wachmann during the original investigation. He slapped it down on the table, scanned it briefly, said, 'On the nineteenth of June 1975, you made a statement to the effect that Gilmore dropped Joan and Helena off at Somerville before driving back to the house you both shared in North Oxford.'

'What about it?'

'Helena Warner never left Marshfield,' said Rigby.

When this produced no response, he pulled the photographs from the file and slapped them on the desk alongside the file.

'Look at them.'

Wachmann made no effort.

'*Look at them.*'

He spread them out before him, and Wachmann glanced at them briefly. They told him what he already knew: that the remains had been almost completely decomposed by the time they were found by the divers, but that what he had sculpted was identical to the photographs in every other respect.

'How do you explain it?' said Rigby.

'I can't.'

'Can't, or won't?'

'Can't.'

'Try.'

Wachmann watched the spools of the tape as they turned.

'You went back to Marshfield in the days prior to the house being submerged.'

'You can't prove that.'

'I don't need to. How else could you have produced the statue?'

No reply.

Driver cut in with, 'Do you remember what it was like to be brought in, day after day, week after week?'

Wachmann hit back, 'I remember watching you giving up by degrees when it didn't get you anywhere.'

Driver smiled. 'And here I am, popping up out of the woodwork, twenty years down the road.' He leaned forward and placed his hands on the desk, palms down. 'Aren't you getting just a little bit bored with it?'

'Aren't you? Besides, you're retired. What authority do you have to question me?'

'He has all the authority he needs with me here,' said Rigby.

'You've got absolutely nothing on me,' said Wachmann.

'That so?' said Driver.

There was something about the tone of his voice, something Wachmann recognised from many years ago. It served as a warning, and he responded to it with caution. 'Like what?'

'Like what was found in the barn at Thornley. The barn where you stored your work. *That's* what we've got on you. That, and *this.*' He stabbed the photos with an index finger.

The barn, thought Wachmann, and, the minute he knew they'd found it, he knew that Driver had him.

He expected to feel something, if only a vague unease

about what the future held, but, strangely enough, it didn't worry him.

At first, he didn't know why. Then he recalled those units at Chaggfords and the bed-and-breakfast existence that would follow. Churchill House was preferable to that, preferable to most things, in fact, and, with his parents dead, he would inherit the farm, and the proceeds of sale would pay the fees for a good many years to come.

Driver instinctively left him to it, Rigby doing the same, each of them watching and waiting, hoping the thoughts that were running through his head would produce the result they wanted.

Wachmann looked up. Smiled. 'I made a deal with my parents. They said that, if I would agree to being admitted to Churchill House, they wouldn't go to the police.'

'What made them want to make a deal of that nature?'

'Fear, I suppose.'

He stopped there, and inevitably Driver asked, 'What had you done to make them afraid?'

'I hung something up to dry.'

'What kind of something?'

No reply.

'What kind of something, Richard?'

Wachmann timed his answer for maximum effect, and got it by saying, 'Something that belonged to my mother. I hung it in a tree.'

'What was it?' said Rigby.

No reply.

'Come on Richard,' said Driver. 'What was it?'

There was a moment's hesitation, and then he replied, 'A cat.'

Driver suffered a flashback to the stone-flagged kitchen, the fawning Siamese, and the tone of Merle's voice as she said, 'I keep my cats in. I don't let them out of my sight . . .'

Wachmann added, 'I think she would have forgotten about it if not for the birds in the paper.'

'What paper?'

'The wallpaper. I used to paper them over.'

The room seemed suddenly colder, a little bleaker, as though some small part of the dismal sky had crept through the mesh to envelop them.

Wachmann smiled, looked at Driver and said, 'She used to strip it down. It made her cry . . .'

47

Softly now, Driver said, 'When did you last see her?' and Wachmann cast his mind back to what had happened shortly after he had arrived at Thornley. He had taken a train to Marshfield and had walked from the station, cutting across the fields that flanked the side of the house, knowing that, from this angle, he couldn't be seen from the kitchen.

When he got to the outbuildings, he had seen Gilmore walking towards his car, and he had kept out of sight until it disappeared down the drive. Then he had walked to the kitchen and had knocked on the door because he had no key.

His mother answered, her skin blotched, her eyes bloodshot, and mud on the hem of her skirt. There was no welcome, no comment, just a blank stare as though she barely recognised him.

'How about letting me in?' he said.

She didn't reply. She merely kept him standing on the doorstep to what, after all, had never been his home. Marshfield had been his home, the flatlands he had loved with a passion that equalled his father's, but for reasons that were very different.

She barred his way to the kitchen, and with the rain driving against his back, Wachmann grew impatient. 'Look,' he said, 'you were the one who phoned. You were the one who wanted me to come. Are you letting me in, or what?'

'Now that you're here, I'm not sure.'

'For God's sake,' said Wachmann. 'It's fucking cold out here . . .'

She stepped back then, opening the door a fraction, Wachmann pushing his way into a kitchen that looked as he'd never seen it before. The stones and surfaces shone in what might almost have amounted to a celebration of his father's death, and the table was devoid of the paperwork that had surrounded his every childhood meal. 'Incredible,' he said, flatly.

He walked to the kettle and filled it, aware that, to his mother, it was almost as though a stranger had walked into the house to make himself at home. Even then, he sensed her fear, and, turning from the kettle, he said, 'Tea?'

'Not for me, thank you.' Her voice shook like the crops that were shrivelled annually.

'Miss him, do you?'

'Who?'

'My father. Miss him?'

She stood by the door as if willing him to leave, and Wachmann indicated the kitchen. 'What do you think he'd have made of all this?'

'All what?'

'The tidiness. Bury him tidily, did you?'

He switched the kettle on, turning as he said, 'Why did you ask me to come?'

'I need to talk to you.'

'What about?'

'You know what about.'

'Sorry, you've lost me.'

'That girl . . . they've found her remains.'

'Which one?'

'Don't. Please Richard, I can't stand it . . .'

'Helena, then. Is that it? Helena Warner?'

She looked as if she were about to collapse and, instinctively, he led her to the table, pulled a chair, and sat her down. 'Shhh,' he said. 'Come on now, no need for that.'

She sobbed the words, 'Once they found her remains, I knew . . . *I knew for certain* . . .'

The silence that followed lasted long enough for the kettle to boil and switch itself off automatically. Even then, Wachmann waited long enough for the steam to become a gentle wisp before he said, 'You always knew. You've lived with the knowledge for years.'

'*I haven't!*'

'*You have.* Oh yes . . .'

Women were so beautiful when they cried, so vulnerable. Sometimes, he'd made a woman cry for the sheer pleasure it gave him to feel that his guts were being ripped out. He reached down, wiped a tear from her cheek and said, 'You're the one woman I've never been able to sculpt. Did you know that?'

She was dumb with the horror of it.

'It wasn't for lack of trying. I used to sculpt you from memory, but the result was never satisfactory. I can't sculpt from memory, you know that.'

She ignored him, as if by doing so she could somehow make him dematerialise.

'You were wasted in places like Marshfield and Thornley.' He smiled to himself. 'People used to sit on the marsh for hours, looking for rare birds, rare plants, a certain light on the water. Nobody looked at you. They didn't even know you existed.'

She allowed the statement to rest, uninterrupted, between them and he added, '"Life's a battle, Richard." Do you remember saying that to me when I was a kid? "A lifelong battle trying live with the consequences of one stupid mistake." I used to think you were referring to marrying my father, but as I grew older . . .' He stopped, and his mother shook her head. 'As I grew older, I realised you were referring to me.'

'I wasn't . . . I . . . Please Richard, I want you to go . . .'

'You had the most beautiful body. Incredible skin.' She drew away from him. 'Cold. Like stone. Like marble.' He smiled. 'I want to come home.'

She stood up, the chair falling back.

'What is it. What did I say?'

She moved away from him, made for the door and opened it.

'I can, can't I? Now that my father's dead. *I can come home?*'

'I'm leaving.'

'You're what?'

'Selling up.'

'But—'

'You belong in an institution.'

For a moment, they merely looked at each other, his mother shaking now, her eyes wild with horror. 'I have to tell the police.'

'Tell them what?'

She pointed in the direction of the barn where he stored his work. 'Those things,' she said. 'Those things in the barn . . .'

For a minute, he hadn't been sure what she meant. 'The barn,' she repeated. 'Full of your things.' Her mouth twisted into an expression of horror. 'You have to move your things.'

She ran out into a rain that was driven by a wind from the north, making for her car, and, after grabbing a torch from the sill, he ran after her, catching her easily, holding her close, stroking her hair. 'Shhh, it's OK, really, it's OK.'

She was shaking with fear and the cold, and he dragged her across the fields, the small resistance she made a mere inconvenience, hardly enough to hold him back as he hauled her along in his wake.

He struggled with the door within a door, the wind fighting him every inch, and then they were inside, and she watched as if rooted to the spot when he shone the torch on the statues. He saw at a glance that nothing had been disturbed. Fine muslin cloths covered most of the pieces, some of them ghostlike with limbs protruding where the cloths had slipped to reveal them.

'Mother . . .' He was gentle now. 'Why won't you let me come home?'

She stared past him at the horror of it all as he put his arms around her. 'Come on,' he said. 'No need . . . no need.'

He let go of her and began to whip the muslin from the statues, his mother shaking her head like an animal shaking off water, trying to rid herself of the apparitions before her. There was a face he knew she would recognise, and when she saw it she put her hand to her mouth.

'Thought so,' said Wachmann. 'Remember her?' He pulled another cloth. 'And her?'

She was white, thought Wachmann, as white as stone. He loved her for that.

'They came to the door when we still lived at Marshfield. Remember?'

She made no reply, and, his patience exhausted, he found himself shouting at her, trying to shake a response from a mouth rigid with terror. '*Do you remember?*'

Her reply was barely audible, more of a whisper, the words falling to the earthen floor of the barn. 'Of course I remember.'

'There now,' said Wachmann. 'That wasn't so hard, was it?'

No reply.

'*Was it?*'

'No . . . no . . .' she replied. 'Not so hard . . .'

It had been the year before he'd gone up to Oxford, his mother in the kitchen, his father in the fields, and two foreign students had come to the door, asking if it was safe to cross the marsh. His mother had told them to keep to the path, and Wachmann had offered to guide them. Even then he had sensed her hesitation, and a look had passed between them. 'I'll guide them,' he said.

'We're just about to eat.'

'Start without me,' said Wachmann, and then he was gone, closing the door behind him, aware that his mother was watching from the window as he led them towards the marsh.

It had been the kind of afternoon you only got at places like Marshfield, the sun baking down, the air, like the ground, cool on the skin. They had sat on the grass by the river, Anja pulling a bottle of wine from one of the rucksacks and handing it to him. He opened it and they drank from the bottle, passing it round. It was good. Very dry. The first good wine he'd ever drunk.

Estelle had stripped out of her clothes to lie on her back in the sun, her breasts bare and brown. Seconds later, Anja had done likewise, and, when she had slipped the jeans down her thighs, he had seen the tattoo. She had touched the butterflies gently, and had looked at him, her English as good as Estelle's was poor. 'Do you like them?'

He had liked them very much, and the painting Joan had seen in North Oxford had been the result of the sketches he had made in the days that followed – sketches that had enabled him to sculpt the statues now confronting his mother. 'Do you like them?' he said.

His mother made no reply.

He led her out of the barn and they walked across the fields towards the house. She didn't speak, but she wept. He didn't know how he knew that. The rain had smashed against their faces, and yet he had known she was crying.

He made for the barn where the cars were kept and she followed him inside. Some instinct told him it was safe to let go of her then, and, when he did so, she stood beneath the beam. She didn't move, and he wasn't surprised. He had seen this condition before, a total submission that rendered the woman unable to think, to comprehend, to escape.

He picked up a rope that was coiled and lying on top of a box of tools. At the time, he had barely noticed what was in the box, but, now that he thought back, he could see the items as clearly as if he had studied them. There was oil in a can that had rusted to uselessness, a cardboard packet of nails, unopened. A hammer which, at some point, had come away from the handle, his father having fixed it by jamming a rag into the end and beating the metal head down onto the wood. He flicked the rope, and found it to be thin, but adequate. 'It's OK,' he said. 'Things change. I understand that.'

She fought in those final few moments. He regretted that. There had been something undignified about it, and he hadn't wanted his last memory of her to be of some deranged and terrified thing, scratching like the Siamese he'd dangled from a tree.

He rose from the interview room chair, extending his arms before him. 'See?' said Wachmann, and Driver saw that years of handling stone, of lifting it into position, of carving it, had given him strength enough. He said, 'Is that how you murdered Helena Warner?' and Wachmann replied, 'No.'

An admission by default, thought Driver.

Mindful of procedure, and slightly disappointed that Wachmann's admission hadn't resulted in his feeling anything even approaching euphoria, he said, 'Let me get this straight. Are you confessing to the murder of Helena Warner?'

'My client—' began his solicitor.

'Your client,' said Wachmann, 'is admitting to murder.'

48

Rigby opened the file and pulled a statement, one that Driver recognised as having been taken from Wachmann during the original investigation. 'Why, after all this time, did she suddenly decide to go to the police?'

'Once Helena's remains were found, she felt she had no option. For years, she and my father had convinced themselves they might just be mistaken.'

'What made them suspect in the first place?'

'I'm not sure. The holiday, probably.'

'Which holiday was this, Richard?'

'The holiday we took during the summer of my fourteenth birthday.'

'Where did you go?'

'France.'

'All of you, your father as well?'

'My father never left the farm.'

'And something happened to make your mother concerned, is that it?'

Wachmann didn't reply immediately. Perhaps he was wondering how best to phrase it, thought Driver, or perhaps he was merely keeping them waiting so that his words would have more impact.

'The daughter of a couple who were staying at our hotel went missing.'

The silence was palpable, and it seemed an age before he added, 'She was never found.'

Rigby felt a chill run through him. 'Were you questioned?'

'Only superficially.'

'And your mother suspected you?'

'No, not really. Not then, at any rate. But the following year we went to Greece, and it happened again. She knew then. She never mentioned it, but she knew. And after that holiday she started to draw away from me. So did my father. It was as though they were watching me from a long way off. They were polite. Helpful. But distant.'

'But they didn't do anything about it?'

'No.'

Driver could imagine the scenario: Merle Wachmann alone in the house, her husband out in the fields, neither of them wanting to face up to the possibility that, between them, they had created some sort of monster, each of them convincing themselves they were wrong, that it would all turn out all right; that Wachmann would go to Oxford, get a brilliant degree, marry, have kids, and be perfectly happy, successful, and above all, ***normal***. He said, 'And then those two students went missing.'

'Precisely,' said Wachmann.

'Where are their bodies?'

'Where do you think?'

On the marsh, thought Driver, and he recalled standing on the embankment to gaze into the water and come to terms with the fact that Helena Warner's remains would never be found. Of course, he hadn't known then what he knew now, that her remains had been buried in the house, but, if Wachmann had buried those girls on the marsh, the same principle applied: the remains would never be found.

Wachmann said, 'Certain types of bog preserve the bodies of the animals that fall into them. Parts of Marshfield were like that. You could bury a bird or a cat, and dig it up months later. Perfect. Hardly any decomposition, just the skin like leather; even the eyes intact.'

Rigby suffered the briefly flitting image of some small, dead, leathery thing dripping with slime. He pushed it out of his mind, saying, 'What was the point?'

'In what?'

'The cats, the birds . . . the women . . . Why did you do it?'

'I should have thought that was obvious,' said Wachmann. 'I liked to sketch them and record the way their bodies were decomposing.'

Thurston said, 'Did you find it sexually arousing?' and there was an edge to Wachmann's reply: 'Why else would I do it?'

Why else? thought Driver. He'd heard it all before. Different deviations, but the sickness that brought them about producing the same result. He said, 'So for years, your parents had their suspicions, but they somehow managed to convince themselves they might just be mistaken.'

'That's about it,' said Wachmann.

'And once Helena's remains were found your mother felt she had no option but to go to the police.'

'For once in her life, she had to face the facts.'

'But, even at the time that Helena disappeared, she must have *known* you were a killer?'

'No, she didn't know for sure. I'd never admitted I'd killed anyone, and none of my victims had ever been found. Suspecting something is a far cry from knowing it for a fact, and they didn't really *want* to know, that was the thing. If they'd known for a *fact* I was a killer, I'm pretty sure they would have felt duty-bound to tell the police, so it suited them better to suspect, but not know. That way, they could absolve themselves for merely putting me out of sight.'

'Didn't they confront you when Helena disappeared?'

'No, but I think they hoped I'd be caught and charged with her murder. When that didn't happen, they realised the responsibility for stopping me from killing anybody else rested entirely with them.'

'For God's sake,' said Driver. '*Why didn't they tell me?*'

'They didn't want anyone to know. They didn't want the shame of it.'

'So they settled for getting you admitted to a psychiatric unit in the hope that you might admit during therapy what you wouldn't admit during questioning.'

Mimicking his mother's voice in a way that was skin-crawlingly accurate, Wachmann replied by saying, 'We only want to help you Richard – we love you, you know that we love you – please darling, please . . .' and Driver suddenly felt deeply cold. It was one of the side effects of old age, he knew that: the sudden loss of heat, an almost inexplicable coldness that gripped the body and threatened to kill the unsuspecting.

'They wanted me out of their lives. Can't say I blame them. Would you?'

No, thought Driver. Not for a minute. He said, 'Why did you play along with it?'

'What choice did I have? I didn't want to go to prison, and I didn't want to go into a mental institution run by the National Health. I still don't.'

Rigby looked up and met Thurston's eye. He held Rigby's gaze for a moment, and then turned away as Rigby said, 'How many others are there?'

Wachmann stared past him to the door.

'How many others?' said Rigby.

Wachmann replied, 'There are plenty of derelict barns in Oxford. Why don't you check them out?'

Rigby felt nothing. Not even surprise. 'Are you willing to tell us where we can find the remains of more of your victims?'

'Yes.'

'Why?'

'Churchill House has been my home for twenty years. I've had six months to decide whether I like the outside world any better, and I don't.'

'You're telling me it won't bother you if you end up spending the rest of your life in a secure unit?'

'There are worse places,' said Wachmann. 'Those units at Chaggfords, for example.'

Rigby hadn't seen their interiors, but he could visualise them, small, drab, cheaply constructed. Prisonlike.

Wachmann added, 'With both my parents dead, I stand to inherit the farm. Once it's sold, the fees will enable me to stay at Churchill House for the rest of my life.'

Rigby suddenly realised Wachmann had no idea the farm was mortgaged twice over. There was nothing to inherit; and, even if there had been, once a court established that he was responsible for the murders he claimed to have committed, he was likely to end up in a secure unit that was a far cry from the near luxury he had grown accustomed to at Churchill House. He said, 'How did you get around?'

'By car.'

'You've got a car?' said Driver.

'I'm a depressive,' said Wachmann, 'not an imbecile. Churchill House let me come and go as I please.'

And why not? thought Rigby. He could see it. That was the tragedy of it. With his parents paying the fees and Wachmann appearing to be of no particular danger to anyone, there would be no reason why he shouldn't be given as much freedom as he could handle. 'DVLA didn't have you on record as owning a vehicle.'

'It was in my mother's name.'

'What kind of vehicle?'

'A Volvo Estate.'

'The one you had twenty years ago?'

'No, but one similar. My parents used to pass them on to me.'

Good strong vehicles, thought Driver; the type farmers so often chose because they could take a battering from deeply rutted tracks. They were cheap to run and maintain, and they lasted forever. More importantly, where Wachmann was concerned, once you put the seats down, you could get anything in there, from the lifesize statue of a body to the real thing. He felt as if someone had pulled a plug in the small of his back, as though every ounce of energy he possessed was being drained. 'There's something I don't understand: you claim your motivation for murdering these women lay in the fact that you derived some sexual satisfaction from keeping a record of the way in which their bodies decomposed.'

'What about it?'

'When you murdered Helena Warner, you knew the water was rising, knew that in all probability you wouldn't be in a position to keep any kind of record.'

'So?'

'So there had to be something more to it.'

'Are you acquainted with the work of Aristide Maillol?'

'You know I'm not,' said Driver. 'What was he, a painter?'

'A sculptor,' said Wachmann. 'His wife was one of the most beautiful women the world has ever seen. Maillol said of her, "I lifted her chemise and found marble," but she died obese.'

'That doesn't help me,' said Driver.

'I'm saying that women lose their beauty,' said Wachmann. 'Painting them is one thing, but by capturing them in stone you can feel them as they were, cool to the touch, skin like marble, muscle and bone as it was when they were alive.' He didn't add that when he had pushed into the butterfly lips he had found that, like the rest of her, and unlike any woman he had ever known, Helena Warner was unnaturally cold. It had been like making love to a statue, and it had terrified him.

'Were you having an affair with her?'

'Yes.'

'Did Gilmore know?'

'He caught us at Marshfield?'

'What was his reaction?'

'He lashed out at us, and she cracked her head against the wall of one of the outbuildings.'

Driver could picture the scene. Erotic, animal, violent.

'Then what?'

'She was stunned, no more than that.'

'What did you do?'

'I ran into one of the barns.'

'What about Gilmore?'

'He just stood there. I don't think he knew what to do. Joan led him back to the house. Helena tried to follow.'

'And you tried to stop her.'

'The only thing she wanted to do was beg him not to leave her.'

'Sexual jealousy can be hard to deal with,' said Thurston.

'No – *you don't understand* . . . In that moment, I saw nothing but decline for her. She would marry him, have his children, and decay in some ordinary existence. That body would be lost to the world. I wanted to preserve it.'

'And just how did you intend to achieve that, under the circumstances?'

'The water was rising. I knew I couldn't bury it on the marsh . . . I wasn't sure what I was going to do to be honest, but I knew I had to kill her.' He glanced up, defiant. 'I *owed* her that much. If she were alive, she'd thank me.'

Rigby didn't know what to say. For once, he would have been grateful if Thurston had made some comment, but it was Driver who broke the silence.

'How did you manage to persuade Gilmore that his action had caused her death?'

'I didn't have to,' said Wachmann. 'He just assumed it.'

'And you let him?' said Driver.

'Why not?'

Why not? thought Rigby. It had been the simplest solution, one that even Gilmore had accepted without question. Quietly now, he said, 'How did you kill her?' and again, Wachmann stretched his forearms out as if their sheer size and strength were a marvel to him. 'I smashed her head against the wall.'

Driver looked past Wachmann to the window beyond. Gilmore was three floors down in the cell he had first been held in over twenty years before, and Driver wanted him out of it. More than that, he wanted to be the one to put him out of what had clearly been twenty years of unnecessary misery.

Rigby ended the interview. 'We'll take a break,' he said.

49

Same interview room, thought Gilmore; same mesh at the windows, same table, same chairs. He was tired, and afraid in the way that he had been afraid at nineteen. The prints that had linked him to Merle Wachmann were probably just the beginning. He had to face facts.

Driver and Rigby walked in, acknowledged the men who had brought Gilmore up from the cells, and each pulled a chair.

'This isn't official,' said Rigby.

It didn't make much difference to Gilmore. Official. Unofficial. It was all the same to him now. 'Certain facts have come to light and I felt you should be made aware of them as soon as possible.'

It was a trick, thought Gilmore. 'I'm listening,' he said.

'What were you doing at Thornley the day Merle Wachmann was murdered?'

For a moment, Gilmore considered denying he was ever there, a reflex action, habit almost, but his prints were all over the glass. There seemed no point. 'I wanted Richard's address.'

'So you admit you were there.'

'You *know* I was there,' replied Gilmore.

'How did she react when you turned up?'

He answered cautiously. 'Well put it this way, she could have phoned the police, but she didn't. She let me in.'

'Meaning?' said Rigby.

'Meaning that if she thought I was likely to kill her she was hardly likely to have let me in.'

'Did she give you his address?'

'She told me he was living in South Africa.'

'Did you believe her?'

'No.'

'Why should she lie?'

'I don't know. At the time, I just got the impression she was lying. I can't say why.'

'There must have been some reason?'

'I knew him, remember; shared a house with him. I just couldn't picture him farming in the Transvaal or anywhere else for that matter.'

'So why do you think she lied?'

'I came to the conclusion she probably didn't want me dragging him into my problems. Turned out I was right. Once she knew why I was there, she asked me to leave, which I did.'

'That doesn't answer why you went there.'

'I've just told you why I went there, I wanted Richard's address.'

'Maybe, but that was a side issue. I think you went to Thornley because you thought she knew something, and you wanted to find out what.'

'I just wanted to get in touch with Richard,' insisted Gilmore, and Driver went with it for the moment, seeing no point in winding him up. In a few, short minutes, he was going to get a monumental shock, one that Driver was still reeling from. It would be better if he received it in a calm frame of mind.

'All right,' he said. 'So you wanted to contact Wachmann. I'll go with that.'

'It's the truth.'

'Like I said, I'll go with that,' said Driver. 'But why, after twenty years, did you suddenly decide you had to see him?'

Gilmore had thought it through. Sitting in the cell, he had tried to anticipate Driver's every question, and he had the reply ready for him. 'Helena's remains had been found at Marshfield. That meant she must have gone back in the days before the house was submerged. I needed to talk to him.'

'Why?'

'Who else could I talk to about it?'

'There was always Joan.'

The look on Gilmore's face said it all, and Driver smiled. 'You owe her.'

'I know.'

'So why not Joan?'

'It's hard to explain how things are between me and Joan. It's complex . . .'

I'll bet, thought Driver. 'Did you two ever meet before that weekend?'

'No,' said Gilmore. 'I'd never set eyes on her prior to Marshfield.'

'Then how come she covered for you?'

It was a question Gilmore had often asked himself in the early days. It was maturity that had provided the answer, experience gained as a result of the sheer number of women who had entered his life only to exit stage left when they realised they were dealing with a man who couldn't commit, couldn't express what he felt – didn't even *know* what he felt. 'What makes you think she did?'

'Don't make this harder than it needs to be. Why did she cover for you?'

Gilmore suddenly wondered what it must feel like to get to Driver's age and to have had a case like Marshfield on your mind for years on end, but it was a sense of his own imminent defeat rather than sympathy for Driver that finally made him reply, 'She thought she was in love with me.'

Again, thought Driver, an admission by default. 'She hardly knew you.'

'No. Maybe if she had, she'd have felt differently.'

'You don't hold a very high opinion of yourself.'

'No, well . . .'

'Ever wondered what it was that attracted her to you?'

Gilmore wondered that about every woman he had ever been involved with.

Driver added, 'Maybe she wanted you simply because you belonged to Helena.'

It was a new one on Gilmore, but he realised there might be something in it. Short of being physically repulsive, it wouldn't have mattered what he'd looked like. Knowing, as he did, how Joan really felt about Helena, the fact that he was Helena's lover might well have been enough.

'So what happened between you the night of the party?'

'I can't answer that.'

'Then let me answer for you,' said Driver, his tone hardening. 'She led you to the outhouse. Right?'

'No,' said Gilmore.

'And you caught Wachmann and Helena having sex . . .'

'No.'

'You lashed out at them and Helena smashed her head against the wall.'

Gilmore stood up. '*No!*'

'Sit down,' said Driver.

Gilmore remained standing, and, softly now, Driver said, 'Humour me, Ian. Let's just suppose, for a moment, that that's what happened. She led you back to the house and led you upstairs to one of the bedrooms. Not for sex. Just to listen. Good listener, Joan. It's inherent in women like her. Before you knew what was happening, you found yourself in bed with her . . .'

'No.'

'You had sex with her . . .'

What was the point? thought Gilmore. He knew. He'd always known.

He suddenly realised what was in store for him. During the weeks and months ahead, much of his time would be spent in that room. Sometimes with Rigby, and sometimes with Driver there too. Whatever the case, between them, and irrespective of whether the questioning was official or unofficial, they would grind him down. They had a body.

They had his prints on the glass. He had no idea what else they had but whatever was needed, they'd get it. Nineteen years ago, Driver had taken him to the brink of a confession. Now, the prospect of what lay in store for him finally tipped him over.

'I killed her,' he said, and it came out flat. A simple statement of fact.

Driver had often imagined what it might be like when Gilmore finally cracked, but, of all the potential scenarios, he hadn't anticipated the small, flat admission that Gilmore had finally delivered. 'You killed her,' he said. 'That it?'

Gilmore sat down. 'What more is there to say?'

Christ, thought Driver. Just like that.

'You've waited a long time to hear me say that,' said Gilmore. 'How does it feel?'

Twenty years ago – even twenty-four hours ago – Driver would have felt triumphant. Now, he merely said, 'Not good, I have to admit.'

He watched the look of confusion that spread across Gilmore's face. 'I don't follow . . .'

Driver stood up and went to the window. 'You didn't kill her,' he said. 'Richard did.'

'What?'

'Wachmann—'

'*What are you trying to pull?*'

Driver kept his back to him. 'It's the truth,' he said.

'I lashed out at her.'

'I know,' said Driver, 'but you didn't kill her. After you went to the house with Joan, Wachmann went back and battered her to death. You assumed you were responsible for her death because he allowed you to assume it.'

Driver turned from the window, wanting, *needing*, to look him in the eye as he said what he had really come to say. 'I'm sorry,' he said. 'I was wrong.'

50

Gilmore came downstairs, groggy from sleep that had been deep but insufficient despite its having been a good nine hours since he had collapsed fully clothed on the bed. He had dreamt of nothing, he was sure of that. No haunting dreams of Joan's beseeching face or Helena's lifeless form. Just blackness. Nothingness. Peace.

There were letters on the mat, bills mostly. He stooped, picked them up, and took them through to the kitchen. Without thinking about it, he reached out for the snowman and plucked it off the fridge, pinging it into the bin and watching the lid snap shut on the smug plaster face. Whatever happened in the future, he was determined he would never find another note under that snowman.

He made himself coffee, sat in the kitchen to drink it, and thought about the future. It made a pleasant change and he suddenly realised just how long he had allowed his mind to dwell persistently on the past. There had never been a tomorrow, or even a today – just Marshfield and water and death.

He cast his mind back to some of the things Driver had said the previous day, and came to the conclusion that he owed it to himself to lighten up a little, to live a little. If only he would allow himself to take it, he now had a chance of building a life for himself, a life that someone like Sue might want to share; an ordinary kind of life, perhaps, but one in which he could start to believe in himself as being all the things that his arrest had made him realise were precious to him. He wanted to believe that he was decent, worthy of love, and able to give his love in return. He wanted also to share his life with someone worthy of that love, someone who wouldn't betray him, lie to him, cheat on him, and ruin what years he had left. If nothing else, Sue looked a promising prospect. Chances were, she'd had him up to the teeth. He wouldn't blame her for that, but he owed her the opportunity to tell him so to his face.

He put the mug of coffee down on the kitchen table and cast his mind back to the way in which he had screwed her letter into a small blue ball before hurtling it into a corner of the room. Whatever he had felt about its contents at the time, he felt differently about it now. Of all the women who'd drifted into his life only to exit it disillusioned, he had felt closest to Sue, and if he didn't phone her now he might never pluck up the courage.

He dialled her office number, and when she answered, said the first thing that came into his mind. 'You wrote to me.'

Nothing. Total silence.

'Sue?'

'Where are you?'

It came out cool. 'Home,' he replied.

The silence returned.

'Sue?'

'Ian, *what do you want?*'

Good question, thought Gilmore. He caught the bitterness in her voice and recalled that the last time they spoke there had been no trace of it. Just desperation that was born of a last-ditch attempt to get through to him.

'I want you back,' he replied.

'Just like that . . .'

'I don't know how else to say it.'

'Why bother saying it at all? This time next week, next month, we'll be back where we are today.'

'No,' said Gilmore. 'We won't.'

He almost expected the phone line to go dead, and had half

a mind to put himself out of his misery, to be the first to hang up. 'We need to talk,' he said.

'What about?'

'The future.'

That magic word. Future. Women set such store on it, and he'd never before known why. There was a pause, a gap he didn't know how to fill, not unless he told the truth. 'I care about you. It's hard for me to say that. Don't make it harder.'

The doorbell rang. 'Sue . . .'

'Phone me later.'

'I have to know . . .'

'Phone me later.'

'Say you'll give me a chance. That's all I'm asking. A chance.'

In the silence that ensued, the doorbell rang again. Gilmore knew it was Driver, and knew he would wait. 'A chance,' he repeated. 'How about it?'

'Things have to change.'

'I know that.'

'If you mean what you say . . .'

'I do.'

'Phone me later.'

She hung up, and he opened the door to find Driver, fresh as a daisy, standing on the step.

'You know how to pick your moments . . .'

'Well I didn't expect the "Hallelujah Chorus", but I think I deserve better than that.'

'Come in,' said Gilmore.

He led him into the living room, Driver's apology still ringing in his ears from the day before. Wrong, he thought. *Sorry, Ian, I was wrong*. It reminded him of the way in which Driver had said, 'Sorry to bother you, Ian, but I could just do with you down at the station this morning. Any objections?'

It wasn't good enough, but then he too had been wrong. How could he blame Driver when he had thought himself guilty?

He wished his father were alive to see him now. Marshfield was a subject they had avoided once the investigation was wound down, but, shortly before his death, his father had said, 'I have to know', and Gilmore, who had known what he was going to ask, had replied, 'I didn't do it.'

His father couldn't have known what it had cost him to say that. It had been his dying wish to know the truth, and Gilmore had lied. He had carried that guilt with him down the years, a guilt that sat beside the greater guilt of having committed a murder.

'Sit down,' he invited, and Driver sat.

'You don't seem too happy,' said Driver.

Gilmore sat down opposite him. 'It's going to take time. For twenty years, I've believed I killed her. I can't just switch that off.'

'No,' said Driver. 'I'm having a spot of bother with that one myself.'

'You were convinced it was me.'

'It was a fair assumption,' replied Driver. 'So were you.'

Gilmore looked back over the years of anguish he'd suffered as a result of believing himself to be a killer and he wondered whether Driver had any idea what he'd been through. His voice held a tinge of bitterness. 'What happens now?'

'There'll be charges relating to evidence you withheld at the time of the original investigation.'

'What about Joan?'

'She'll also be charged,' replied Driver. When Gilmore made no comment, he added, 'If Wachmann hadn't killed her, would you have taken her back?'

He didn't even have to think about it. 'No.'

'Why not?'

'Pride.'

'That all?'

'No, not pride. More a defence mechanism. I couldn't have let her get close enough to hurt me again.'

That was fair, thought Driver. Most men would feel the same.

'So Wachmann was worrying unnecessarily.'

'What about?'

'He told us he couldn't stand the thought of her decaying in some mindless existence.'

'Is that how he saw her future with me?'

'It's how he sees the future of any woman he deems beautiful enough to warrant his attentions,' said Driver, adding, 'You lived with him, shared a house. Wasn't there any indication that something was wrong?'

Gilmore thought back to a painting by Wachmann. He had seen it at the house in North Oxford, and that had been so long ago he couldn't recall the details. All he could recall was the fact that it depicted a woman eating a pear, and that it was possibly one of the most sensual paintings he had ever seen. He was gripped by it, but wasn't sure whether he liked it, or even wanted to see it again. There had been something about it, something that disturbed him, but he doubted he could explain that to Driver. A man like Driver wouldn't understand. Or maybe he was doing him an injustice: maybe Driver would know *instinctively* what it was that had troubled him.

'Well?' said Driver, and Gilmore replied, 'He was reading fine art. Most of his friends made *him* look positively normal.'

'Artists,' said Driver, 'are a bit that way inclined, so I'm told. Don't know many, personally. The force doesn't tend to attract that type of person.'

Looking at Driver, Gilmore could believe it. 'So what happens now?'

'In what regard?'

'To Wachmann?'

'We've got to prove a case against him, but that shouldn't be difficult.'

'What then?'

'He's probably looking at spending the rest of his natural in a secure unit.'

'Christ,' said Gilmore. 'Why didn't his mother confide in you?'

'Why didn't you?'

'You know why. I thought I'd killed her. If I'd told you that, I'd have got life.'

'No,' said Driver. 'What you'd have got was justice, a thorough investigation to establish the facts. The body would have been brought to the surface, and a post-mortem would have established that she died as a result of having had her head battered against a wall. *Repeatedly* battered, Ian. You hit her once, and it wasn't even enough to knock her out. What Wachmann did caused a massive haemorrhage.'

'What are you saying?'

'I'm saying that, once we'd established that, it wouldn't have fitted in with the stories given by Wachmann and Joan Poole. They would each have said you lashed out at her, and we would have known it wasn't enough, so we would have probed further. Chances are, we'd have looked at the possibilities and found that the people still in the house at the time were out of the frame. The only person we could have pointed a finger at was Wachmann, so we'd have worked on him and got to the truth. Even if he hadn't obliged us with a confession, I'm pretty sure that, once she knew Helena was dead, his morher would have come forward.'

'It was all a waste of time, then. A waste of our lives, mine, and Joan's.'

'And the lives of the women Wachmann subsequently murdered.'

'How many are there?'

'We don't know. Several, at Rigby's last count, but Wachmann's still coming up with locations. Barns, mostly.'

'What about names?'

'He chose his victims cleverly. Women passing through. Women who needed a roof for the night. Women who wouldn't be missed.'

'I didn't realise it was so easy to get away with murder?'

'Coming from you, that's a good one,' said Driver. 'People are murdered every day. The fact that they've disappeared is only reported to the police if they're missed. You any idea how many bodies go unidentified every year? Some of them homeless. Some of them elderly people abandoned by kids who now live abroad and don't contact them from one Christmas to the next; or women who bump into people like Wachmann. Then there are the winos, the drug addicts, the runaway teenagers. I could go on.'

'Was there ever a time you thought Helena was a runaway?'

'No,' said Driver. 'I knew from the start she was dead. Knew from the start that she never left Marshfield.'

Gilmore made no comment, and, as if needing confirmation that Wachmann must have seen the body in order to sculpt the statue at a later date, Driver added, 'What's your opinion, Ian? Could Richard have gone back to Marshfield in the days following the party?'

Gilmore thought back and recalled that he wouldn't have known for sure where Wachmann was from the Monday to the Wednesday. 'I don't know, but knowing the way he used to work, I'd say he wouldn't have done it from memory. He must have gone back, opened the wardrobe, and sketched the remains for future reference.'

It was Driver's turn to sit silently and absorb what he'd just been told. Gilmore left him to it, lost in his own thoughts, thoughts that seemed increasingly to concentrate on the future and what it might now hold. It was new to him, this concept of having a future, a frightening prospect, yet one that was beginning to hold some appeal.

'There's something I don't understand,' said Driver. 'Something I've been asking myself for twenty years if I'm honest.'

'What?'

Driver cast his mind back to the day he'd stared into the water, convinced that Helena's body would never be found. He said, 'Why the house instead of the marsh?'

For a moment, Gilmore didn't see what he was getting at. 'Does it matter?'

'It does to me,' said Driver. 'Considering you knew the marsh was about to be submerged, it seemed a stupid thing to do, but I know there had to be a reason.'

Gilmore couldn't believe it wasn't obvious. In Driver's shoes, it would have been the first thing he thought of, but then, Driver didn't know what Ernst had done prior to leaving Marshfield.

He saw himself back in the kitchen with Joan, the glare of the bulb bright, a thin film of scum on water that lay in the sink. She had pulled the plug and watched it drain to leave the crockery coated, and then she had run the tap and demanded his hands.

He held them out to her, and she soaped the blood away, her thumbs strong and rubbing the palms in the spot he had always associated with nails. The pressure sent a sensation up his arms, a pain, almost; and then, in an act that was as bizarre as it was erotic, she dried his hands on her hair.

'Don't,' he said, softly, but she clung to him, her fingers like steel, and he knew even then that those fingers would reach down the years.

She led him out of the kitchen and into the room where the doe-eyed print stared down from the wall. It was dimly lit, the air thick with smoke gone stale, and as he walked in Wachmann looked up, but the moment for recriminations had passed without either of them taking the initiative. 'We'd better call the police,' he said, but Wachmann was against it.

'Do you really want to go through all that crap? I don't – and it won't bring her back. Nothing that any of us can do will bring her back.'

Gilmore said, 'That isn't the point,' but Joan backed Wachmann up.

'Maybe he's right. Think about how it might look. It would all come out about Richard and Helena and me and you, and it would also come out about Helena sleeping around. Think how her parents will feel when the press gets hold of that.'

'So what do you suggest?'

Nobody suggested anything and yet the thought of burying the body on the marsh hung heavy on the air.

It was the horror of it that Gilmore couldn't stand. To dig a hole and put Helena in it would have been utterly beyond him, but it was academic in any case. They couldn't bury her because Richard's father had stripped the form of tools. There wasn't a spade or anything even closely resembling one anywhere on the property.

Joan looked down at the long wooden boards beneath their feet, and didn't say a word, but Wachmann said, 'We'd never get them up, not without tools.'

'Whatever we do, they'll find her,' said Gilmore, and, turning to Wachmann, Joan said, 'Maybe not. How long will it be before the water starts to rise?'

'It's started already. It'll be up to the door by Wednesday.'

There seemed no point in saying it was the first that Gilmore had heard of it. 'I thought we had longer,' he said.

'Well you don't,' said Wachmann. 'I thought . . .' He had been going to say he thought that Helena had told him, but he changed this to, 'I thought you knew.'

'Why do we have to do anything?' he pleaded. 'Why can't we just leave her there?'

Joan responded with a coolness that gave him some inkling of what she was capable of if pushed. 'She'll float to the surface.'

It was a nightmare, thought Gilmore. Here they were, calmly discussing how best to dispose of a body. And not just a body. *Helena's* body. It was murderers who wondered what to do with bodies, not normal, sane, everyday people. But what was normal and sane about having killed someone in the first place? What did it matter what they did with the body? And yet it mattered greatly. It mattered to him, and he couldn't bury her. He just couldn't.

As if knowing what was passing through his mind, Joan said, 'Let us handle it. You stay here. You need never know what we did if you prefer it that way.' And she took Wachmann with her, Wachmann, who was calmer and was handling it better.

He left them to it, and in many respects, that had been the most horrific thing of all, to sit on that mock-Turkish blanket, not seeing, but hearing the body being dragged across the hall and up those stairs to the bedroom above his head. He had covered his ears and had sat like that for an age, but finally, he had listened and there was . . . nothing.

He had stood up then, had walked into the hall and had found the silence terrifying. He had run up the stairs to the bedroom, and would never forget what he saw: the hand, the half-open door, Joan pushing it closed, and the look that had been on her face as she turned the brass knob.

'We didn't have tools,' he said 'Richard's father took them.'

'As simple as that,' said Driver.

'As simple as that,' replied Gilmore.

CONTINUE READING FOR AN EXCERPT FROM JULIA WALLIS MARTIN'S NEXT BOOK

THE BIRD YARD

AVAILABLE FROM ST. MARTIN'S PRESS

Roger Hardman had spent his life on the land, and although this particular job was new to him, the land, as such, was not. It was a different county, that's all, one that was unfamiliar, the shape of the trees as new to him as the shape of the people he found himself thrust among.

He put the scythe down for a moment, wiped his brow with the back of his hand and looked up. The position of the sun told him it was lunchtime, just as it told him that the path wound east, which meant he'd reached half-way. If he could find a spot to sit a moment, have a bite to eat . . . but there was nowhere suitable, just trees, darkness and a treehouse of sorts, well off the path to his left.

He felt the ground, found that it was damp, and reasoned that in an hour or so, with luck, he'd have the job finished. Lunch could wait, he decided, so he lifted the scythe and continued, stopping only when curiosity caused him to wonder who might have built the treehouse.

Kids, he decided, but Fenwick had died without issue, so it must have been built by the children of a family that had once owned the estate. Colbourne House was prestigious enough for minor gentry, and it had no doubt accommodated more than its share in its two-hundred-year history. Still, to build a treehouse so far from the gardens struck him as strange, and he tried to picture the children who had built it, seeing them in breeches and those odd buttoned boots, a snatch of lace or velvet at their pale, slender throats. He wouldn't have wanted to be a child a hundred years ago, privileged or not, and if he had been, he wouldn't have built a treehouse in a wood where the trees were gnarled into shapes that could seem almost demonic to a child's eyes.

In leaving the path to take a closer look, he realized he'd

been wrong. Whatever it was, this thing, it wasn't a treehouse. Its shape and proportions were difficult to discern, ivy having distorted it and made it part of the background so effectively that he might not have seen it at all if he hadn't just happened to glance at it from a particular angle.

It was supported on poles that had been stripped of bark, planed smooth, and driven into the ground to form a rectangular construction. It looked like some kind of scaffold or the frame to a four-poster bed, but the base, instead of being at a level that would make it possible for a person to climb in, was at shoulder height. Ivy had smothered the base with a mattress of green; the leaves moving softly, a bird dipping down and swooping its length, then fluttering into the trees, and on the soft, still wind, he caught the sound of a dog's single bark from many miles away.

He stretched out the hand that still held the scythe and used the arc of steel to touch the ivy. The tip of it lifted a tentacle of green, and in a nervous, jerking movement, he whipped it away to reveal what it concealed.

He knew, of course, that what he'd found were bones, and he wasn't a stranger to death, so it wasn't of death itself that he was afraid. What he feared was the fact that he had reached out, and had revealed with his scythe, a thing that was touched by evil, and he threw the scythe to the ground. He would never retrieve it again, feeling it to be tainted, unlucky, and all the more likely to carve through his flesh and bring about his own untimely demise.

Poor young bugger, he thought, for even as he stepped back and away from the scaffold he knew the remains were small. Boy or girl, he didn't know, but this had been a child.

He turned now, and ran, stumbling down the path, feeling the trees closing in, feeling that he was in danger. Death had been to this place, had visited a child there, had left its remains to the birds, and he ran as if that thing on the scaffold might lift itself from the bed and beckon him back, the teeth grinning, the voice child-like: *You'll never forget me you know. Every day for the rest of your life, you'll remember the way you found me, and it will haunt you, Roger Hardman, that I promise . . .*